Advance Praise for
TORCH

"*Torch* immerses readers in the lives of a group of teenagers in Czechoslovakia after the 1968 Soviet invasion. Rather than live without freedom, one of them decides to protest the regime's oppression by setting himself on fire—and as a consequence, the dreams of his best friends go up in flames too. I was immediately hooked and couldn't put this down. Incredibly relevant for today's teens, especially with the current surge of authoritarianism around the globe."

—Kip Wilson, author of *White Rose* and
The Most Dazzling Girl in Berlin

"With meticulous attention to detail, Miller-Lachmann recreates a terrifying and excruciating chapter in our shared human history. A work of historical fiction about an almost forgotten time that is frighteningly relevant in today's world."

—Padma Venkatraman, author of
The Bridge Home and *Born Behind Bars*

"Lyn Miller-Lachmann's *Torch* manages to accomplish the nearly impossible—a novel that is not only intensively researched and informative, but also riveting and deeply heartfelt. Readers will learn and care in equal measure."

—Cynthia Levinson, author of the Robert J. Sibert Medal-winning
The People's Painter: How Ben Shahn Fought for Justice with Art

"A magnificently rendered novel that feels especially timely, *Torch* packs an emotional punch with its intriguing characters and compelling setting. Lyn Miller-Lachmann has written an outstanding work of historical fiction that achieves the unique distinction of being both sensitively drawn and impeccably researched. I was swept away."

—Carly Heath, author of *The Reckless Kind*

TORCH

LYN MILLER-LACHMANN

Carolrhoda LAB

MINNEAPOLIS

For Richard

Carolrhoda Lab®
An imprint of Lerner Publishing Group, Inc.
241 First Avenue North
Minneapolis, MN 55401 USA

For reading levels and more information, look up this title at www.lernerbooks.com.

Design elements by: Makmur Jaya/Shutterstock.com (phoenix); Filip Bjorkman/Shutterstock.com (flag); Nosyrevy/Shutterstock.com (forest); nomadFra/Shutterstock.com (wire); STILLFX/Shutterstock.com (texture).

Main body text set in Minion Pro.
Typeface provided by Adobe Systems.

Library of Congress Cataloging-in-Publication Data

Names: Miller-Lachmann, Lyn, 1956– author.
Title: Torch / Lyn Miller-Lachmann.
Description: Minneapolis : Carolrhoda Lab, [2022] | Includes author's note. | Audience: Ages 13–18. | Audience: Grades 10–12. | Summary: "When 17-year-old Pavol fatally sets himself on fire in Prague in 1969 to protest the Soviet invasion of Czechoslovakia, his three best friends must figure out how to survive an oppressive regime without him" —Provided by publisher.
Identifiers: LCCN 2021050161 (print) | LCCN 2021050162 (ebook) | ISBN 9781728415680 (lib. bdg.) | ISBN 9781728460741 (eb pdf)
Subjects: CYAC: Communism—Fiction. | Suicide—Fiction. | Defectors—Fiction. | Czechoslovakia—History—1968–1989—Fiction. | LCGFT: Novels. | Historical fiction.
Classification: LCC PZ7.M6392 To 2022 (print) | LCC PZ7.M6392 (ebook) | DDC [Fic]—dc23

LC record available at https://lccn.loc.gov/2021050161
LC ebook record available at https://lccn.loc.gov/2021050162

Manufactured in the United States of America
1-48684-49102-5/6/2022

NOTE TO READERS

This book contains references to suicide. If you are thinking about suicide or worried about a loved one, call the National Suicide Prevention Lifeline at 988 or at 1-800-273-8255, or text HELLO to 741741. Both services provide 24/7 free and confidential support and resources.

JAN PALACH'S MARTYRDOM

Yesterday's death of Jan Palach has deeply moved the people of Czechoslovakia, as well as many outside that country. . . . And still unanswered is the question of whether young Czechs and Slovaks will turn themselves into human torches in a similar effort to strengthen Czechoslovak resistance to Soviet tyranny.

—*New York Times*, January 20, 1969

ROZCESTÍ: THE CROSSROADS

MARCH 10–15, 1969

CHAPTER 1: PAVOL

The letter was Pavol's last chance for a future. He paced Štěpán's living room, secrets like carpenter ants burrowing into him, eating him from the inside out. Štěpán's wisecracks thudded in his ears. Tomáš hunched on the sofa, pen tap-tapping against a blank notebook page.

"Let's get started," Pavol said. "To the Central Committee of the Czechoslovak Communist Party: We are secondary school students, the future of our country." He stopped to let Tomáš write.

"We're not the only ones writing a letter, are we?" Tomáš set down his pen and picked at loose skin on his thumb.

Sprawled on the rug, Štěpán rolled his hockey stick back and forth. "I thought we cleared this up already."

"It's all right," Pavol said to Štěpán before turning to Tomáš. "Thousands of people have been writing. Famous people. Even KSČ members." His throat was parched despite the Kofola cola he'd downed in two gulps. "Remember the newspaper editorial telling people to fight for their freedom?" He didn't remind Tomáš that afterward the Russians shut the paper down.

"I bet the people who wrote are in prison now." Tomáš squeezed his thumb until a ruby drop formed.

"Don't be a baby, Tomáš," Štěpán snapped. He unfolded

himself from the floor, checked that the windows were shut tight, and padded to the wooden hi-fi console. "My father's in the Party and he signed a petition to reopen the newspapers and the radio stations. If he can do it, so can we." But Štěpán's father wasn't as high up in the Party as Tomáš's. Comrade Kuchař would probably murder Tomáš if he found out about this letter.

Pavol tugged at his hair while Štěpán flicked through the stack of now-banned Western albums in the cabinet. "Next line: We believe that having freedom to speak and read and listen to music and debate politics last year made our country stronger."

"Wait, that's not how you say it." Tomáš raised his pen. "It's *strengthened our glorious socialist revolution.*"

Štěpán let out a harsh laugh. "Is that the crap your father says?"

Tomáš flinched. "They're the words we're supposed to use, if we want them to take us seriously."

"Tomáš is right," Pavol said. "His father made him take the political classes."

"Complete waste, but I guess you had no choice."

Štěpán lifted a record, wiped it with a cloth, set it on the turntable, and lowered the needle. After a few pops and clicks, the opening drumbeat of the Zombies' "Time of the Season" wafted through the speaker. Štěpán lowered the volume while humming the melody.

Pavol rubbed the back of his neck. His hands shook. "Focus, guys. We need to get this done today. And Tomáš?"

"Yes?" Tomáš peered through his black-rimmed glasses with the mixture of trust and awe that reminded Pavol of the farm dogs he'd played with back in his village in Slovakia, before his family had come to live in this northern Bohemian town of factories and coal mines. Before those mines killed his father and threatened to one day kill him.

"When you put in that we want freedom, an end to censorship of books, newspapers, music, and movies, and the Russians to go home . . ." Pavol swallowed, his throat sawdust. "Say we want amnesty for everyone arrested for protesting the invasion last August. No expulsions. No blacklists."

Tomáš squinted at the paper. "How's this? We accept the absolute authority of the KSČ but also request mercy for those who protested the troops that took action on 21 August 1968 to protect world socialism. Please do not let their talent and enthusiasm go to waste because of youthful indiscretion." He pushed up his glasses and grimaced. "They expect abject submission. We have to pretend to give it to them."

A chill rippled through Pavol's body. "Perfect." He couldn't bring himself to explain why this part mattered so much to him. Nobody knew that he'd been arrested for smashing road signs to keep the tanks from reaching Prague. That the police had beaten him on the spot and released him with a warning. That he'd thought it was a lucky break . . . until early January, when the government rejected his application to Czech Technical University in Prague and assigned him instead to a black-lung-shortened life in the mines.

They hadn't said they'd turned him down for political reasons. They'd found out what he wanted most and snatched it away without giving any reason at all.

"I can get this typed up," he said instead. He took a deep breath. "Also, I need you to get me into Prague Castle. So I can deliver the letter personally and they can see my face." Because he was the one without a future, unless he could look them in the eye and convince them.

Tomáš could get him in. He'd been inside with his father for Party meetings. Pavol could take it from there.

Behind his glasses Tomáš's left eyelid twitched. "But I thought the letter was supposed to be anonymous. Mailed, in the name of all Rozcestí's secondary students."

Štěpán lifted the needle from the record, casting a hush over the room. "Listen to him, Tomáš. If anyone's pretty face could charm the Party heads, it's Pavol's."

Pavol held his fist to his lips. What he would ask his friends to do, what he'd ask them to risk—especially Tomáš—sat uneasily in his gut like one too many shots of slivovice. But he needed this letter to work. He needed to open closed minds and hardened hearts. Because the only other way out of his ruined life and his occupied nation was a torch.

The first warm days of March brought back memories of the previous spring. Snow melting into muddy puddles. Sunshine warming his hair. Later, the lingering scent of raindrops, linden, and honeysuckle; pink and white blossoms scattered on the grass and cobblestones of the town.

And music. Long-forbidden songs had blasted into the narrow streets and broad squares that spring. Pavol's tongue had twisted around the foreign words: "She Loves You" . . . "Like a Rolling Stone" . . . "Wild Thing" . . .

The girls wove flowers into their hair and fashioned them into necklaces. Pavol and the other boys let their hair grow as long as the girls'. They read poetry of love and sex and rebellion that would've shocked the Party old guard and at times shocked him, raised Catholic in secret. They debated in classrooms and living rooms the meaning of *socialism with a human face*.

That was the spring he met Lída Pekárová.

He fell in love with her to the scream of the electric guitar, the heartbeat of bass and drums, the Beatles song he would sing over and over: "I Want to Hold Your Hand."

That was then: 1968, the spring of freedom.

Now was an overcast Thursday, three days after he, Tomáš, and Štěpán had finished the letter. The morning was unseasonably warm but with a chill in the air that signaled a coming cold snap. In front of the old church in Rozcestí's main square—turned into an auditorium for Party events—Pavol squeezed Lída's hand. They often met here before he headed for the No. 3 Secondary Railway Technical School next to the train station and she reported to the squat brick shoe factory at the western edge of town.

"Where's Ondřej?" Pavol had already searched the square for Lída's father, whose red-rimmed eyes were a force field keeping him from kissing Lída the way he wanted to.

"He came home a mess. He's going to be late for work again." She blew out her breath and tucked a strand of chestnut hair behind her ear. "As long as our machines don't need fixing, he'll get away with it."

Pavol winced, head throbbing from lack of sleep and his own evenings in the taverns. Lída counted on him to take her away from a father hell-bent on drinking himself to death—as if it wouldn't happen if she were in Prague and not there to see it.

The letter . . . the last chance.

Lída's voice brightened. "They're showing a Cuban film here tomorrow night." She glanced toward the former church. "Let's meet when I get off work."

"I'm going to Prague tomorrow." He ran his tongue along his upper lip and stared into gunmetal skies heavy with clouds and coal dust, picturing the faraway city on the horizon. A cold sore was emerging inside the lip, and it stung when he touched it.

"We're spending the weekend there, me and a couple of other guys from school. Delivering a letter."

"What kind of letter?" Lída shook away the unruly strand that had fallen back over one eye. Her face seemed rounder than usual, her cheeks rosier, but maybe he was imagining it because he'd miss her.

"To students at the university, to collaborate on some technical projects. So next year I'll be ready for the advanced classes." Forcing himself to look into her large brown eyes, he held his breath, not sure she'd believe him.

"Be careful, Pavol. You know those university students like to . . ."

Drink. She worried about that for him too. "Of course. I've learned my lesson." He leaned into her, sniffed her spearmint breath, pressed his lips to hers. The sting in his mouth melted away. He had to do this for her. Deliver the message. Win back their freedom . . . and his place in the university.

"I love you, Lída," he murmured between kisses.

He burrowed his hands under her shawl and wrapped his arms around her soft body. He wished he could hold her forever, freeze time in this moment of their embrace rather than watch it march onward like soldiers with their tanks and guns.

On the railway platform the next morning Pavol listened to the whistle from the east. The letter, two pages on onionskin paper he'd typed on the sly in the school's business office, was in his satchel. Štěpán stood beside him, canvas knapsack dangling from one shoulder.

"Figured Tomáš would crap out on us," Štěpán said.

Pavol shivered. It had turned cold the night before, catching him unprepared when he stumbled home from the bar, and he hadn't been able to get warm since.

"Do you want to do this?" Štěpán pressed. "I mean without him?"

After he sucked back the mucus in his nose and throat, Pavol nodded. "I'll get us in. With my pretty face, like you said."

"Right." Štěpán's smile and hand on Pavol's shoulder chased away a bit of the chill. Yes, they could do it.

They boarded the train, leaving the platform empty of people except for the white-haired couple working the coffee-and-news-paper kiosk. Along with the local Party-approved papers, the kiosk now displayed the Czech edition of *Pravda*—the news direct from their Soviet masters.

Štěpán tossed his knapsack on the empty seat across from him. Pavol hugged his satchel and stared out the window at the whitewashed station with its steep pitched roof and scattered bits of moss on the shingles, decay that ran all the way to the top. Beyond the station stood a dense forest—magnificent, mysterious, doomed. All over this region, forests waited silently for machines to chew them up in worship of the false gods of heavy industry and soft coal.

Pavol pressed his cheek to the window. The condemned forest beckoned him to save it—to save himself and his country. To take a stand against more censorship, more rules, more occupiers making the rules.

Štěpán ran his fingers through his short blond hair and pressed the gelled ends into spikes. "The freak was probably more interested in riding the train than helping us out anyway," he said, just loud enough for Pavol to hear over the *clack-clack-clack* of wheels on rough track.

"Lay off him, brácha. He's a good kid."

"His father knows people. That's all."

"Which is probably why he didn't show up." The town and forest surrendered to a desolate landscape of open-pit mines and processing plants. Pavol turned to his friend. "Would've taken a lot of guts to stand up to your father like that."

Better that he didn't show up. Less weight in Pavol's gut.

He pressed his tongue against the cold sore that had blossomed inside his mouth. The paste that he'd tapped on that morning to numb it had worn off, but the reflection from the window glass showed no redness, no swelling. All the pain on the inside.

In Prague Pavol and Štěpán approached the iron gate of the castle—the seat of the Czechoslovak government, an impenetrable Gothic beast looming over the Vltava River with stone turrets that clawed the sky. Inside, brown-uniformed Russians milled, keeping their distance from the Czechoslovak soldiers in their shiny green uniforms.

This is the moment. Clutching his satchel in a sweaty hand, Pavol stepped up to the nearest Czechoslovak guard. His heart raced, and his churning stomach sent sour liquid into his throat. He swallowed. Sucked in a breath. "We're here to visit the castle, comrade." He cleared his throat. "We have a letter."

"No one is allowed inside," the guard said.

A broad Russian stepped up, heels clicking on the stone, machine gun strapped across his back. "What's the problem?" he asked the guard in accented Czech.

The guard gestured at the junior hockey team patch on Štěpán's coat. "Couple of kiddies from the countryside. Want to get a gander." Pavol's heart sank into his stomach.

"Tell the bumpkins to get lost," the Russian ordered.

"Wait, sir! Please let us in." Pavol's throat burned. "This summer when I turn eighteen, I'm joining the Party." A lie, a bargain he'd never make, but it was all he could think to say, the only thing that might soften them. Štěpán stared at him, openmouthed.

The Russian flicked the back of his hand at them and said, "Good for you. Now go home, both of you."

"You heard him," said the Czechoslovak guard. "Scram. Your mama's teats are dripping." He wagged his machine gun at Pavol. Pain clenched Pavol's ribs, an echo of the beating from a similar weapon last August.

As the laughing soldiers retreated behind the gate, his muscles relaxed, leaving his body loose and quivery. They hadn't taken names.

"Come on," said Štěpán, yanking his skinny tie from his neck and stuffing it into his coat pocket. "I'm not missing another hockey practice for this. Let's take the next train home."

"Isn't your brother expecting us for the weekend?" Pavol asked, the air sucked from him as he thought of the only two options he had left.

"I'll phone him. He'll be thrilled he doesn't have to kick his latest girlfriend out of his bed."

As they walked back across the Charles Bridge toward Old Town, an ache seeped through Pavol's chest. He gazed up at the statues in their scaffolding cages that lined the bridge. Tattered signs on the rusted metal announced a multiyear reconstruction. The carved-stone historical and religious figures seemed to shrug at him, as silent and helpless as the grim-faced pedestrians trudging the patchwork of asphalt and cobblestone. The letter smoldered in his satchel like pieces of charcoal—too small to cook with but enough to sear flesh.

Pavol stepped off the bridge onto a narrow street. A streetcar clanged. He jumped backward to the curb and coughed out the smog that hung over the city. His knees wobbled.

"Too slow, *bumpkin*." Štěpán made a show of dusting off Pavol's shoulder. Pavol flinched. He didn't understand how his friend could think any of this was funny, but Štěpán's jokes always had bite, a remnant of his bully past.

The tall, dirt-streaked buildings closed in on Pavol, gray and menacing. "Yeah, I don't belong here." If only he hadn't come to this cruel city, if he'd stayed home with Lída even though it tore him apart to be with her and not tell her the truth.

They stopped at a café that advertised a public phone inside. The café was noisy and stuffy, full of restless students. Gone from ice-cold to broiling, Pavol unbuttoned his brown cloth jacket and fanned his face. He listened to Štěpán's side of the conversation— no letter or building mentioned, the phone certainly tapped. At one point, Štěpán put his hand over the mouthpiece and turned to Pavol.

"He said you could still stay with him. What do you want to do?"

Pavol ran the toe of his hiking boot along the sticky floor. "I'll come back with you." He pictured the faces of his mother, his sisters, Lída. He'd have to tell them the truth now.

His heartbeat stuttered.

Because, unlike Štěpán and Tomáš, he couldn't go back to the way things were, pretending this day never happened.

Because his family had counted on him, supported his studies year after year in the hope of a better life for all of them, and now that hope was gone.

Because he and Lída had planned their future together, and he couldn't be sure she'd stay with him if he no longer had that future.

Because when Jan Palach set himself on fire in January, two weeks after Pavol learned of his own fate, his university's rector begged others not to follow in his footsteps. *We need the strength, the hearts, the minds, the arms of all of you. Our country is small, and we cannot afford to lose a single man, a single woman . . .* And yet the new rulers had thrown Pavol away, as if his life, his dreams, his intelligence and hard work meant nothing.

Jan Palach's letter, signed "Torch No. 1," claimed there were more young people—*torches*, he called them—ready to set themselves on fire for freedom, although so far only Jan Zajíc, a secondary student, had done it. Newspapers called Jan Palach a madman. The government banned visitors from his grave. Nevertheless, people came by the hundreds.

Somebody else had to do this. Somebody else had to pay the price for freedom. And maybe this time, the third time flames consumed a kid with his whole life ahead of him, hearts would unharden. His people would stand up to the invaders.

Outside again, Pavol buttoned his jacket all the way to his throat, flipped up the collar, and folded his arms across his body to keep warm. He followed Štěpán through Old Town's narrow streets to the long boulevard of Wenceslas Square. In the middle of the afternoon, it was half-filled with shoppers and students. He fixed in his mind the windswept plaza in front of the National Museum where Jan Palach had collapsed. Now, only a pile of stones remained—tokens from mourners.

Will people leave stones for me? Will they rise and say, "Enough"?

As he stared at passing trams, he wished he'd paid more attention to the forest on the way, imprinted it in his mind instead of this cold city. He thought of the people he would never see again: Mama. Alžbeta, Nika, and Tereza. Tomáš, Štěpán, his other school friends. Lída. He regretted not giving them a proper goodbye.

From the square it was a few short blocks to the rail station. Štěpán bought two sandwiches while they waited for the train. Pavol took one bite of his ham and cheese and handed it over to his friend.

When the train pulled into the station, Štěpán stood and threw his knapsack over one shoulder. Pavol remained on the weathered bench.

"Coming?"

Pavol shook his head. "I changed my mind. I've never seen Prague outside a school trip."

"You gave up your place to stay." The squeal of air brakes nearly drowned out Štěpán's words, the hint of worry in them.

"I'll figure something out."

Štěpán reached into his back pocket. Pavol waved him away.

"I'm fine. I have all the money I need."

"Stop by my house when you get back. We'll go kick Tomáš's ass together." Štěpán punched his fist into the palm of his other hand. The sharp *pow!* startled Pavol.

"Don't blame him. He didn't know." Pavol's mouth was so dry he could barely get the words out. He needed a drink, something strong.

"Didn't know what?" Štěpán demanded.

Pavol stood, close enough to Štěpán that no one else in the station could overhear. "The part of the letter where we asked for a general amnesty . . ." He swallowed. "It wasn't in the abstract. I got arrested last August for trying to stop the invasion. And I didn't get into the technical university."

Štěpán gaped, and his knapsack slid down his arm. "Why didn't you say something?"

"I didn't tell anyone. Not my family, not even Lída. They all think I'm coming here in the fall." He touched his finger to his lips. His cheeks burned. "So this is my last chance to have fun in the city."

Štěpán stepped forward, a hand's length from Pavol. "Party your brains out. We can fix this when you get home. I'll talk to my father and brother. I'll even talk to Comrade Kuchař. And I promise I won't beat up Tomáš, ever."

"Yeah. Forgiveness is good."

Štěpán smiled. "The true words of Saint Pavol." He embraced Pavol and patted his back. Pavol's hand trembled against his friend's shoulder. He wanted to make the sign of the cross, to murmur a prayer of forgiveness for Tomáš . . . and for himself.

Count not my transgressions, but, rather, my tears of repentance . . . my sorrow for the offenses I have committed against You.

He had drifted away after the tanks rolled in, gone through the motions at home because of his mother, but let his faith grow hollow. Still, God would forgive him for all that he'd done, all that he was about to do. Because among those freedoms he fought for was the freedom to worship Him not only at home in secret but in the public square.

The conductor announced the final boarding call. Štěpán kept holding on to him, so long and so tightly that Pavol thought his friend suspected his plan. "Go. You'll miss your train," he said.

Štěpán lowered his arms and handed Pavol the city map from his coat pocket. "Tell me all about it when you get back." He hummed a few bars of The Doors' "Break on Through" and snapped his fingers in time to the beat.

As the train rumbled out of the chilly station, Pavol pictured his family, his friends, and Lída. In death he would lose everything.

But in their lives, he'd be one person torn away, like his father was for him. The passing years and God's grace would comfort and eventually heal.

The haunting opening of "The End"—his and Tomáš's favorite song—echoed in his mind. He blew on his fingers, which had stiffened and turned pale. After flexing them once more, he reached in his satchel for the letter and his silver mechanical pencil, the second-place prize from his school's math competition.

He pushed his hair from his face. The sore in his mouth throbbed. What he'd soon do to himself would hurt worse than anything.

At Wenceslas Square he'd make the sign of the cross . . . a final act of defiance, a prayer for forgiveness . . . and let the phoenix rise from the ashes and fly.

CHAPTER 2: ŠTĚPÁN

The train rolled north past blocky red-roofed buildings, past Vítkov Hill with its well-tended gardens and huge national monument. Štěpán turned from the window and twisted his knapsack's strap around his wrist until the circulation cut off. *Why didn't Pavol tell me about not getting into the university? I'm his best friend.*

Then again, he never told his father or brother about flubbed passes and missed shots that cost his team the game. Show weakness, and the strong fed on your carcass.

As the train crossed the Vltava River, Štěpán recalled the first day of school after the invasion, when Pavol showed up moving slowly as if each step pained him.

Štěpán had tried to embrace his friend, but Pavol edged backward. *Sorry, brácha, no hugs. I was helping my mother carry stuff for her cleaning job and fell down the stairs. I think I busted some ribs.*

At the time Štěpán couldn't help suspecting there was more to Pavol's story, just as he couldn't ignore the two sandwiches hardening into concrete in his stomach right now. He'd left Pavol alone in the city.

Štěpán dug his fingernails into his palms, thumbs out, the way he'd do before beating up some other kid. He rapped his fists against the sides of his head, squeezed his eyes shut, and tried not to scream. He hadn't slept well the night before—or any other night that week—counting down the days until their trip. Because if the Party leaders and their Soviet overlords didn't listen to poets and scholars and university students, why would they listen to schoolboys from a town in the middle of nowhere, where the train tracks split to take them, their coal, and their factory goods somewhere else?

Behind Štěpán's closed eyes, black-and-white images flickered as if on television: police whacking protestors' bodies with nightsticks, kicking them in the ribs while they lay on the ground. When the tanks rolled in, Štěpán had twice-a-day hockey practice, his world reduced to home and the ice rink. But Pavol had gone to the demonstrations all summer long. Pavol said he would have stopped the tanks with his own body if he could.

I have to fix this for him. Pavol had worked hard to get into university, and to make a better life for his family. Besides, they were supposed to be in Prague together next year.

Štěpán still waited to hear from the army hockey team. It was his lifelong dream to make the team, try out for the Olympics, and travel the world playing the sport he loved. Unlike Pavol, though, he had a backup: the literature and pedagogy program at Charles University, where he'd never have to take a math class again.

At least Pavol had the map, and on it was the phone number of Anton's dorm. Maybe there was no reason to worry. Pavol would return to the student café. Pavol was good at meeting people, fitting in, having people buy him stuff. The university students would get him drunk, take him to a dorm room to sleep it off, and send him back home with stories.

Štěpán leaned back in his seat and remembered the warmth of

Pavol's body during their long embrace in the station, so long he'd almost missed his train. He'd savored the faint aroma of sulfur in Pavol's windblown hair, a remnant of the haze that hung over their town. He smiled at the way Pavol buttoned his jacket and turned up his collar, more interested in keeping warm on this late winter day than looking sharp in the big city.

Štěpán's eyelids drooped and he dozed off until the train pulled into Most. A squad of police officers boarded, pistols in their belt holsters. They shuffled down the aisle checking everyone's tickets and identity booklets. Not yet fully awake, Štěpán passed his to them.

The young policeman motioned for him to stand.

Now alert, with knees shaking and no chance to run, Štěpán bumped the passenger next to him, mumbled an apology, and wobbled behind the uniformed man to the front of the car. Two more officers blocked the open door to the platform. Behind them hovered the gloom of coal dust and incoming night. Sweat streamed down Štěpán's body under his layers of clothing.

"School ID, Citizen Jelínek." Fingers numb, Štěpán fumbled in his wallet and handed over the laminated card. The officer was only a few years older than he was, with the build of an athlete and a smooth baby face. He could've been a hockey rival, but the uniform and gun meant he could do anything he wanted to Štěpán. Beat him. Arrest him. Have him kicked out of school or barred from the university like they did to Pavol. "Today is not a holiday. Why are you on this train?"

Štěpán fought to make his tongue say whatever the man wanted so they'd let him go. "I went to Prague to see my brother."

"Your brother. What is his name, and what does he do?"

Štěpán took a deep breath, let the air fill his tight stomach, and released it slowly, feeling its warmth in his nostrils. He did this to relax in the moments before he skated onto the ice with his team-mates for the opening faceoff.

This time it wasn't a game.

"Antonín Jelínek. He's in his second year at Czech Technical University. I'm starting university in the fall and wanted him to show me around the city."

"Cutting school then."

"You could say that, comrade."

"Did anyone travel with you?"

Štěpán's throat twitched. Had someone followed him and Pavol to the castle, or after? He'd looked for cops on the way across the bridge and back, while Pavol gazed at the statues of saints and kings as if he still lived in a country that worshipped them.

Štěpán couldn't snitch on his friend and have the police find the letter in his possession. "No, comrade. I was alone."

The officer wrote something in a small notebook. Drying sweat itched under Štěpán's collar. They were writing down his name, his hometown, his brother's name. With that information, they could learn almost everything about him if they wanted to.

Standing there at the policemen's mercy, Štěpán realized he could do nothing to fix things for Pavol. *They* had all the power. There was no such thing as fairness in their world.

The man gave back the documents. "Have a good trip, Jelínek."

"Didn't you say you'd be gone all weekend?" his co-captain, Petr Kolodny, asked when Štěpán pulled into a parking space for their predawn practice. Living a quarter kilometer away, Petr had walked in darkness to the modern school and regional athletic complex and now shone his flashlight in Štěpán's face as if conducting his own interrogation. Štěpán shuddered. His friend's military-style haircut reminded him of the officer on the train.

Štěpán lifted his equipment from the trunk of his parents' pocked and faded blue Trabi, bought secondhand after they joined the Party eight years ago and put their names on a long waiting list. "Anton's girlfriend made other plans for him."

"Bummer. Hope she's cute for all that," Petr said.

"I wouldn't know. She's from Prague. She won't come out to the sticks."

As usual, Štěpán told a half-truth. Anton had brought her home once. Yet seeing her holding hands and snuggling with his brother felt as distant and unreal as watching a romantic drama on a black-and-white television. Everyone agreed she looked fine, but she didn't move anything inside him.

When Štěpán was with his teammates, it was like being in the theater—the movie on a large screen and in color. Take the same movie and add music, rock music, so loud it made his body pulse—that's what it was like to be with Pavol, just the two of them.

He couldn't risk revealing that, of course. Anyway, Pavol wouldn't reciprocate. He had that dark-eyed girlfriend, Lída. The one everyone called Gypsy.

He'd called her that until Pavol told him: *She's not Roma. Her mother died when she was young, and she moved around a lot with her father. Even if she were, it doesn't matter. We're all the same in the eyes of God.*

That was last year, when they could listen to loud rock music and Pavol could talk about God and what he believed. Štěpán didn't believe, but Pavol's stories about the creation of the world and God sending His son to die for humanity's sins captivated him the way a great novel did.

Some things Štěpán could never talk about, though, not even with a once-in-a-lifetime best friend. He couldn't be sure Pavol's God considered him *all the same*.

For as long as he could remember, he and his teammates passed around the slurs like candy, whenever someone messed up or backed off a hard check or a fight on the ice. By hitting the hardest Štěpán proved himself. But at the junior national tournament in Prague that beautiful spring, he'd followed a couple of older players from Holešovice to an underground club after their team had kicked his team's asses.

In a basement near Wenceslas Square, men danced together, their bodies so close they could've been joined. The rival hockey players told him about a bookstore in Prague where he could buy Czech translations of a great American poet who was like them.

Like him.

The next day, Štěpán tracked down those books that Comrade Dubček had allowed into the country for the first time. The American poet Walt Whitman became his guide.

I celebrate myself, and sing myself,
And what I assume you shall assume,
For every atom belonging to me as good belongs to you.

In practice jersey and pads, Štěpán skated onto the ice, the verses still running through his head. Coach Hájek's voice drowned them out. "Jelínek, I see you've decided to show up after all."

Štěpán tapped the ice with his stick. "Yes, Coach. Tournament's too important to skip practice."

"He's lying," Petr said. "He got shipped home on the next train because Anton's girlfriend said he's too ugly."

"It's not like you're getting any, Comrade No Teeth." Štěpán skated past Petr, quickly pivoted, and shot shards of ice toward his co-captain's face. He shoved in his mouth guard. Petr refused to wear one and had lost two front teeth while Štěpán still had all his.

Girls like guys with teeth, Štěpán told Petr last year.

No they don't. Real men get theirs knocked out playing hard, Petr answered.

They'd made a bet on who would score with the girls, teeth or no teeth. So far, they'd tied: 0–0. Not that he was searching, but Petr was, so Štěpán counted it a win for the teeth.

"Let's get it together, guys. We have work to do." Coach Hájek skated toward them, pointed Petr to the center and Štěpán to the left wing. They ran through the plays and skirmished with the second line. Alternating with the right wing, Štěpán swatted the puck to Petr and scooped up the rebounds with such precision that he could've done it blindfolded. *We are a machine.* He imagined his team against Russians, dismantling the enemy on the ice.

Everyone was on edge because in one week, the Rozcestí squad would defend their regional championship against seven other teams. A tournament victory would give Štěpán one more trophy than Anton ever won, one more victory in a rivalry that began the day of his birth.

Follow-the-rules-do-what-they-say Anton. Younger, and for many years smaller, Štěpán learned early on that he had to break the rules, fight on his own terms, and it made every win that much sweeter.

At eight the team finished practice. Štěpán followed the others into the locker room, taking his time so that most of them would finish and leave before he stepped into the shower. He needed his space alone, eyes focused on the cinderblock wall. During practice, he'd put the police officer out of his mind, but now the young officer's sneering face popped up like a propaganda poster on the wall. *He wrote down my name.*

Under the hot water Štěpán conjured Pavol in the man's place. At that moment, what was Pavol doing? Was he curled up in his underwear on a dorm room floor, sleeping off a night of partying? Or stumbling through Prague's streets shoulder to shoulder with his new friends, singing folk songs to greet the sunrise?

"Coming to breakfast, Štěpán?" Petr called.

"Yeah, give me a minute." Štěpán turned off the faucet and quickly wrapped the towel around his middle.

Another voice came from above and behind Petr. Squeaky, like one of the younger kids on the second line. "Someone says he's here to see Jelínek."

The police? Muscles tense, Štěpán dressed, grabbed his gear, and raced upstairs.

Several hockey players surrounded skinny Tomáš, whose dark brown hair fell into his face. Behind his glasses, his eyes were red and swollen. He clutched a calculus textbook to his chest.

"What's that loser doing here?" Petr asked.

Cold dread trickled down Štěpán's spine. He glanced between his teammates and the school's number one social outcast, who didn't show up when he should have and now turned up when he shouldn't. "Tutoring me." He winked, a forced gesture. "'Cause I'm a dumbass jock."

"So no breakfast for you," Petr said.

"Yeah. I guess I'll feed my mind instead." Štěpán waved the black-taped knob of his stick toward them, and the group lumbered off.

As soon as they were out of earshot, Štěpán lowered his voice. "Why are you here?"

Tears welled in the corners of Tomáš's eyes. His glasses slid down his nose. "It's Pavol. He set himself on fire in Prague."

"Wait, what do you mean? He was in an accident?" Štěpán squeezed his gear bag so hard his fingernails dug into his palm.

"Not an accident. He did it at the same place as Jan Palach." With the back of one hand Tomáš pushed his glasses into place. "He died at the hospital."

Štěpán dropped his bag. His stick clattered on the floor. "No!" His voice echoed in the cavernous lobby, all concrete floors and walls. "That can't be."

No way. Impossible. He'd left Pavol in the train station. Alive. Planning a fun weekend. "You're making this up."

"I'm not. His sister—the oldest one—came over an hour ago and she told me."

Štěpán grabbed Tomáš's shoulders. "Bullshit. Where is he?"

Tomáš trembled. "I don't know. Prague. His mother left for Prague."

Štěpán's heart wrenched. Though Pavol had refused his money and the offer to stay with Anton, he'd taken the map. *I'll figure something out*, he'd said. While flashing his luminous smile like he was about to have a grand adventure.

Štěpán tightened his grip on Tomáš's scrawny body. "You're lying, you little turd!"

"I swear I'm not." Tomáš's eyes bulged. "He was my friend too!"

I have all the money I need. Pavol never had enough money, not for a whole weekend. Štěpán hadn't thought to press him.

No one needs money when they're about to die.

Blood simmered in Štěpán's brain. "Damn you, Tomáš. You could have gotten us in with the letter. But no, you had to be the baby you are, and now he's dead."

Štěpán shoved Tomáš, whose back and head smacked against the concrete wall below the mural of a smiling railway construction crew. His book crashed to the floor.

"You killed him!" Štěpán stepped forward and swung. His fist connected, and the impact reverberated through his arm. Tomáš's glasses flew from his face. Blood spurted from his nose. Štěpán didn't care. He didn't need to forgive Tomáš. Pavol would never return.

Tomáš raised his hands to protect his face. His next words were barely more than a whisper. "You're here. You left him too."

Štěpán froze, fist in midair.

Why did I leave him alone right after he'd told me about the university? His life was over, and I couldn't fix it, not when they wouldn't even take the letter. But I could've at least been there for him.

"What's going on?" Štěpán recognized Petr's voice, low and harsh. He was supposed to have left for breakfast.

"Nothing."

Petr and others grabbed his arms and pulled him from Tomáš. "Doesn't look like nothing to me."

Štěpán tried to wriggle free, but the pain in his shoulders and elbows stopped him. At the edge of his vision, Tomáš scooped up his glasses and textbook and fled, leaving drops of blood to mark his trail.

"Better not let Coach Hájek see what you did," Petr said, pushing Štěpán against Moučka, the goalie. "You get suspended, we're screwed next week."

"Tomáš won't say anything," Štěpán said.

"He'd better not." Petr glanced toward the door. "Good thing I forgot my flashlight and came back before you killed him."

Štěpán let his body go limp. He could tell by the way they glared at him what they were thinking: *Bully. Punk. He'll never change, no matter what he claims.* He *had* changed, but sometimes, it was so hard to show it.

25

Petr shoved Štěpán's bag into his midsection. "Clean it up."

His teammates walked away, leaving him holding his bag and wondering what, if anything, to say. Did they overhear? Did they know already and not care?

"Petr," he called out, because they did care. Everyone liked Pavol. Petr turned, hand on the door latch.

Štěpán choked back the cry in his throat. "Pavol Bartoš is dead."

CHAPTER 3: TOMÁŠ

Tomáš rushed outside the building into the chill gray morning. If the other hockey players hadn't shown up, Štěpán would have killed him, and he deserved it.

He tipped his head back and squeezed his nostrils shut with his fingers until the blood stopped dripping. His nose and left cheek throbbed, a pulsing heat in his body shaking with cold and terror. He wiped his glasses with his shirt, dropped his textbook into the basket of his bicycle, and walked the bike toward home. He didn't trust himself to stay upright on Rozcestí's cobblestoned and rutted roads. Sulfuric coal smoke mixed with the metallic scent of his blood.

Never again would he listen to The Doors' "The End" with his first and one true friend.

He used to give Pavol money to buy albums from the older kids at school. They stashed them at Pavol's apartment because Tomáš's father didn't permit any music except classical and military marches.

Don't let that boy use you, Tomáš's older sister warned when she came home from university last summer and found out how much he'd spent.

He's not using me. He really is my friend.

Sofie gave him the big-sister-knows-best eye roll, but when their father left town for Party meetings, she lingered in the living room to listen with him and Pavol.

Tomáš passed the rail station, a neighborhood with tall stucco row houses turned into apartments, and the main square with people going about their business as if nothing had happened. He wanted to grab them, shake them, and shout, *Stop! This is not a normal day.*

At each newsstand he scanned the headlines, papers from Prague, from Most, from Ústí. No mention of a seventeen-year-old student from Rozcestí who set himself on fire and would never walk these streets again.

He clenched his fists, wanting to shout into the empty sky: *Why did you do it? Didn't you care about who you left behind?*

His tender, swollen nose reminded him that wasn't the whole story. He'd promised to go with Pavol and Štěpán, make sure they got into the castle to deliver the letter. He knew some of the guards, the ones who'd tried to muss his hair when he was little and laughed when he squirmed away. They would've remembered him and let all of them in.

Pavol's oldest sister, Alžbeta, had said the authorities found a satchel leaning against the wall of an arcade facing Wenceslas Square. That's how they'd identified Pavol's body. She'd called it an accident, like a toddler careless with matches. She'd said nothing about the letter.

But Štěpán had.

If I'd gone to Prague, you'd still be alive.

Tomáš leaned his bicycle against the iron fence surrounding the garden in front of his family's whitewashed two-story house, one of the largest in Rozcestí, built on a hill overlooking the town's red and gray rooftops. *The walled garden*, Pavol called it, as if it were the paradise from his Bible stories.

Inside, the aroma of coffee filled the living room, along with Dvořák's Symphony no. 7 in D Minor His father awaited him, unshaven and in pajamas. His gray hair was disheveled, his eyes narrow slits.

Tomáš's breath caught in his throat. He'd expected his father to still be asleep.

After Alžbeta had arrived, sobbing, he'd dressed in a rush, snatched the thick calculus textbook that he took everywhere, and jumped on his bicycle. Hoping to find Štěpán at hockey practice because . . .

He should have gone to Prague with them.

He didn't know what else to do. He was, in his father's words, *borderline antisocial*, despite his perfect scores and his efforts to tutor anyone who would have him.

Alžbeta's tears had unnerved him. He didn't understand death. How did it feel to have flesh burn? How long before a heart stopped beating?

"I was worried when you left," his mother said.

"Where were you?" his father growled.

"Tutoring." Tomáš wrapped his arms around the textbook with its crumpled and ruined pages.

"You're lying," his father said. "Who beat you up?"

"No one."

Comrade Kuchař snatched the book and slammed it on the end table. The needle skipped on the record. Tomáš cringed. "It was one of the hockey players, right?"

Of course his father had guessed. Why else would he have gone to the school-and-recreation complex early on a Saturday morning? Tomáš pressed his trembling lower lip with a bloody finger.

"What were you doing with those boys? You know what they think of you."

"I was helping . . ." He glanced toward the book.

"Which one? That ox Jelínek?"

"Yes," Tomáš mumbled. The teachers called Štěpán an ox, though Jelínek actually meant *stag*, a name he wore with pride. For years Štěpán had been the ringleader, the first to trip Tomáš in class, shove him into the coat closet, or yank his pants down in gym.

"I'll get you some ice," his mother said. She slipped into the kitchen.

Tomáš didn't want the ice. He wanted her there, to protect him from his father's fury.

Comrade Kuchař stepped forward, carrying with him the stench of stale beer that overpowered the coffee. "Did you even fight back?"

Tomáš averted his eyes. Dvořák's symphony reached a crescendo.

The slap, across his bruised cheek and battered nose, knocked off his glasses. His face exploded in agony. Salty, metallic saliva filled his mouth, and when he exhaled, blood flecked his shirt.

"Pansy. Stop embarrassing me."

Comrade Kuchař hurled Tomáš against the front door. A spike of pain shot down his arm.

Tomáš pulled himself up straight, his back to the door. He gripped the doorknob and waited for his father to hit him again, to beat him to a bloody pulp. He wanted to feel some of what Pavol felt—Pavol, who had suffered and died to stop injustice.

Instead, Comrade Kuchař spat at his feet and said, "Go to your room."

Tomáš picked up his glasses and plodded up the stairs. His face stung. When he touched it, his fingers came away shiny with fresh blood. In the bathroom, he scrubbed his upper lip and rinsed his face over and over with cold water. His left cheek was swollen and bright red. He ripped a paper tissue in half, wadded it into his nostril to stop the bleeding, and put his glasses back on.

His mother came upstairs with the ice pack. "I'm sorry," she said. "I'll talk to him."

"Won't do any good. Never has," he muttered. Always the nurse, his mother. Trying to fix things after the damage had been done.

His bedroom under the eaves was large but crowded with a bed, desk, waist-high shelves packed with books, and—atop four folding tables pushed together in the middle of the room—the train set he'd collected since he was six years old. When he was little, his father had spared no expense, buying trains, tracks, two stations, and houses and storefronts imported from Germany. But once he turned twelve, Comrade Kuchař said he was too old for children's things.

Let's make a deal. You sign up for the youth leadership classes, and I'll buy you one piece for your set each year.

Tomáš took the Marxist-Leninist classes, even convincing his father to buy extra track and buildings for his perfect test scores. He liked studying the theories, the ideas organized neatly and scientifically like a perfectly calibrated machine. Or like a puzzle that he could solve, one that made life less messy and scary and confusing.

When Pavol first talked about socialism with a human face, Tomáš didn't understand, much as he didn't recognize actual faces.

The machine was predictable. Comforting. Safe.

He was so much better with problem sets and the grammar of foreign languages than with people. Now, the one person he understood—the one person who understood and liked *him*—was gone forever.

31

He glanced toward the blank wall above his bed. Last week his father had ordered him to remove the black-and-white poster of Marta Kubišová—the image of her standing in a forest wearing tight jeans, her dark hair windblown. According to his father, the singer's work was now considered pornography. When she won the national song contest two years ago, Pavol had helped him put up the poster. They'd been friends from math club for months already, and Pavol didn't mind when Tomáš insisted it had to be lined up correctly.

We're engineers. We're supposed to be precise. Otherwise our buildings collapse, Pavol had said with a nod.

Tomáš switched on the train's power supply. He tracked the cars as they hummed and clicked past the buildings, through the fake-grass-topped tunnels. Moving perfectly along their closed circular track, no complications. He slowed at the station.

"All aboard!" he called, muffling his words with one hand.

He imagined the small, brightly painted people climbing onto the train, bound for other lands.

He should've boarded that train. Pavol would still be alive, maybe in his room moving the little people around the village and countryside while discussing Comrade Dubček's ideas.

Socialism with a human face means we get a say in our lives. We aren't pieces of a machine but human beings who feel and think. We care about each other, and we care for the woods, the river, the creatures, and the air we breathe.

Pavol would always hesitate before saying the next thing, even during the brief time when they had the freedom to say it aloud.

We have the right to worship God. The Creator of all.

Tomáš didn't know much about God or religion, and Pavol's praying to the Virgin Mary but then spending his nights with a girlfriend baffled him even more. Tomáš had never met Lída, didn't know her last name, hadn't seen her house in the woods—which sounded like something out of a fairy tale. But he'd seen the effect she had on Pavol.

Early in January, Pavol had caught up to Tomáš at the end of school and said, *If my mother asks, tell her I'm spending the night with you.*

It was the first of many times. Once Mrs. Bartošová did ask him, and he answered the way Pavol had instructed him while staring at his loafers.

Anything happen that I should know about?

He hadn't expected a follow-up question. He hadn't rehearsed that possibility with Pavol.

No, Mrs. Bartošová. He shifted from one foot to the other.

He came home green around the gills. Were you two drinking?

No, ma'am. I don't drink.

Would Alžbeta tell Lída what had happened to Pavol? The memory of Štěpán's fist made Tomáš grateful he didn't have to be the bearer of bad news again.

A rap came at the door. He cut the power to his train set so his father wouldn't see him playing with it. The engine coasted to a stop before the tunnel, in front of a ski chalet.

He opened the door, grateful his father hadn't simply burst in. This was also their deal, to help him become more *socially adept.* When Tomáš was younger, he'd barge into his parents' or sister's room unannounced. They'd agreed to make the same rule for everyone: knock before entering. He could refuse to let Sofie in, but not his parents.

Comrade Kuchař sat at the desk and motioned for Tomáš to sit on the bed. Ordering him around in his own room. An anxious pang coursed through his body as he waited for his father to mete out a punishment, to make him pay for not fighting back against a bully.

Comrade Kuchař cleared his throat. "I apologize for hitting you. Something has happened."

Tomáš touched his tender cheek. Along with the apology was always the *but*—whatever he'd done wrong to make his father rage.

This time, though, his father lowered his head. "Your friend, the one who used to come to dinner. He passed away last night."

It sounded so peaceful, *passed away*. Not like how Alžbeta described it.

"I'm sorry, son. I thought he was a solid young man."

Tomáš's jaw tightened. He covered his mouth and bit the heel of his hand to keep a scream from bursting out.

His father continued. "Sometimes we don't know people as well as we think. They have secret lives. Problems they don't share with us." His salt-and-pepper mustache moved up and down as he spoke. It made Tomáš think of the soft-bristled paintbrushes he used to dust his train set. Grown out and bushy, it bore a not-so-faint resemblance to Stalin's mustache, but Tomáš couldn't be sure because at one point when he was young, all the pictures of Stalin vanished from books and billboards.

Tomáš lowered his hand and spoke through gritted teeth. "Papa, my friend is dead. What does this have to do with anything?"

His father leaned forward in the chair, rested his elbows on his knees, and fixed his eyes on Tomáš's. That's what a man did when things got serious, looked other men in the eye. But eyes drilled through Tomáš and faces twisted and faded into a blur.

Tomáš forced his gaze to remain on his father's eyes, bloodshot inside puffy lids. Last night he'd heard broken bottles, his father shouting, his mother pleading.

"Pavol Bartoš set himself on fire in Prague. Some people will say he did it as an act of protest against the normalization.

Understand, son, that we're doing what we must to defend our socialist revolution against dangerous revisionism."

I wrote the letter with Pavol and Štěpán. I promised to go with them. Tomáš pressed his lips together to keep from blurting out the words.

"That boy was no hero. In fact, the opposite." His father rubbed his eyes. "At best, he was a copycat, following the degenerate Jan Palach, letting himself be influenced by reactionary imperialist forces."

He leaned back in his chair, sighed, rested his forearms on his thick belly.

"At worst, he was an agent of capitalism, deliberately undermining the revolution and demoralizing our young people." He paused. "Which was it, son? You knew him."

Tomáš's mouth was parched when he spoke. His father had that way of grinding all his anger, all his resolve, into dust. "I-I don't know. Like you said, he didn't share his problems with me."

"You spent a lot of time with him."

Tomáš sucked in his breath. "We didn't talk politics." He hated lying. But he'd learned years ago that lying meant survival. All he had to do was tell himself it was another kind of truth, like solving one math problem for x and the same problem for x^{-1}.

"Sofie said you bought record albums for him. How many times have I told you not to let people like him take advantage of you?"

"A . . . lot." Because it didn't start with Pavol. All the way through primary school, he bought candy and toys for the other kids so they would play with him. Pavol was different, though. He didn't just take the stuff. They listened to the albums together. Pavol explained the world to him.

"You need to testify at the local Party meeting that Pavol

Bartoš was mentally ill. That he killed himself because he suffered from depression. We will make the letters disappear."

"Letters? There were letters?" *More than one?*

"He wrote a suicide note on the back of a typed letter full of reactionary propaganda."

Tomáš's stomach clenched, as tight as his father's fist. "What did it say?" He could scarcely get the words out.

"The typed letter, the usual counter-revolutionary claptrap."

Tomáš's eyelid twitched, and his cheek throbbed along with it. *Those were my words!* Words Pavol and Štěpán convinced him would make a difference. Words he'd learned in his political leadership classes, where for seven months they got to debate what Comrade Dubček meant when he said they had *not only the right, but the duty, to act according to your conscience.*

"And the note—something about loving life so much that he had to give it up." Comrade Kuchař waved a hand. "What do you expect? He was obviously disturbed."

We are created in the image of God, and life is precious, Pavol had said. Had Tomáš's father made the whole thing up? Or misread the note so it didn't make sense?

"You don't need me, Papa. You can tell them. He came over for dinner all the time."

His father shook his head. "I don't think you're following me." Comrade Kuchař turned to face the train set, the engine parked in front of the tunnel, awaiting its fate. He held up a finger. "One. It would carry a lot more weight coming from you. Someone who saw him in school every day, not twice a month for a meal."

"You can ask his teachers. They'll give you his test scores and conduct reports."

A second finger went up. "Two, he had other friends whose reputations could be on the line. Like Comrade Jelínek's boy—"

"You mean the one who beat me up this morning?" Tomáš wasn't supposed to interrupt, but he couldn't stop himself.

"His father is my subordinate. I have a duty to him."

Comrade Jelínek worked for the state railway. That was all Tomáš really knew about the man.

"He's a good accountant," his father went on, "but the Party suspects he's unreliable. If his son was involved in this, that would reflect badly on Comrade Jelínek."

Just because he signed a petition?

Tomáš shook his head. His gaze wandered to the blank spot on the wall, the missing poster of the singer his father had suddenly accused of pornography. None of this made sense. "On the other hand, if Pavol acted alone, there'll be no need to investigate the Jelínek family."

Now Tomáš understood. By painting Pavol as a lone madman, he'd be protecting others. Not just Štěpán but Štěpán's parents and brother, and even the railway's operations.

His father raised a third finger. "Finally, you need to clear your own name."

"Me?"

"People have seen you two together. I'm not going to sugarcoat it. You've had problems getting along with others. Your behavior might be considered antisocial."

That word again.

"We let you get away with a lot of things, like spending time with that boy even though he concerned us. We invited him over in part to keep an eye on him."

Tomáš gulped. His parents had always acted so nice toward Pavol. Whenever he came for dinner, Tomáš's mother would wrap leftovers for Pavol to take to his family. Had they been faking it all along?

"Now that you're turning eighteen, son, the consequences are far more serious."

"Consequences? They can't send me to prison because of Pavol, can they?"

"We don't send people to prison for psychopathy. There are hospitals for that purpose."

The words were a knife twisting in Tomáš's gut. His father would describe people sent away *for their own good*, as a warning. The kids in school and youth camp talked about it to taunt him. He wanted to crawl under his table, wrap himself into a tight ball, rock himself until he calmed down, but it would only prove his unfitness to live in society.

Comrade Kuchař glanced toward the train set. "If you testify, I'll make it worth your while."

Tomáš squeezed his eyes shut. Was that what Pavol's life meant—another piece for his train set?

"When do I have to do this?"

"We'll investigate first." The chair squeaked as his father rose to his feet. "I expect we'll finish next week, so be ready."

"Yes, sir ... *Comrade*," Tomáš whispered to his departing back.

THREE MONTHS BEFORE

DECEMBER 22, 1968

CHAPTER 4: LÍDA

The Sunday before Christmas, Pavol's mother invited Lída and her father for dinner. Pavol's family lived on the ground floor of a subdivided building near the town center—a solid, well-lit space so different from the wood-and-stone cottage in the woods where Lída and her father had moved two summers ago. In some ways, Pavol's family was even poorer than hers. Their two rooms, not counting the shared kitchen and bathroom, had little furniture, and meat thickened the potato stew only because of the rabbit that Lída had trapped and brought to them. But it was a foundation. A piece of a community. A place where someone could grow up strong.

It was the life Lída wanted with Pavol: to read his books over his shoulder in a student apartment in Prague, learn his family's Slovak language, show she wasn't the kráva her aunt and everyone at school had called her.

After Pavol's mother served the meal and sat at the head of the table, they clasped hands. Lída squeezed Pavol's smooth warm palm and her father's fingers, knobby and twisted from a lifetime of battles.

Accustomed to saying grace from previous invitations to their home, Lída joined Pavol, his mother, and his three sisters as they recited, "Bless us, O Lord, and these, Thy gifts, which we are about to receive from Thy bounty, through Christ, our Lord. Amen."

Her father grunted.

"Pa, *please*," she whispered.

Lída wondered if the youngest sister, Tereza, eight years old and sitting right next to him, detected the caustic odor on Ondřej Pekár's breath and skin. He had started early, or maybe never finished from the night before. Had the Christmas season not meant so much to Pavol's family, Lída would've once again come alone and made excuses for him.

If anyone noticed her father's condition, they said nothing, and Sunday dinner passed without incident. Ondřej scraped his share of meat onto Tereza's plate, winning a smile from her and a glare from Nika, her next-older sister. They talked about winter's early start that year, all three sisters on the honor roll at their primary school, the math contests Pavol had entered, and his plans to become a civil engineer, building railroad tracks over rivers and through mountains.

Like the Soviet occupation, Lída's job—or the fact that she had a job instead of finishing school—was one of those things they didn't talk about. Even though as many girls left school at sixteen to work in the factories as boys did to extract the brown coal that lay under the hills on the way to Most, she'd never planned to be one of them. But she didn't have high test scores to protect her from a government that had turned her father's work absences into her problem.

Days after she'd started her final year at the girls' school, the principal escorted her to the office, where a Party functionary waited. *Ondřej Pekár is a fine mechanic*, he said while her principal looked on, silent. *We need you to make sure he gets to the factory to do his work. The only way we can do it is have you show up with him.*

Her principal added, *For unusual academic talent, we could've made an exception. We encourage you to continue your studies in night school.* She handed Lída a schedule of evening classes at the town library, classes she'd never be able to take without electricity at home to do her assignments after working all day.

The schedule offered nothing for her real dreams, to direct the kind of movies shown at the community center. Movies filmed all over the world, from the deserts of Siberia to the tropical forests of Cuba. In the spring before the tanks, a woman director, Věra Chytilová, had even come to Rozcestí to talk about the movies she'd made.

A girl like her had to be practical, though. Lída would study nursing if she had the chance.

She and Pavol had come up with a plan to go to Prague together. *A five-year plan*, he joked, but for her, a plan for life.

After dinner ended and Lída helped Pavol's mother and sisters carry the dishes out to the kitchen, her father stood and rested his hand on Pavol's shoulder.

"Walk back with Lída and me." His gravelly voice still carried a commander's authority from his years in the Czech Resistance during the Nazi occupation.

Lída pressed her lips together in a weak smile. Until now, her father had withheld his approval, even though she'd introduced Pavol to him in the spring and they'd met several times over the summer at rallies to support Comrade Dubček's reform government. Since she wasn't yet eighteen, she needed her father's permission to go to Prague with Pavol in September. She also needed to make sure he could get along without her.

The three of them crossed the main square and walked along slick cobblestones to the muddy uphill path on the town's northern edge. Lída's father edged closer to Pavol. "Call me Ondřej."

"Yes, sir, Mr. Pekár."

Lída laughed and took Pavol's hand. So polite. So endearing.

It was bitterly cold, light fading fast on the shortest day of the year, coal dust turning the sun a bloody orange on the horizon. Lída pressed herself against Pavol for warmth, crunching through the thin icy crust of puddles rather than let him go. She wanted her father to see how much she loved Pavol.

As he followed her inside the cottage, Pavol ducked to avoid hitting his head on the lintel. Lída pushed her rolled-up mattress and blankets against the front wall under the window to create a makeshift sofa. It faced the handmade pine table, four chairs, and two stacked cupboards—keepsakes from her father's years working on collective farms. Behind the wood stove next to the dining area, a plastic curtain hid his bedroom.

Ondřej lit the wood stove, fanning the flames with a newspaper that he tossed into the firebox before slamming the metal door.

"I guess I'd better be getting back to town, Mr. Pekár," Pavol said, bowing slightly as if he was already exiting through the front door. "I'm meeting some friends from school."

"Ondřej."

"Right." Pavol hesitated. "Ondřej."

Lída's father opened the bottom cupboard and brought out an unlabeled bottle of homebrew slivovice along with two shot glasses. He set the bottle and glasses next to a candle on the table.

"Pa, no."

"Sit, kid." Ondřej held his hand, palm up, over one of the chairs. "I see you're surrounded by women. I'll show you how to be a man."

He filled both glasses to the brim. Lída shuddered.

How do you plan to support my daughter? Will you help her go back to school and finish her education? Those were the questions a father should have asked. Not *How much can you drink before you pass out?*

43

She stood on tiptoe and whispered in Pavol's ear, "You don't have to do this."

Pavol touched his lips to her cheek. The lightest of pressure melted the chill inside her. "My mother isn't expecting me," he said. "And my friends can wait because there's no school tomorrow."

A pang shot through Lída's heart. The shoe factory didn't have the day off. They would work right up to Christmas and if needed, on the day itself. Christmas meant nothing to the invaders.

Ondřej drained his glass and poured another. "Okay, I've had a head start. I assume this isn't your first time."

With a shake of his head, Pavol sat at the table and lifted his glass. Lída had seen him drink a few beers with his friends while she pretended to sip the bitter liquid from her bottle. She kept track of Pavol whenever they went to parties and taverns. Back when she lived with her aunt and uncle in Znojmo, Aunt Irina—herself an expert on how to choose shitty men—warned her never to marry someone who drank. *I tell you this because girls gravitate to boys like their fathers.*

Lída wanted the opposite of her father. Someone stable, who could move to a place and grow roots. Make friends. Be the kindest one among their friends.

Pavol Bartoš is the kindest boy in Rozcestí. Not bad-looking either. She'd heard that from Daria, the Roma girl in her class, the one who befriended her when she arrived from Znojmo via Pardubice and Liberec and Ústí nad Labem and Most.

Yet he seemed to want to take her father's test, and Lída didn't know how to stop him.

"I'm going out for water and kindling. We're running low," she told them. She would need to heat water for coffee in the morning, to make sure her father showed up at the factory along with her. So he wouldn't lose yet another job and force them to move again.

44

Lída filled and lit a kerosene lantern and picked up the bucket. The creek where she fetched water, scrubbed their clothes, and bathed in warmer weather ran parallel to the road, an easy walk. After breaking a thin coating of ice, scooping up water, and leaving the bucket by her door, she followed a narrow trail through the woods in the opposite direction, past the latrine, to the railroad tracks. Her shoes left prints in the shallow snow that lingered on the sunless path long after it had melted everywhere else. She sat on the track where she and Pavol had spent so many hours over the summer, trading *I love you*s and talking about their future in freedom. Puffs of snow on the underbrush refracted the lantern's flickering orange light.

They'd met at a poorly chaperoned dance in the cafeteria of the all-boys' technical school in February 1968. Daria had talked Lída into going, along with Daria's twin brother Grigor, a student there. Lída stood with the Roma kids against one wall while other kids danced to the booming music they called *rock 'n' roll*. Lída tapped her foot in time to the rhythm, then shook her hips when she thought no one was looking. Grigor and two of his friends smoked skinny hand-rolled cigarettes. A harsh laugh made her stiffen.

"Well if it isn't the track sweepers." The voice above her was slurred, its owner's face bright red and beaded with perspiration. His gelled-up blond hair glistened. He stepped so close Lída could breathe in the stench, like her father's acrid sweat when he staggered home late. She pressed her back to the wall.

Behind the boy were two others—dark-haired, tall, and solid. They wrapped their arms around each other's shoulders, a human snowplow. Grigor and his friends, so much smaller, held their palms out in a gesture of submission. Caught where they didn't belong, even though the Roma boys in the special integration program were also invited to the dance.

A gangly boy approached with a purposeful expression. His hair, the color of wet sand, covered the tips of his ears and crept down his neck. Like the others, he'd taken off his jacket, loosened his tie, and unbuttoned his shirt collar. His neck was pale and pimply, and below his Adam's apple a wooden cross dangled from a leather cord. The Communists had banned displays of religion. He was the first boy she'd seen with a cross.

He's a brave one.

He tapped the drunk boy's forearm with his fist. "What's up, brácha?"—though they didn't look at all like brothers.

"A bunch of dirty gypsies stinking the place up."

Lída noticed how the new boy looked Grigor in the eye as he said, "How's that our business, Štěpán? We came here to have fun. Listen to music. Dance."

"Get drunk." One of the darker-haired boys held up a metal flask.

"Meet girls," the skinny boy said.

"Lot of good that'll do you, Saint Pavol." The drunk one in the middle pointed to the cross. Its wearer grinned as if the name suited him.

He stepped forward and bowed to Lída and Daria. "Ladies . . . gentlemen. I am so sorry for the behavior of my friends this evening. I promise that it will not happen again. Please excuse us."

His friends laughed and slapped his back as they moved toward the dance floor.

"That's Pavol Bartoš," Daria told Lída as soon as he and the others left. "The only decent one of the bunch."

Grigor said, "There's another gadjo who doesn't mess with us, but he's not here. He never comes to parties."

"Neither would I, if I didn't get points for being here," one of Grigor's friends said.

Lída chewed the inside of her lip. She didn't belong here. She should never have let Daria convince her to come. The Roma kids had to prove they'd integrated into society even though they'd never be accepted as equals. And here she was, the only one among them who wasn't Roma, doing nothing to keep away the kids who wanted to mess with them.

Because the others would only mess with her too.

Daria elbowed Lída's upper arm, urging her forward. "Pavol's cute. You should dance with him."

"Oh, no. Not me." Lída's voice wavered. She'd never danced with a boy before. Constantly moving, living alone with her father in forest cottages abandoned by Party officials as soon as the government gave them better ones, she'd become invisible, ghost-like. As if she could come and go and leave no footprints.

With delicate hands, Daria pushed her toward the center of the room. She could've resisted, but she didn't. She found herself at the snack table, facing Pavol.

"Thank you for your help with my friends," she shouted over the music.

He smiled. His Adam's apple bobbed up and down. "You're new here, right?"

Blood rushed to her face. "How do you know?"

"I go to all the dances. This is the first time I've seen you."

He spoke Czech with an accent. "You're not from Rozcestí either," she said.

"Slovakia. A village near Banská Bystrica."

Lída pictured his village on a map. Her father had fought with the partisans there during the Second World War. "So you're used to a whole different language."

Pavol shrugged. "It hasn't been too hard to adjust. In Slovak, *Rozcestí* means the same thing as in Czech: 'a fork in the road' or 'a parting of the ways.'" He shook his hair back. "Kind of ominous, don't you think?"

"So do you think romance is doomed for people in this town? Like one of those tragic movies?" She clapped her hand over her mouth. What a ridiculous thing to say.

He laughed, then pointed at the loudspeaker. "Do you like the Beatles?"

Lída nodded. The music was wild, aggressive, and free, the words as foreign as the instruments and rhythms.

"This music was banned here until a few weeks ago. Now we're dancing to it. Pretty amazing." In the low light, his eyes were deep blue like the sky at dusk. Sincere eyes.

It was her time to act. To control her own course rather than letting the whims of others blow her in their directions. She reached for Pavol's wrist.

Her words would be a betrayal of Daria, her only friend. Even so, she wanted this chance.

"You can dance with me. I'm not a gypsy."

CHAPTER 5: LÍDA AND PAVOL

Lída gathered kindling in the woods next to the tracks. Twigs dropped from her unsteady arms. Did her father approve of Pavol? Could she tell him her plans for next year?

On her way home she thought she heard an animal keening, so she checked the traps. All of them were empty.

Inside the cottage, her father sat alone at the table, the bottle of slivovice on its side and glasses empty. "Where's Pavol?" Lída asked, a hitch of dread in her voice.

"Nice kid but can't hold his liquor. I told him to take his problem outside." Her father's tone signaled amusement rather than contempt. He placed both hands on the table and pushed himself to his feet. "I'm going to town."

For more drink. Nothing she could do but let him go. Lída stepped aside as he passed and glared at his back until the door swung shut.

Grabbing her lantern, she noticed Pavol's coat on the chair. "You didn't have to do this," she repeated under her breath as she rushed to the road.

She shouted his name into the darkness. Beyond the light from her lantern, uneven footsteps squished in the mud. Her father's or Pavol's, headed to town?

An owl hooted overhead, followed by retching behind her.

"Pavol!"

"Over here," came the faint reply.

If he'd tried to walk back, he'd taken a wrong turn. Without a coat, exposure would kill him. Cursing her father, Lída thrashed through brush that caught on the sleeves of her wool coat and slapped her face. She raised her lantern.

Pavol leaned into a tree trunk, his head against the bark, threads of slime dangling from his mouth. His shoulders rose and fell with his labored breaths. "Not like my family has so much food that I should go puking it up."

He tried to laugh, but when he turned his face to her, it was slick, as if he'd been crying. His eyes were watery and bloodshot behind drooping lids. He took two steps forward, away from the tree, and dropped to his hands and knees.

Lída set her lantern on the ground, crouched next to him, and rubbed his back. "Go on. Get it out." How many times had her father crawled in the dirt, mumbling *Get it out* over and over to himself?

Pavol gagged and spat. "I'm a pathetic loser, Lída. You don't deserve me."

Lída wrapped her arms around his trembling body. "There's no shame in my father outdrinking you. It doesn't mean he thinks you're unworthy." She pulled him closer, taking in the mixture of damp soil, cheap brandy, and vomit. The familiar odor of loss and sadness.

"No. It wasn't that. He said we'll never win back our freedom. We aren't even trying." Pavol rocked backward onto his heels, sat up, and pressed his crossed arms to his stomach. Half-speaking, half-crying, his words ran together, and Lída strained to understand them. "I told him I tried. When the Russians invaded, I turned the road signs in the opposite direction. The ones that wouldn't turn, I smashed. The police arrested me and beat me up. He said that was nothing."

Despite the stench, she sucked in her breath. Why hadn't he told her? "You were arrested?"

"Remember when I said I fell down stairs helping my mother?"

Lída slipped her hand between his arm and his body and flattened her palm against once-broken and taped ribs. It had taken weeks after the accident for him to let her hug him. "You were brave. They really hurt you."

"Did it stop the invasion?" Pavol shouted into the forest. "Did it keep them from Prague? Yeah, for about two hours."

She had no answer. She too had been amazed at how useless their resistance had been. The students in Prague blocked streets and leapt onto the tanks in the morning, but by afternoon they'd scattered from the tear gas, police batons, and gunfire. It seemed as if everyone wanted their freedom, but after the tanks rolled in, they could only watch helplessly as books and record albums disappeared from store shelves and censorship returned to newspapers, television, and radio.

Pavol's voice faded to a whisper. "He killed people for this country when he was our age."

"He wasn't our age. He was twenty already. He joined the Czech Resistance when the Nazis closed the university in Brno." Her father had no right to put all this on Pavol.

Beneath her hand, Pavol shivered. "And the Nazis destroyed his village while he was in hiding. It made him fight harder. Not give up like we did."

Her father's village . . . She'd only heard about it from her aunt, who'd married and moved to Znojmo before the war. He never talked about the place where he grew up. He made it sound like he'd never had a childhood home and because of that would never find another home for the rest of his life.

We might as well be Roma. Except that she didn't fit in with the Roma kids either. Daria had never invited her to wherever she lived, nor come to Lída's home in the woods.

"I can't kill the invaders the way he did," Pavol slurred. "I can't take the life of another human being." He toppled away from her and curled into a fetal position with his knees to his face.

Lída scooted closer to pat his head. "My dear sweet Pavol." She ran her fingers through his damp, matted hair and picked out bits of leaves, twigs, and bark.

"I'm a coward."

"You're not. We live to fight another day." That's what they'd told themselves in August.

"If we were alone in this world . . ." He sucked in his breath with a moan that squeezed Lída's heart. He grabbed a clump of his hair and yanked. Fine strands glistened from his fist in the lantern's weak light. "What was I saying? I can't even think straight."

"If we were alone," she repeated, voice shaky.

"Right. If we were alone, we could live the way we want." He hiccupped. "But we're not alone, and they're so much stronger." Another hiccup. "I don't know what more to do."

Leaning against Lída, he struggled to his feet. Mud streaked his sweater and pants. His teeth chattered, and his damp body against hers chilled Lída to her core.

"I should go home," he mumbled.

"Come back to the cottage first. You left your coat inside." His coordination was shot, but he'd freeze if he stayed in the woods much longer. She'd keep him for the night; her father wouldn't be back until morning anyway.

Lída scooped up the lantern and wrapped her other arm around his waist. With a hand pressed against his back, she guided his clumsy steps, steering him clear of roots and vines. Despite the chill inside her, sweat streamed down her face and back as she helped him to the path.

Lída paused by the woodpile next to the door to rest, then

stumbled inside with Pavol. Her face flushed in the heated-through room, and she stripped off her coat before setting a saucepan of water on top of the stove. She unlaced Pavol's boots the way she'd unlaced her father's, but with her father she always stopped there. Pavol's sweater and pants were soaked and stiff. She couldn't leave him filthy like that.

She stripped him down to his underwear, and washed his face, neck, and hands with lukewarm water. He reached for her hands, and she thought she heard him say, "Let's go swimming," as if in his drunken state he had no idea where he was. Golden hair stood like miniature wheat fields from the goosebumps on his arms. She rummaged through the cupboards for linden tea, gentler on his stomach than coffee. The tin was empty, so she filled a metal cup with the water that bubbled on its way to boiling.

After blowing on it and testing it, she said, "Drink this."

Pavol slumped in the chair, his head in his hands. Sliding her fingers under his chin, Lída lifted his head and kissed his freshly scrubbed cheek that smelled of soap mixed with brandy. He wrapped his hands around the cup and inhaled the steam before taking his first sip.

"Thank you." Another sip. Pavol sat upright. His dusky blue eyes met hers. "I love you so much, Lída."

"I love you too." Her voice broke, the way it had when they first pledged their love by the railroad tracks, back when even the impossible seemed within reach.

She slid her hands under Pavol's T-shirt, and stroked his ribs and chest, all skin and bones of a boy who never had enough to eat. She and her father hunted birds and squirrels and rabbits, but the townspeople were lucky if they had a small garden to supplement their meager wages and the bare store shelves.

As she caressed him, it occurred to her that he was no longer wearing his leather necklace with the cross. Had he lost it in the woods? Left it at home?

She traced where the necklace would have hung, until he clasped her hand.

"What time is it?" he asked, his words coming more slowly now.

Lída checked the wind-up alarm clock on the windowsill. It had been dark for hours. "Nine thirty."

He rubbed his temples. "May I lie down for a while?"

Lída unrolled the mattress and covered Pavol with a blanket. She squeezed next to him, wrapped her arms around his sad, helpless body, and fell into a dreamless sleep.

Pavol awoke with a pounding headache and a gnawing deep inside him. His eyes adjusted to the darkness. He lay between Lída and the wall, her body the only source of warmth. Across the room, dark red embers flickered inside the stove.

He vaguely remembered making a fool of himself in front of Lída and her father. Crying. Showing weakness.

You're surrounded by women. I'll show you how to be a man.

A man would relight the stove.

Pavol sat upright. His stomach flipped inside out. He scrambled outside in his underwear.

Afterward, he leaned against the woodpile gasping frigid air, bare feet tingling, diaphragm and barely-healed ribs throbbing.

Jaw clenched against another wave of nausea, he lifted the tarp and picked out a single log along with slats and twigs. Entering the cabin, he banged his shoulder on the doorframe. Lída stirred.

"Pa?"

Pavol cleared his throat. "It's me. Getting more wood."

He crouched in front of the stove to feed it. A profound weakness swept through him, as if he hadn't eaten in days. He sipped water from the metal cup to soothe his throat.

Lída knelt next to him and rubbed his back. His insides quivered and relaxed. The fire roared as it filled the box, and he stripped off his T-shirt to wipe his sweaty face.

Lída kissed the back of his neck, little butterfly kisses. "Feel better, sweet Pavol?"

He shut the iron door and let her pull him back onto the mattress. She made figure eights with her index finger on his bare stomach. She'd taken off her sweater, and her breasts stretched her camisole. His stomach fluttered at the unfamiliar sight. "Sorry I woke you," he said, even though now he wasn't.

The drilling in his head and ribs diminished, and in its place was an electric buzz. He reached down to cover the lump in his briefs between his damp thighs.

"Where are my clothes?"

"They're kind of a mess," she said. "You can wear my father's overalls when you go home."

"Do I have to go?" How much time before Ondřej returned? Would Ondřej, who'd already killed a bunch of people in his life, kill him for sharing a bed with Lída?

"He won't be back until he and I leave for work. Hide in the woods by the train tracks and go home after." She flashed him a conspiratorial smile. Steaming blood coursed through him.

She leaned over to kiss him. He held one hand over his mouth. "Is my breath disgusting?"

She pushed his hand aside. Her open-mouthed kiss was his answer. He held his breath to keep his insides in place.

After the kiss ended and she propped herself on one arm

beside him, he said, "I swear I'm never drinking like that again. I don't know why"—he gulped—"I did it."

But he had known why, realized it the instant Lída's father had challenged him. He wanted to obliterate the churning in his mind. To die without physically dying.

And now, here he was. Alive. Ashamed. Naked in front of Lída. She still loved him.

He reached for her, kissed each of her delicious breasts. She unbuttoned her camisole and wrapped her arms around him. She buried her fingers in his hair and massaged his scalp.

He'd never seen her like this. They'd never touched each other this way. His head and stomach grew calm, as if he hadn't poured nearly half a bottle of homemade plum brandy down his throat earlier that evening and would never need to again, not with the girl he loved making him feel so good.

It was his first time, but he didn't know if it was hers. She didn't seem to hesitate at all, and clumsy from drink and inexperience, he followed her lead. She acted as if she knew what to do, but it could have been instinct. The same instinct of their village ancestors up in haylofts and behind woodpiles, surviving their hard lives by making love to each other.

The Bible set down rules: No sex before marriage. God's laws separated human beings, created in His image, from the rest of His creatures. For this reason, God gave humans dominion over nature.

The Communist government said there was no God, no Church, no rules except those of the Party. The teachers made them recite the words of Lenin: *All worship of a divinity is a necrophilia.* A worship of death.

After the invasion, he'd come to realize his teachers were right. His faith hadn't helped him. God hadn't answered his prayers. And the necklace he wore openly all spring and summer could have again landed him in a police interrogation room.

At the beginning of September, he'd wrapped the necklace in an outgrown school-uniform shirt and buried it at the bottom of his drawer.

Over the next three months Lída fought against Pavol's despair. No matter in what state he arrived in, for the hours they spent together his gloom seemed to lift. Her dreams of a life with him blossomed in the words left unsaid, in the joy they found in each other's bodies. He remained awkward and gentle and respectful, and with him, her uncle's damage faded as if Pavol's love made her reborn.

By the end of January she was taking her own problems outside early in the morning when she should have been making her father's coffee. A flu, she thought, or a rabbit she hadn't pulled from the trap in time or cooked thoroughly enough.

She'd been five years old when her own mother died giving birth to her younger brother, Michal, who survived less than a day. For seven years, she'd lived in Znojmo with her aunt and uncle while her father worked for the forest service and on collective farms nearby. Her aunt and uncle had no children. *Who in their right mind would bring a child into this world, in this country?* Aunt Irina would ask.

In Znojmo she learned that a grown man could do anything he wanted to a girl. In the Middle Ages, the townspeople had broken through the walls of their cellars to build giant catacombs, where they hid from their enemies like animals hiding from predators. Centuries later she, too, had to hide there.

After Lída told her father what Uncle Ludvík had done to her, what her uncle demanded she keep secret, her father took her away from that place to live with him, alone, for the next five years.

So when Lída fainted one morning at work at the beginning of March, it was Yulia, the plump, gray-haired Russian woman next to her on the production line, who thought to ask, "When was the last time you had your monthly bleeding?"

Lída couldn't remember. She hadn't kept track. Her bleeding had started later than her classmates' and rarely came on the day it was supposed to.

Yulia invited her over after work the following Monday, asked her to pee in a cup, and spread her urine over wheat and barley seeds. Yulia waved her hand above the damp seeds as if performing magic.

"If you are with child, the seeds will sprout," Yulia said when Lída asked what the ritual meant. "Wheat for a girl. Barley for a boy."

"Why?"

"It's how a woman's body nourishes a child. It's different for girls and boys."

An hour after Pavol told Lída that he couldn't go to the movie with her, that he and his friends were going to Prague for the weekend instead, Yulia arrived at the factory with the tray of seeds. Half had tiny green shoots.

"My dear girl, you're pregnant," Yulia said. "And you're going to have a boy."

THE RECKONING

MARCH 17–24, 1969

CHAPTER 6: LÍDA

Yulia told Lída how she could get rid of it. *Get rid of it* were the words Yulia used. "The hospital has a special department just for this."

Lída wrapped her arms around herself and shivered. In the twenty months they'd been living in Rozcestí, her father had ended up in that gray stone building behind the main square twice for alcohol poisoning. She'd had to collect him when enough of the poison had cleared his body—had to endure the stares and laughter of her classmates while she helped him home.

Would they stare and laugh at her again now? Would they even remember her?

"I can take you after work on Monday if you don't want to go alone," Yulia said.

It seemed so simple. Sign in. Wait in the queue until the nurse called her name for the procedure.

"Does it hurt?" Lída asked. She wasn't one to complain about pain, but she remembered her mother screaming in agony for three days, struggling to give birth to her brother until her body gave out.

"A little. You'll have bleeding and cramping for a few days, but then you'll be as good as new."

"Not like giving birth." Lída's mind flashed to her mother's motionless gray body on the bed and the midwife holding bloody, limp Michal.

"No, dear, not at all." Yulia smiled and patted Lída's shoulder. "You should decide what you'll tell the boy. *If* you tell him."

If we love each other, there should be no secrets between us. A year ago, she and Pavol had agreed on that, but was it a secret if he never asked?

Lída waited all weekend for Pavol to return, debating whether she would say anything to him. Several times she packed her shoulder bag, preparing to walk down the muddy road to the town library for a book explaining all those things a mother would've explained to a daughter. Instead, she unpacked and hiked in the woods.

Too many curious eyes in the library.

Now that she knew, all the other changes made sense: her heavy swollen breasts like fully loaded water balloons, the small bulge in her belly, the late-in-the-day hunger that led her to finish her father's rejected supper every night.

If she told Pavol, he would not want her to go to the clinic. Even though he no longer wore the cross around his neck, he prayed with his family before their meals. He believed all life, even life that had not yet made itself apparent in the world, was sacred.

If she told him, he would marry her. That had been their plan anyway, just not so soon.

They could survive. The government would give them a ration card for the baby along with the student apartment in Prague, maybe even a bigger apartment than they would've had for just the two of them. She could take the boy—if Yulia was right, a boy—to the infant care center at the new job they'd assign her while Pavol attended classes. In five years Pavol would have his degree in engineering, their child would start kindergarten, and she'd finish secondary school and study to become a nurse. After a day of work and school, they'd have supper together and spend the rest of the evening playing or doing homework, she and the child together.

Lída Bartošová. That would be her new name.

But if her dreams turned to domestic life with Pavol, her nightmares echoed her mother's wails, the smell of fresh blood turning brown and cold, the thud of dirt on two pine boxes. She'd never seen a woman give birth, only death.

Maybe when we're older, when we're ready. That's what she decided on Monday morning when she left for work with her father. Along with five years of classes, Pavol would need to do months of national service to receive his degree, leaving her alone with the baby in a big, unfamiliar city.

If he didn't know, if he didn't ask, her decision wasn't a lie—or a secret. She wouldn't have to hurt him. They'd still be together as before.

When Lída and her father arrived at the factory, the buzz of conversations instantly ceased. The hair on the back of her neck prickled, and her stomach cramped. She glanced toward her father. The nick from his morning shave was angry red in a face drained of color.

Two men in business suits stepped forward. One was bald on top with close-cropped salt-and-paprika hair on the sides above and behind his ears. The other had darker hair combed over the top of his head. "Ondřej Pekár," the bald one said, holding up a badge. State Security. "We're conducting an investigation."

Her father's jaw clenched. Lída's pulse hammered in her temples. *Is Pa in trouble?*

The bald man nodded in her direction. "You too, Miss Pekárová. Please come with us."

And what could I have done?

Her knees wobbled as she followed the policemen into the break room, her father at her side. She reached for his hand the way she'd done back in Znojmo before their nighttime escape. But his hands were buried deep in the pockets of his overalls, leaving her fingers exposed, icy and trembling.

They sat at the metal table. "May I ask what this is about?" Her father's voice quivered.

"Yes." The bald StB officer reached into his briefcase on the floor and pulled out a manila folder that he left unopened on the table. "A young man named Pavol Bartoš. I believe both of you know him."

The shudder came from deep within Lída. "Why?"

"He got into a spot of trouble in Prague." The man drummed his fingers on the folder while glaring at her with steel-gray eyes. "Did he tell you why he was going?"

She opened her mouth, but no words came out. Had the university students lured him into something that had landed him in prison?

"I expect the truth, Miss Pekárová."

"He said he was working on a technical project between his school and the university. He's in his last year at the secondary school. Number Three—"

"We know his school. Did he say anything about a letter?"

"Yes. It was about the project."

The comb-over man stepped to the door, blocking any chance of their leaving or of any coworkers entering. He crossed his arms over his chest. Lída's hands shook and her mouth went dry.

The bald officer cleared his throat. "Did he travel to Prague with anyone else?"

"Friends. He didn't say who."

"And who are his friends?"

Lída pushed the words past her parched throat. "I don't know." The rude hockey players didn't seem likely to go to Prague for any reason except a sports tournament. She'd never met Tomáš Kuchař, the other friend he'd talked about.

Besides, what had her father told her? *This is how you survive with your soul intact. Never name anyone. You saw nothing. You heard nothing. You have nothing to say.*

The officer's eyes flitted from Lída to her father. Above his tightly buttoned shirt and snug tie, his face had the shape of an egg. An Easter egg, painted pinkish orange. "Comrade Pekár, when was the last time you saw Pavol Bartoš?"

At our place. For supper a week ago. You'd shot a wild boar by the tracks, and he took some of the meat to his family.

"Thursday night," her father answered.

You saw Pavol without me? While I lay awake at home, wondering if I should tell him? She bit back the words. The less they revealed about themselves, the better. And her father didn't know about the baby either . . . nor would he.

"Where did you see him?"

Ondřej's head drooped like that of a whipped animal. "Bar Šťastny." The ironically-named Lucky Bar, a dank, dirt-encrusted basement room that she'd hauled him out of multiple times.

"Did he say anything about a trip the next day?"

"No, comrade."

Lída's fingers curled, as if she could finish this interrogation with her hands around her father's neck. *What were you doing in a bar with Pavol? Wasn't one drinking contest enough for you?*

How many other times did you meet there?

Because Pavol must've met *someone* at a bar in town. Several nights in January and early February he'd stumbled, reeking, into her little house and passed out on the floor before she could unroll her mattress. Or he never showed up at all when he'd promised to visit but appeared the next night, sheepish and full of apologies. In mid-February, she, Ondřej, and Pavol had gone on a camping trip together and he'd promised to quit, but another no-show happened after that.

The bald officer scraped his chair forward, rested his arms on the table, and leaned over the manila folder. He was so close to Lída's face that when he spoke, his coffee breath wafted up her nose and made her stomach twist. "This question is for both of you. Did Pavol Bartoš express any opinions against the socialist revolution? Repeat any imperialist propaganda?"

How could she begin to answer that one? Ever since the first days of the reforms last January, freedom had pulsed through their veins, to the beat of rock 'n' roll and the chants of demonstrators. *We want freedom! Russians out! Ivan go home!*

After the invasion, they'd stopped speaking openly and only mouthed those words, because the walls had ears and spies were everywhere.

"You arrested him?" Her insides tightened. People who were arrested—they came back from prison changed. Their eyes haunted. Trembling as if they had the palsy. Afraid to be touched.

"No, Miss Pekárová." The StB officer opened the folder and laid a grainy color photo on the table.

Lída gasped. The face had been burned black, the eyes deep pools of emptiness. Where the fire had not devoured it, the skin was swollen and red. Even though nothing remained of his sand-colored hair, she saw Pavol.

What was left of him.

She screamed. Everything around her seemed to vibrate, the world on the verge of breaking in half and swallowing her whole. She pressed her hand to her mouth to stop the rush from her stomach, nothing but air after the sickness had emptied her out that morning. She leapt to her feet and dashed to the rust-stained sink in the corner, her belly heaving and Pavol's charred, disfigured face seared into her mind—the final image she would have of him.

When she caught her breath, she forced out the only question that came to her: "What did you people do to him?"

Her father jumped up—perhaps to come to her aid, perhaps to stop her outburst before she said things she'd later regret. The StB officer standing at the door gripped his shoulder and pressed him back into his seat.

"He did it to himself," the bald man said, his voice calm. Cold. Like he didn't care about the boy who only days ago was so alive in her arms, pink flesh and warm blood. Excited about his weekend in the city and in love with her.

Her guts wrapped in a tight knot, as if to protect that one piece of Pavol, Lída sank to the floor and raised her knees to her face. She squeezed her eyes shut as sobs shook her body. Tears dampened the knee patches of her overalls and chilled her inside.

This can't be happening. Maybe the picture was a fake to get her to name names. They did things like that. The person in the photo had no hair, no eyes. It might not have even been a boy but an old man whose photo they showed to everyone.

The bald StB officer flipped his chair around to face her. She shrank backward toward the wall, the bottom of the sink touching her head and the metal drainpipe pressed against her shoulders. "Your boyfriend—I'm guessing he *was* your boyfriend—poured vodka and gasoline over himself and set himself on fire like that madman Palach."

Not a madman. A hero. Pavol had called him a hero. The officer's words wrenched Lída's insides.

The man continued. "Perhaps young Bartoš, intoxicated by the big city, had far too much to drink Friday afternoon and didn't know what the hell he was doing." He returned to the table and nodded toward Lída's father. "Comrade Pekár, I'm sure you know all about that."

Lída slid forward and leapt to her feet. "Get out! Leave us alone!" She no longer cared if they took her to the State Security headquarters and she returned as one of those shattered, trembling ghosts.

"Emotional over that boy, aren't we, Miss Pekárová?" He winked toward his fellow officer at the door.

"Please sit and calm down, Lída," Ondřej said.

Shaking, she returned to her seat. Her father was right—she needed to control herself. Any more of a scene would mean trouble for both of them.

"Thank you, Comrade Pekár," the bald man said, something Lída hadn't expected. He scooped up the photo and folder and dropped them into his briefcase. "We'll be in touch again soon."

The two men left, shutting the door behind them.

Lída wept, her head cradled in her folded arms on the table. The StB officer had called her *emotional*. Did he have no one in his life whom he loved?

There would be no apartment shared with Pavol. No moment of joy seeing each other after a long day of school or work, no pleasure in each other's bodies.

The kindest boy in Rozcestí, with dreams and plans of his own.

Sure, he'd talked about Jan Palach, but he'd said nothing about following in his footsteps. Spots flashed in her vision. Had he kept that secret from her, after promising no secrets?

She would've stopped him. But perhaps he *had* said something and she hadn't listened . . . or hadn't given him enough reason to live.

Her father patted her shoulder. She twisted away from him. "Go away." She glared into his bloodshot, yellowed eyes. "After you did everything you could to ruin him." She rose to her feet. "Why did you take him out drinking?"

"I didn't take him. He was already there with his friends." He met her gaze. "Big guys, but lightweights too."

The hockey players. "More people to defeat in a drinking contest, right?" Her throat burned, and her voice cracked. "Does that make you feel important? Does it? Because everything you touch dies."

Lída brushed past her father, out of the break room, and across the factory floor, where she caught the eyes of her coworkers. Confused? Amused? Pitying? Did they have any idea?

Outside Lída screamed into the cold, cloudless sky above the brown haze—the sky into which Pavol had ascended, if the Heaven that he believed in truly existed.

She ran. The ends of her hair slapped her neck, and her feet thudded against cobblestones and pavement, sending shock waves through her body along with a strange new churning inside her belly.

No. She would not go to the hospital with Yulia. This child-to-be was all that remained of her Pavol, and no matter what secrets he'd kept from her, she would never give up this piece of him.

In front of Town Hall, in the center of the main square, she stopped to catch her breath. She gazed upward, beyond the clock tower with the date *1882* carved in sandstone, beyond the rooftops and hills of Rozcestí.

If you'd known, Pavol . . . if I could've told you . . . would you have done it?

CHAPTER 7: ŠTĚPÁN

Štěpán's parents said nothing about Pavol. His death wasn't reported in the newspapers or on radio or TV. And Štěpán wouldn't be the one to tell them, to provoke his father's temper or shatter his mother's faith that her nine-year-old students would one day usher in the Marxist utopia.

Nor did his friends mention it at Sunday's hockey practice, those few sweet hours when Štěpán could forget that he'd never see Pavol again. Nor did the school administration make an announcement over the intercom on Monday, as if they could pretend Pavol was out with the flu every day until graduation.

But word spread, whispered in the moments before class, in the cafeteria when no monitors were listening, on sidewalks and in squares after the dismissal bell.

Did you hear Pavol Bartoš set himself on fire like Jan Palach?

Braver than I'll ever be.

That was his point, brácha. We can't accept this as normal. We have to stop them from taking our freedom.

To those kids, who didn't really know him, Pavol was a hero. Not a beautiful, brilliant human being who ended his life because he'd been blacklisted from the university and his closest friends weren't there when he needed them most.

Was there hope for any of them in this occupied country?

Brooklyn. A year ago, Štěpán had bought two copies of the translation of Walt Whitman's poetry at that bookstore in Prague and given one of them to Pavol. Lying in bed Monday night, he savored the memory of Pavol opening it, face brightening, voice excited with questions. *Who is this guy? Why don't his verses rhyme like the ones we read in school?*

In Brooklyn, the poet could be himself. Love men as well as women. Write free verse and live in freedom.

On Tuesday Dr. Navrátil, the school director, summoned Štěpán to the office before the first bell. Inside, two plainclothes officers stood. One was tall, slender, and balding. The other was stocky and had dark brown hair and a pouty lower lip.

"We're taking you for questioning. About the incident last Friday," the slender one said.

As if he were a machine already set in motion, Dr. Navrátil narrowed his eyes and frowned. "Officers, I apologize again for the conduct of our two students and will take steps to ferret out similar sentiment." Turning to Štěpán, he picked up a ruler and slapped it against his palm. "Štěpán Jelínek, I cannot begin to express my disappointment. I thought you cared about your future. Effective now, you are expelled."

"The hockey tournament . . ." Štěpán blurted out.

"I will inform Coach Hájek of your expulsion so he can replace you immediately."

The officers grabbed Štěpán's arms and shoved him out of the room.

Pain shot through his elbows. "What about my books? My skates? The rest of my gear?"

The stocky officer replied, "They belong to the State now."

My parents . . . ? He closed his eyes and let the men drag him wherever they wanted. His parents couldn't help him. They also belonged to the State. Even though they'd joined the Party—his father organizing physical education events, his mother herding the children in her class into the Young Pioneers—it hadn't protected him.

The men chained him to the floor inside the back of a livestock delivery truck that stank of piss and manure and pig sweat. Splinters and bits of hay poked through his clothing and scratched his butt and thighs. He tried to muffle the foul odor by twisting his neck and pressing his nose against his school jacket. Tears stung his eyelids. His heart hammered.

He counted to sixty over and over to calm himself. After twenty times doing this his neck cramped. He stretched it from side to side, surprised at how quickly he'd adjusted to the stench. The ventilation slits were too narrow for him to see where he was, though he guessed the StB men were taking him to Prague. Most of the road was smooth, until the end when the truck stopped and started abruptly, causing him to slide on the floor while the cuffs and chains dug into his skin. His fingers went numb.

How will I survive interrogation? Torture? That was what they did, tortured people to force names from them, to ruin more lives.

He needed a strategy. His own future was over—expelled, no army team, no backup plan for the university.

Was this how Pavol felt?

The truck stopped. The door opened like gates to the underworld, and the two officers unchained him and yanked him out. He fell onto the cement, banging his knee. He yelled. The stocky man lifted him up by his collar, and the slender man slapped him across the face. His cheek stung.

Štěpán's bladder ached as he half-walked up the stairs to a loading dock. With each footstep he heard Pavol's voice in his head, like a command from the world beyond: *Whatever you do, don't rat out Tomáš.*

His insides pulsed. He had to take a piss. "May I go to the lavatory?" he rasped.

"Last chance. Do it now," the thin one said.

Both of them went into the dingy unheated room with him and whistled outside the stall. Half-naked on the toilet, he shook uncontrollably. His intestines revolted. Diarrhea rushed from him along with urine, his body purging itself like he was a wild animal about to die.

"I'm done," he said between chattering teeth.

They let him wash his hands in freezing water, no soap, while they cursed him for the stink he left behind. After cuffing his wet wrists in front of him, they led him to a windowless basement office. As cold as the lavatory, the room smelled so strongly of bleach that Štěpán's eyelids and nostrils burned. A single bright bulb shone over a bare metal desk with a low stool in front of it. Two regular policemen stood in separate corners slapping truncheons against gloved hands. *Thunk. Thunk.* Štěpán steeled himself.

The man seated behind the desk wore a shiny green uniform and glasses. He had close-shaven brown hair and a goatee that made him look like the young V.I. Lenin on the poster behind him. "Sit, Jelínek," he said.

Knees weak, Štěpán lowered himself to the metal stool. It wobbled on four uneven legs, making him dizzy. A fog descended over him, as if someone else were sitting in this room while the real Štěpán Jelínek fooled around in class with his friends.

The man flipped open a manila folder. Štěpán strained to read the contents, but the edge of the desk blocked it.

"The sooner you come clean with us, the easier it will be for you."

Tell them nothing. Stay strong like Pavol.

On the stool, Štěpán's knees came to his chest. His cuffed wrists itched, and his arms cramped.

The questions came at machine-gun pace. Even if he'd wanted to answer, he didn't have time.

"Why did you skip school and take the train to Prague?"

"Did you intend to set fire to yourself like Bartoš and then chicken out?"

"Who wrote the letters?"

There were two letters. The one they carried to the castle, and Pavol's suicide note. The StB officer didn't read him the suicide note, and Štěpán couldn't see it. His gaze froze on the lip of the desk.

Rust lined the metal strip. Or was it blood?

"Who taught you reactionary propaganda?"

"Who helped you?"

"What degenerate books did you read?"

"What degenerate music did you listen to?"

"Why didn't you join the KSČ like your parents and brother?"

"Do you have a girlfriend?"

"We talked to your coach and teammates. They told us you've never had a girlfriend. Your teammates also said you didn't go back to Rozcestí with them when you were eliminated in the junior national tournament in Prague last year. Where did you go?"

Sweat broke out on Štěpán's face. Those rats. They'd been the ones who played like shit and lost the game. At least the guy didn't mention Anton, who'd let him stay over without asking questions.

"They think you're a homosexual. Are you a homosexual?"

Sweat tickled as it streamed down his cheeks, but he couldn't raise his arms to wipe it or react in any way. Coach Hájek and his teammates had guessed his secret and sold him out.

"Was Bartoš a homosexual?"

He wouldn't confess, nor would he denounce anyone else: not the snitches on his team, not whiny baby Tomáš, not even the dead.

The interrogator stood and left, on his way out passing a large man with short, curly black hair. The new interrogator's upper lip was split and crudely sewn together, leaving a white scar on his ruddy skin and a mouthful of broken and missing teeth. Štěpán's empty stomach lurched. He swallowed and rubbed the crawly skin of his forearm on his pant leg.

The new interrogator glanced quickly at the folder the other one had left behind. "They tell me you're a hockey player."

Štěpán pressed his lips together, dreading to the bottom of his queasy stomach what else his teammates had said.

"I played hockey too. Defense for the army team, alongside Jan Suchý. Did you see him in the Olympics last year?"

Štěpán closed his eyes, his own dreams of Olympic glory evaporated like ice shards. *Tell him nothing.* Even though the ugly man appeared friendly, he was still StB.

"Silver medal. Next time, gold."

Štěpán held his tongue between his teeth.

The man pushed the folder aside. "Look, kid, I don't know what that other guy said, but he's a bastard. I'm on your side." He leaned forward and folded his hands. "Good kids get caught up in bad situations all the time, and I want to make it easy for you. Get you out of here and back on the ice."

Štěpán's loneliness reverberated like a body slam against the boards.

"What position do you play, kid?"

Talk about hockey, nothing else. "Left wing." After hours of silence, his croaked-out words sounded like a stranger's in his ears.

"Stats?"

"I averaged 1.5 points per game, with 1.2 assists."

"Good player on a good team." The man kept his lips together when he smiled.

"We won the regional championship two years in a row. And this season, we've only lost one game, so we're top seed." A spike pierced Štěpán's heart at the thought of the tournament he'd miss—his final season ended six days too soon.

"So who's your favorite player?"

"Jiří Holík. Plays left wing like me."

"Good pick." The officer leafed through the file. "Why didn't you join the Party? You wouldn't have had to try out for the army team; you'd already be on it."

"It ate up a lot of time. My brother joined, and I saw that he didn't get a chance to practice as much as he should have. It hurt his game, and now he doesn't play at all."

After his father joined the Party, he'd brought the two of them to meetings. The men took turns reading boring passages from Karl Marx's books. They listened to speeches. In a corner of the room, weird Tomáš picked his nose and stashed his boogers in the cuffs of his slacks. Štěpán counted the hours he could've been working out, getting stronger and better.

Or he could've been reading and dreaming—under a government that detested dreamers.

"And you thought you'd be good enough to qualify on skill alone."

"Yes, comrade. I wanted to be the best hockey player I could. I figured it was more important to win and it wouldn't matter whether or not I joined."

"You'd think that's how it works," the man said, shaking his head. "Though sometimes being the best isn't enough."

Štěpán's jaw dropped. Had he heard correctly—a police officer complain about the way things were, the corruption that made it possible for second-rate players to win spots on the first team?

"Nice teeth," the man said.

"I believe in the mouth guard."

"Want to look good for the girls."

"That's right." Štěpán forced a grin, the way he always did with Petr when they joked about girls. Would Petr now get a slot on the army team for ratting on him?

The officer doodled on his pad for what seemed like forever, though Štěpán had long ago lost track of time. His bladder prickled. He squirmed, legs pressed together. The man had coffee and water sent in, but only for himself. The coffee aroma made Štěpán's stomach grumble.

"They told me you couldn't have anything to eat or drink," the man said.

Better I don't drink. I'd piss my pants for sure.

After making a show of drinking the coffee, the officer leaned forward, arms folded on the desk. "I want to go back to that tournament in Prague last April. You didn't take the train home with your team after you lost. I'd like you to walk me through what you did instead."

"I-I wanted to watch. Learn from the winners." It was what he'd told Anton too.

"At three in the morning?"

How did he—? A wave of dizziness came over Štěpán, and he fell off the stool. Warm liquid soaked his pants, and in the next moment, a truncheon thudded against his spine. He bit back a scream. Through pins and needles, he peered up at the interrogator. *The one who promised to help.* The man was writing notes.

The truncheon-wielding policeman kicked Štěpán's thigh, grabbed his upper arm, and yanked him back onto the stool. Pain from his wrenched shoulder zipped down his arm.

In the freezing room, his urine turned cold and rank. His pants squished on the metal stool every time the uneven legs rocked. New questions came, rapid-fire, and he said he didn't remember, as if he could get away with silence after talking so much already.

His head ached. His eyes burned from lack of sleep. His empty stomach turned in on itself, sending acid to his esophagus and throat. Everywhere, his body throbbed.

"Why did you leave Bartoš, if he really was your friend?"

Štěpán licked crusted lips. "He said he wanted to see the city. He'd only been once on a field trip." *Why did I leave him? How did I not see his desperation?* Štěpán tried to push from his mind those evenings in the bars around town. Him and Pavol . . . Him and Pavol and their friends . . . Him and Pavol and the old men who bought them drinks.

"Do you know how we figured out you'd gone with Bartoš to Prague?" The interrogator waved the map Štěpán had given Pavol, with the phone number of Anton's dorm.

His own brother had denounced him. That's why the police had singled him out on the train at Most. Had Anton also told them how late Štěpán had gotten back last year, when he'd gone to that club near Wenceslas Square?

"You lied to our officer that day. You said you traveled alone. That's six months in prison right there."

They'd nailed him, thanks to Anton, who'd snitched out of jealousy or pure meanness or to save his own skin. "I admit it. I lied," Štěpán said. "I'll sign the confession, and you can take me to my cell." His insides unclenched at the thought of an empty concrete cell, where at least he could rot away undisturbed.

"We're not done with you." The interrogator flipped the manila folder open and shut, over and over. *Whoosh. Slap. Whoosh. Slap.* Štěpán's vision blurred. He tilted sideways.

Whack! This time the policemen hit him on the side of his head, and he crumpled. When he straightened up, his ears rang, a school bell on the inside of his skull. His left eye stung. He wiped it with his cuffed hands, and his wrist came away streaked with blood.

A new interrogator entered the room, joining the ex-hockey player. "Citizen Jelínek"—he stepped forward and stood over Štěpán—"I've read it multiple times, and I don't think you wrote the letter you and Bartoš attempted to deliver to the Central Committee of the KSČ."

"Agreed," said the interrogator who'd been there already. "The person who wrote this letter has a political education. Neither you nor Bartoš were Party members or attended classes on Marxist-Leninist theory."

The new one again: "Who wrote it?"

"Pavol Bartoš and I did. We learn these things in regular school too."

"You've admitted already that you lied. How can we believe anything from you?"

They wouldn't let him leave the room until they forced Tomáš's name from him.

He'd already spoken after pledging silence.

He'd told the second interrogator of his love for hockey and his reasons for not joining the Party, and the man had used it against him.

He'd confessed to a crime against the State.

Where do I draw the line?

Ondřej, the former Resistance fighter who was always hanging out in the local bars, once told him: *Do not fear death or pain, but betrayal. You will not be able to live with yourself if you betray your comrades.*

Fighting the pain in his side, he sucked in the room's stale piss-and-blood-tinged air. He was ready to die. Though he'd broken his promise not to kick Tomáš's ass, he could, and he would, be the one to save it.

He would be brave like Pavol. He would be a patriot like Pavol. Not a collaborator with an inhuman system like his brother.

"Pavol Bartoš and I wrote the letter. There was no one else."

Štěpán repeated it dozens of times.

He repeated it when the officers kicked his ribs until they cracked.

He repeated it when they crushed his balls into the floor with a boot heel. When they lifted him up, screaming from the fire that consumed his groin and belly.

He repeated it in the moments before they smashed his face into the desk's metal edge, pushing his teeth through his upper lip. Pain ripped through his face. Blood spurted into his throat, choking him. Someone grabbed him by the hair, yanked his head back, and slammed a truncheon against his mouth.

Three teeth, teeth he was so proud of, lay in a puddle of blood on the floor next to the desk—the last thing he saw before his world went dark.

CHAPTER 8: TOMÁŠ

Tomáš thought it would take at least a month to examine all the evidence, but on the Thursday evening after Pavol's death, he sat at the head of the table next to his father in the top-floor conference room of the district KSČ headquarters, a stolid sky-blue building on the main square between Town Hall and the auditorium. Among those in attendance were two Russians dressed in brown uniforms with red stars on the epaulets.

Tomáš wasn't good with identifying faces and putting them with names, but he recognized the comrades who often visited his home. Comrade Kolodny, Petr's father, stood behind the seated officials at the opposite end of the table, beside the flags of Czechoslovakia and the KSČ. In front of him sat Dr. Navrátil, the director of No. 3 Secondary Railway Technical School. Across the table from the director was Comrade Moučka, the chemistry teacher whose son played goalie for the hockey team.

Where was Comrade Jelínek?

At lunch on Tuesday a puny first-year student named Filip whispered to Tomáš in the library, where the two often ate to escape the bullies, "Bet you're glad Štěpán Jelínek's not coming back."

"What?"

"I heard they expelled him." Filip blew out his breath, a sound like a horse's whinny. "We're going to lose this weekend's tournament."

Tomáš didn't care about the hockey team whose members tormented him, at least until they needed homework help. But Štěpán . . . kicked out of school?

"Did anyone say why?" he asked Filip. Would the other players think he snitched on Štěpán for beating him up? Would *they* beat him up, now that they might lose the tournament?

"Something about that kid who set himself on fire. Didn't you two run math club together?"

Tomáš nodded, his eyes focused on the brown linoleum floor. He slipped his hand into the pocket of his school jacket and stroked the two-centimeter-tall lead figure from his train set—the hiker with the backpack that Pavol would move to different places on the mountain whenever he came over.

He squeezed the hiker in his sweaty hand, as if he could bring to life his friend who loved the forests and the mountains.

"Did you have any idea?" Filip asked.

"No."

Now, Party officials were asking him the same question. His father had coached him on how to answer. His fingers and his left eyelid twitched. He rubbed his nose, straightened his glasses and then his tie, in that order. Always in that order when he didn't have his textbook to shield him.

"He never said anything directly to me about suicide." Tomáš had negotiated this answer with his father, in return for not mentioning Jan Palach's name. "But he was depressed."

"How could you tell?" a Russian asked.

"He was sad. I saw him cry once. Boys aren't supposed to cry." Tomáš blinked rapidly. It happened a month after the tanks rolled in, and two weeks after school started. In the living room with both his parents out of the house and the windows once again shut tightly, Tomáš had cued up the album with the song they liked so much. "The End." Listening to the words, Pavol had sobbed, tears leaking through his fingers covering his face.

Tomáš had cried too.

"Go on," the Russian said.

Tomáš's voice quivered. "His grades were going down. We used to study together. He was one of the top students in our year. Well, except for me."

The men in the room laughed. Good. They approved of what he'd said, so far. Maybe he could hold some things back and still satisfy them.

"After we returned from winter break in January, he stopped doing these special math problem sets with me. They're an extension of our calculus class. We'd send off for these workbooks from Moscow and solve the problems together. But he said he didn't want to do them, that it didn't matter anymore." A stabbing pain pierced Tomáš's chest. Those words were true, and a betrayal. Had he crossed the fine line he'd invented to make his father happy while not defiling the memory of his only friend?

He reached into his pocket for his little hiker but had left it at home.

Dr. Navrátil held up a sheet of paper. "All his grades declined between January and March. His math scores slid the most because that was his best subject before then, but they all fell, and suddenly. In addition, his teachers reported that he came to class late, skipped class, and didn't turn in homework. Several teachers thought he'd been drinking before school or else arrived hung over."

Tomáš squeezed his empty hand into a fist. Why hadn't Dr. Navrátil tried to defend one of his best students? Or, if it was that bad, tried to help him before it came to this?

An unfamiliar man in a green Czechoslovak military uniform asked, "Young Comrade Kuchař, did your friend drink heavily?"

Tomáš had figured this one out in advance: not a lie if he only told them what he witnessed with his own eyes. "I never saw him drink. If he went to a party or out to a bar, I wasn't there." He glanced at his tightly clasped hands. "I don't go out much at night because I'm pretty busy with studying and Youth Union meetings."

All true, and safer to make it about himself. Tomáš had never attended a school party. He detested the noise—a hundred conversations at once that chafed his nerves and made him want to curl up in a whimpering ball. The same with the bars in town, where the sickly odor of stale beer overwhelmed his senses. During the day he always hurried past their doors and alleyways to avoid the lingering stench. He couldn't understand why his father and just about everyone else in Rozcestí spent all night there.

The military man shifted in his chair. Tomáš eyed his ribbons and medals—the red star, the black cross, the lion standing on its hind legs. "Let's change the subject for a moment. Štěpán Jelínek. How well do you know him?"

"Not that well." Tomáš glanced toward Comrade Kolodny. Why hadn't they called Petr in to answer these questions?

"Tell them what happened last Saturday," his father said.

Tomáš stared at his father, confused. Waiting for clearer instructions. Five days ago, his father had told him he wanted to protect Štěpán's father. But now he wanted Tomáš to speak ill of Štěpán?

Comrade Kuchař nodded as if to say, *go on.*

"When I told Štěpán I heard Pavol had died, he . . . became violent, as though he'd lost his mind." Tomáš lowered his gaze to the gray laminated table. "He bloodied my nose and gave me a black eye."

He pointed to the bruises on his face and under his left eye. A few of the men murmured.

"Could you say he had a highly emotional reaction to Pavol Bartoš's death?"

"Yes, comrade."

The Czechoslovak military officer opened a folder. "Štěpán Jelínek has been in police custody for the past two and a half days. We have learned during this time that he is a liar, a counter-revolutionary, and a homosexual."

Tomáš reached for his necktie. *Štěpán, the toughest, meanest kid in the school? A homosexual? No way.*

He swallowed against the sinking feeling in his stomach. He couldn't read his father's face, to know where he stood.

"Young Comrade Kuchař, were you aware of Štěpán Jelínek's sexual deviation?"

"No. No, I was not." He forced himself to look the stranger in the eye. One second . . . two seconds . . . three seconds. Would the man believe him, the one time tonight he told the complete and honest truth?

Eyelid twitching and mind clouding, he looked away.

The next questions came one after the other, without time for his rattled brain to form an answer. "Was Pavol Bartoš a homosexual too? Were the two of them involved in a secret relationship? According to police, they'd sneaked off to Prague together and then split up; could a lovers' quarrel have caused the suicide?"

Finally, Tomáš leaned forward to answer in a shaky voice, "I was never in their bedrooms." A few men laughed. He didn't tell them Pavol had been in *his* bedroom and nothing happened except playing with trains and putting up a poster of a pretty woman singer the Party now accused of pornography. Before the questions could rain down on him again, he said, "Pavol had a girlfriend, so no, I don't think that's true."

"Did you ever meet her?" someone asked.

"No, but . . ." He trailed off. He only knew the girl's first name, Lída. Pavol had invited him to parties, said he wanted him to meet her, but Tomáš made excuses every time. He didn't dare go to the demonstrations for the reform government that Pavol and Lída attended, nor did Pavol ever ask him to.

"Maybe he invented the relationship to hide who he really was."

Could the comrade be right? Tomáš didn't know what to think now. People—their thoughts, their inner lives—were as unreadable as a book in the dark.

"My son doesn't know anything," Comrade Kuchař said. "He and Štěpán Jelínek were not friends, as you can plainly see. Pavol Bartoš was mentally unstable and deteriorating over the past few months, so much so that a reversal, a spat with his homosexual lover, sent him over the edge and led him to commit this criminal act."

Tomáš stared at his fingernails, already chewed to the quick. They had made up a story perfect in its logic but, judging by everything he'd seen with his own eyes, false.

On the way home inside the dark, silent car, Tomáš dreaded his father's words. If he considered it rationally, scientifically, the way he preferred to do, his goals at the meeting had been incompatible. He couldn't give the Party officials what they wanted without trampling the memory of his friend.

He'd done neither. His father hadn't thanked him for his answers. And everyone in town would forever think of Pavol as a drunk, a madman, and a deviant.

A block from the main square a man with a worker's cap and overalls leaned against a street lamp, smoking a cigarette. A couple entered a bar, the man's arm around the woman's waist. Another couple walked up the hill hand in hand.

The image of the solitary man lingered in Tomáš's mind. He'd never had a girlfriend, never attended dances with the girls' school. He'd read books about people in love, listened to music about love. "Can't Buy Me Love" . . . "All You Need is Love" . . . "She Loves You (Yea, Yea, Yea)" . . .

I think I'm in love with this girl, Lída, Pavol had confessed a year ago, while they listened to their new Beatles albums in Tomáš's living room. All the songs told him boys fell in love with girls. Everything else was a deviation. Antisocial.

His father parked the Škoda station wagon in the half-circle driveway in front of their door but made no move to get out. His lips were pressed together, a grim line under his bushy mustache.

Tomáš rubbed his nose, straightened his glasses and tie, and said, "I did what I was supposed to do, right, Papa?"

"I don't think you appreciate the seriousness of this situation." Comrade Kuchař glared at Tomáš. "Joking around like that. I'm disgusted."

Heat rose to Tomáš's face. "But they laughed. Twice. When I said I was at the top of the class, and then about not being in their bedroom."

"They were laughing *at* you, fool. How can someone so smart be so stupid?"

So often he'd heard that line from his father, from the youth group and camp leaders, from the other kids. So many things he didn't understand.

"This is a criminal investigation, not a comedy show or a play for popularity. Fortunately for you, it appears that Štěpán is the problem. He corrupted a vulnerable classmate, encouraged his reactionary impulses, and drove him to commit a decadent, self-destructive act."

Wait. Wasn't the goal to protect the Jelínek family? Or had the goal and the rules once again changed without explanation? Tomáš thought of Comrade Dubček's call for people to follow their consciences. But ever since last year's *military exercise*, as his father called it, no one seemed to be thinking about anything except saving themselves.

"That you stayed true to your principles and resisted infection speaks well of you and your family," his father went on. "But you need to be more careful choosing friends in the future." He yanked the key from the ignition. "I've been thinking about what to do with you this summer, and another year at Youth Union camp is the answer."

"Again?" Last year, while Tomáš's classmates in Rozcestí enjoyed their summer of freedom, he'd spent half the camp session in the infirmary, between a nasty strep throat and a mosquito bite that became infected. He'd told the staff he was allergic to all bugs, but they hadn't listened. Anyway, the only other thing he'd learned at camp over the years was that kids devoted to the glorious socialist revolution—girls as well as boys—could be just as much bullies as the kids in his school.

"Yes. Those are the people you should have as friends."

It would be useless for him to resist his father's summer plans, though. The thundering inside him told him he had far bigger problems now.

"Will Štěpán go to prison?" After his father nodded, he asked, "For what?"

"Writing that counter-revolutionary letter with Pavol. Lying to an official of the State. Corrupting a minor. Pavol was only seventeen."

The letter. It was only a matter of time. Tomáš hugged himself and pressed his back to the seat, to keep from rocking in front of his father. He'd betrayed Štěpán in the meeting. He'd betrayed both of them by not showing up at the train station. Štěpán had every reason to betray him, under far worse interrogation.

Comrade Kuchař twirled the car keys around his index finger as he spoke again. "He won't be charged with homosexuality, even though it contributed to Pavol's death, because it was decriminalized a few years ago. People are born that way, and punishment won't change it."

Was I also born the way I am?

Tomáš covered his twitchy eyelid. "But you're friends with his father. You said you had a duty to Comrade Jelínek. Can't you get the charges thrown out?"

His father reached toward him, but he shrank toward the door, and his father drew back his hand. "Son, we're a nation of laws, and the laws have to be followed in every case. No exceptions."

The weight of his father's words crushed all hope that his life could continue as before. As soon as Štěpán named him for the letter, they'd follow the law. Tomáš's father would disappear from the meeting as Comrade Jelínek had. Lose his position with the Party, maybe even his regular job as the lawyer for the town. And if he didn't kill Tomáš first, the interrogators or the other prisoners would.

Or else his father would ship him to a psychiatric hospital as soon as he turned eighteen. Claim he'd done everything he could, and maybe they'd let him keep his district leadership position out of pity for having an antisocial son who couldn't be fixed.

After saying goodnight to his parents, Tomáš trudged upstairs to his room and his train set. His gaze locked on the hiker with the backpack, the one he hadn't brought to the meeting but left at the top of the mountain with the tunnel beneath.

It's time you gave up childish things.

His eyelids stung. He couldn't swallow the lump in his throat or banish the aching that filled his chest. He had already lost his only friend. In a way, this loss would be equally hard to bear.

Tomáš considered taking his trains on one final journey along the tracks through the tunnels and town, but he knew one journey would turn into two, and ten, and he wouldn't be able to do what he had to do.

Keep busy and you won't feel the pain.

He gathered the original packaging of his train cars, buildings, tunnels, and tracks and piled the little boxes outside the curtain of green velvet fabric that covered the four pushed-together tables. He was six years old when his father set up the first table, laying an oval track of twelve pieces and adding an engine, a middle car, and a caboose. The train going around and around mesmerized and calmed Tomáš. And underneath the table was his special place where he would spend hours hiding from the world.

As he packed his set into the boxes, piece by piece, Tomáš recalled every new addition of track, train, and building. The birthdays and national holidays and grade report days that brought them. Every major expansion that required a new folding table.

Over the weekend, he cleared the town and train tracks from the tables, stacked the boxes from largest to smallest, folded the fabric covering, and leaned the tables against the wall. He kept his door closed the whole time, so his father wouldn't ask him what had changed his mind and his mother wouldn't try to talk him out of it.

"Are you sure you want to do this?" she said on Saturday night, after he'd brought the first boxes downstairs to the living room. Too late to do anything about it at this point.

"I'm ready to move on," he said.

"But why?"

"I'm leaving soon." He added, to reassure her, "For university." She hadn't attended the meeting at the KSČ headquarters, hadn't heard what his father had told him afterward. She didn't know that a Sword of Damocles hung over him—that his life depended on his chief bully's willingness to endure torture rather than denounce him.

The more he thought about it, the more it nagged at him: *What kind of government forces people to act against their conscience, like turn their friends in for interrogation and torture?* That was what the capitalists did, according to Marx and Engels. That's what the Nazis had done when they invaded. *We're supposed to be better.*

Those were the things he'd talked about with Pavol, when they were free to question.

His mother patted the box on top of the stack. "Your father and I can keep your set in the basement. You may have children one day who'll want it."

If I live long enough to have children.

"Or Sofie," his mother said, filling the silence.

"If Sofie's children turn out like her, they'll want volleyballs and sneakers. Not trains."

His mother laughed, and Tomáš smiled for the first time since the Party meeting. He liked to make his mother laugh, especially since he could never amuse his father.

If he made her laugh, he wouldn't cry.

"I'd like to donate it to the town library," he said.

"That's nice of you, but do you think you might regret it?"

Tomáš twisted the toe of his sneaker against the dark wood floor from the late 1800s when the house, and much of the town, had risen along with the railroad, factories, and mines. Germans once lived in their house, his father had told him, before the Czechs expelled them at the end of the war because of the terrible things they'd done.

In the short time we have in a place, how would we want others to remember us?

"If the train set's at the library, lots of kids will get to enjoy it. There are probably other kids like me who'd watch the trains go around, and it would make them calm and happy." Tomáš swallowed the salty mass in his throat. "I want it to have a good home."

After school on Monday Tomáš's mother drove him to the new concrete-and-glass library two blocks from Town Hall, with the boxed-up set in the back seat of the station wagon and the tables sticking out the rear with the tailgate tied to the bumper. After carrying everything inside, he helped the librarians set up the tracks and the little town. He placed Pavol's hiker at the top of the mountain.

The library director tried to hug him, but he stepped back. She shook his hand instead. "Thank you in the name of the people of Rozcestí and the Czechoslovak Socialist Republic, young Comrade Kuchař. You're an honor to our country and our socialist revolution."

He avoided her eyes.

THE GATHERING

APRIL–MAY 1969

CHAPTER 9: TOMÁŠ

Days, then weeks, passed. Štěpán didn't return to Rozcestí, and the police didn't come for Tomáš. At first, the huge empty space in his room disoriented him. He would awaken at night and pace the carpet, as if he were the train circling his town. One day, while helping his mother straighten the basement pantry, he found some of his father's old exercise equipment—barbells and a bench press—and brought them upstairs while his father nodded approval.

In mid-April Tomáš turned eighteen. His birthday fell on a Saturday, and after breakfast on that raw, drizzly morning his parents asked him to step outside. He had both anticipated and dreaded this moment. Becoming an adult meant he had to fit in and follow the rules even more—or face the consequences the way Štěpán had.

Have they let me off because I was underage? The thought had occurred to him many times in the weeks since the Party meeting.

"Close your eyes and hold out your hand," his father said. Tomáš strained to keep his hand from shaking. What could this strange surprise be?

Something cold and metallic dropped into his palm. He opened his eyes to see the keys for the green station wagon. "For me?"

His father nodded. "We're so proud of you, how you gave up your childhood things and donated them to the library so that all the people will enjoy them. That was a fine socialist thing to do."

A car. It hadn't occurred to him that he'd ever drive a car, even though he could get his license at eighteen and a few of the boys at school already had cars. Like Štěpán, who honked for attention every time he drove his parents' rattletrap Trabi.

"What about you?" Tomáš asked.

"Our new Škoda coupe will be here in June."

His mother added, "We won't need a station wagon anymore, with you and Sofie away at university. I can't believe how fast you've grown up."

"About time," his father said.

Tomáš's eyelid twitched.

"Now get in. You need to learn to drive."

Tap the brake with your right foot.

Push down the clutch with your left foot.

Shift the gear with your right hand.

Let up on the clutch while you press the accelerator with your right foot.

No matter how much his father repeated the instructions, Tomáš couldn't figure out the sequence. The clutch popped and the engine stalled before they left the circular driveway. He came within centimeters of hitting the wall between the garden and the street.

Keep your eye on the road!

Look both ways before turning.

At the first intersection, a horn startled him. He let go of the wheel. A small pickup screeched and swerved. Its front tires sank into the mud beside the road.

"What did I tell you? Look what you did."

The other driver got out of his truck to examine the mess. Tomáš's father climbed out as well. "My apologies, comrade," Tomáš heard him say. "I'm teaching my boy to drive, and he's a bit of a slow learner."

The man bowed slightly. "No problem, Comrade Kuchař. I have some cardboard I can put under those wheels."

Tomáš's father waved his hand. "No need for you to get muddy." He motioned for Tomáš to join them. "Son, you're going to apologize and get this man back on the road."

"I'm sorry."

"Look him in the eye."

Tomáš forced his gaze upward. "I'm sorry, comrade."

"As I said, slow learner."

Hot blood rushed to Tomáš's face, leaving the rest of his body chilled and shaky. His father could turn from friend to foe in an instant—and turn him from almost-adult back to a child.

After he freed the man's truck, Tomáš rinsed his hands with rivulets of coal-tinged water that zigzagged down the hood of the Škoda. He returned to the driver's seat, shoes and pant legs heavy with mud.

On the downhill he held the clutch while pumping the brake. As he stopped, started, and jerked along, his father pressed his hands to his head. "I can't take this, son. You're making me nauseous."

"Should I stop?" Tomáš slammed the brakes with a squeal. The car stalled.

"No, get out. You're never going to learn." His father reached for the steering wheel.

"Another chance?" He had to get this right. Even with all the stopping and stalling, Tomáš saw how quickly a car could take him places compared to walking or biking.

It would take him to university, away from his father.

"Fine. Turn around and drive back to the house."

Hand trembling, Tomáš shifted from first to second gear on the uphill but forgot to disengage the clutch first. The transmission screeched beneath him, and he let go of the shuddering gearshift. The smell of scorched metal and rubber filled the car, and with a final grind and groan the Škoda quit in the middle of the road.

"Fool!" His father jabbed with his thumb. "Out!"

Tomáš's stomach jumped to his throat. "I'm sorry, Papa!" he cried, though it was a worthless apology. The harder he tried to please his father, the more he screwed it up.

Comrade Kuchař raised his hand. To slap him? Tomáš wasn't going to stay long enough to find out. Banging his knee on the steering wheel, he scrambled out into the rain and started to limp up the hill.

"Not so fast!"

Tomáš turned around. His father stood next to the car and gestured toward it. "You're pushing it."

Head hanging, Tomáš trotted toward his father and the car. "Up the hill?" He calculated the slope of the incline and the probability that the car would roll backward and flatten him.

"To the side of the road. Then you're walking into town and finding a tow truck."

Comrade Kuchař sat in the driver's seat. Rain pelted Tomáš's face and beaded on his glasses as he pushed the car to the curb. Nuts, bolts, and jagged shards of metal lay on the pavement. Tomáš picked them up and dropped them into the front pouch of his nylon Youth Union pullover.

A stocky man in a shiny black raincoat and matching hat popped out of his house, jogged up to the driver's side window, and tapped it. "Comrade Kuchař, do you need help?"

97

"I'm going for a tow truck," Tomáš said before his father could roll down the window and answer.

"No need." The man knocked on a few of his neighbors' doors, and soon half a dozen men appeared wearing slickers. Together they helped Tomáš push the car up the hill while Comrade Kuchař steered, windows up, apart from their conversation.

"Let me guess. You stripped the transmission," one of the men said as they approached the last street before Tomáš's house.

"How did you know?"

"I did it too, once upon a time."

Someone else jumped in. "Yeah, old man. Once upon a time is right." A few of the men laughed.

"Is this your first driving lesson?" another one asked.

"Yes. I turned eighteen today."

The men slapped Tomáš on his rain-soaked back, and this time he didn't flinch. Pushing the car uphill along with them, he felt as if he belonged somewhere. In his town. With grown men who'd taken his side and treated him as one of them.

The next day Tomáš rode his bicycle into town to stand in line for meat and pick up his father's suits that the tailor had let out. He returned home to find a toolbox next to the broken-down Škoda and a pair of legs with work boots sticking out from underneath the car.

Tools clinked on the cobblestone driveway. A man crab-walked out and struggled to his feet.

"You must be Tomáš. Alias, the culprit." The man listed from side to side, as if he'd stood too quickly and become dizzy. His tousled dark-brown hair was shot through with gray, and his teeth were crooked and yellowed. He squinted in the sunlight, and the wrinkles around his eyes merged on one side with a scar near his hairline. He wore grease-stained overalls and a T-shirt underneath. Tomáš thought he'd seen him before.

The man scratched the stubble on his cheek with his left hand, leaving behind a black streak. "Ondřej Pekár." He held out his right hand for Tomáš to shake. His hand was warm and damp. Tomáš smelled liquor on the man's breath as he spoke. "I think I fixed it, but let's take it for a drive to make sure."

Tomáš stepped back and pointed to himself. "Me?"

"Yes, you." The man took a half-liter bottle from the chest pocket of his overalls, uncapped it with his thumb, and drank the rest of the amber liquid. "I'm your new driving teacher. Your father told me to prepare myself well."

Tomáš lowered his eyes to the man's workboots. Yes, he'd seen the man various times when his father drove him home from youth meetings. It was the stubble, the overalls, the round belly and skinny arms—the way this Ondřej held the bottle in his left hand, his thumb on the neck, as he drank directly from it. A year ago, during the time of the reforms, Tomáš had noticed him sprawled in the doorway of the tailor shop after it had closed for the night, an empty bottle beside him. His feet were wedged in the corner of the doorframe, and his head was tilted back, his mouth wide open, like a baby bird waiting for its mother to feed it.

He'd tugged his father's sleeve. *Papa, I think that man needs help.* He wanted to help. Socialism with a human face meant you looked out for your neighbor. That was another thing he and Pavol had talked about.

His father had glanced quickly at the man, then back to the road. *I know him. He'll be fine in the morning.*

Forcing his mind back to the present, Tomáš adjusted the

packages in his arms. "I'll drop these inside and get my father." Despite what Ondřej had said about a driving lesson, Tomáš expected his father to pay for the repair—or not, because many townspeople worked for his father for free, for favors—and send the man on his way.

He put away the groceries and handed his father the suits, folded and wrapped in brown tissue paper. "Papa, that guy outside says he's supposed to teach me to drive, but I don't think so." Tomáš's eyelid twitched, and he rubbed his nose. "He's the town drunk, isn't he?"

His father's slap came out of nowhere. "Don't you ever call him that!"

"But we've seen him."

Comrade Kuchař grabbed Tomáš's shoulders and shook him. "I can take away that car as fast as I gave it to you. You are going with him. *You* are driving. Not him."

Tomáš nodded, teeth still clacking. "I understand."

This time he did understand. If he got someone killed because of the way he drove, it would be the town drunk and not the district Party leader.

Outside, Ondřej asked Tomáš for a piece of paper. Confused, Tomáš dug into his pants pocket and pulled out the receipt from the tailor. Ondřej flipped it over and took a pencil from his toolbox.

"Kid, I'm going to draw it out for you." In crooked stick figures smudged by his left hand, he showed Tomáš how to shift the clutch while slowing down or speeding up. "Now practice it," he said.

"In the car?"

"No, here."

Tomáš pantomimed the movements. Ondřej laughed.

"I know. It looks silly," Tomáš said.

"I was joking. I meant in the car. But if it works, what the hell."

After Tomáš had practiced for a while, they got into the car. Ondřej took a swig from the fresh bottle he'd dug out of his toolbox and said, "Let's go, kid."

Tomáš started the car. He pushed down the clutch pedal, shifted into first gear, and eased it up while tapping the accelerator. The first time, the car jerked forward and stalled. He tried again, felt the transmission engage and the car move forward slowly. Smoothly. When the driveway met the road, he pressed down the clutch pedal, then the brake. Looked both ways.

He was driving. Down the hill and into town. He wanted to shout at the townspeople, *I can do this!*

Ondřej leaned against the door, eyes closed and mouth gaping. Snoring.

Tomáš wished his father could see him now, driving on his own and not wrecking the car. Would he take back everything he'd said?

CHAPTER 10: LÍDA

A few days after the StB agents told Lída of Pavol's death, Pavol's oldest sister, Alžbeta, met her and her father at the end of their factory shift. "Mama says you're welcome any Sunday at noon for dinner. You don't need to tell us in advance." The thirteen-year-old sniffled and blew her nose into a wadded-up handkerchief. "Mama told me to tell you: Don't become a stranger."

But as the weeks went by, Lída found herself less and less able to imagine going over to the Bartoš family's apartment. After her sickness ended, she grew plump, so much so that she had to unbutton one side of her work overalls. She nurtured this piece of Pavol in secret, telling no one except the nurses and doctors at the clinic because she needed them to help it flourish.

She'd asked them not to tell her father, and they went along with it. *So many girls—their fathers beat them or throw them out of the house,* the doctor said. Lída didn't correct her, didn't say her father never struck her, not even during his worst nightmares or binges.

Nor did she speak of the baby's father. Not yet. Not until she had to.

She would handle this alone, make her own decisions, decide the course of her life with what little freedom she had.

For every kilo that she gained, Ondřej seemed to lose one. His cheeks hollowed, and skin sagged from his arm bones, though his belly remained round and solid. He had no appetite for meat, so he and Lída traded meat to their factory coworkers for ration coupons at the bakery. Lída winced at the irony: a family whose name meant *baker* needing to trade for bread.

In April, though, her father took a weekend job teaching Comrade Kuchař's son to drive. Lída recognized the name—knew the son must be Tomáš, Pavol's friend, though she didn't mention this to her father. Apparently the boy was a menace on the road, but Kuchař paid in the most delicious bread and butter Lída had eaten in Rozcestí.

"You look... radiant," Ondřej said at supper the final Saturday in April. He cut a slice and handed it to her, slathered with butter.

"I'm worried about you, Pa. You can't live on bread."

"I've done it before." He finished his bottle of beer in one swallow, kneaded his stomach, and released a loud belch. "That's better."

"And your drinking. You're not pouring water on a fire. You're pouring gasoline." She stopped there. Her lower lip quivered.

Pavol, where are you now and why did you leave me?

She pressed her hand against her belly. The fluttering inside was not even strong enough for her expectant fingertips to detect. Let her father think she'd gained weight from finishing his supper every night.

Ondřej pushed his plate toward her. He'd eaten half of the small portion of rabbit she'd cut for him and mashed his potato on the plate so she couldn't tell how much he'd left behind.

"Tomorrow, I'm taking you to the clinic," she said. She would return to the women's clinic while he was seeing his doctor. Make sure that all she had left of Pavol remained safe and growing inside her.

"Can't. I'm teaching that boy again."

"What time?"

"Ten in the morning."

"We'll go afterward."

Her father smiled, and the crows' feet around his eyes crinkled, hiding his scar. "If he doesn't get me killed first."

After the examination, the ponytailed young doctor patted Lída's shoulder. "The baby's coming along nicely. But there's something else we need to discuss." She checked some items on her clipboard and lifted the paper to reveal a letter with an official seal. "We have to resolve this soon, so you can apply for your benefits."

Lída chewed her lower lip. The baby's last name. As an unwed mother, she could use her own name, or the father's. She wanted Bartoš. She'd already decided not to name him Pavol because no one could ever replace Pavol. The first name could be Michal, for her brother who never had a chance. But the child deserved to carry some piece of his father.

"The police stopped by a couple of days ago, and it appears that your situation is a bit . . . complicated."

Lída pressed her heels against the leg of the examination table, the cold metal clashing with the explosive mix of fury and shame that bubbled up inside her. "Why is it police business that I'm having a baby?"

The two StB officers and Pavol's scorched face clicked into her mind. Her stomach heaved, sending air and a hideous barking sound past her throat.

The doctor handed her a plastic basin and rubbed her back while murmuring, "I know it's hard."

Lída swallowed, over and over, to keep the basin empty and the tears from flowing. The doctor's gentle hand seemed to say, *Let it out. Let it all out.*

No! You've escaped from worse. You live in the woods and survive by your wits. You're too strong to fall apart now.

"I'm not getting rid of it if that's what they want. I'm not giving it up for adoption either."

The doctor stepped around to look at Lída. Her eyes were blue. Earnest eyes. "I understand. You've been so conscientious with your appointments and milestones. You do have choices, but you need to make good ones for your future and your child's."

Lída flattened her hand against her belly. "What *are* my choices?"

"You can decline to name a father. That way, you'll receive all your social benefits." The doctor ticked them off on slim, smooth fingers. "Day care at your factory. A spot on the wait list for housing."

Lída nodded. It would be so easy—an apartment in the new high-rise housing estate on the northwest edge of town, where buses stopped to take men west to the mines and women south to the factories. Still . . . "You know who he is. People will make assumptions about me." As they already had, calling her a gypsy and a cow as soon as she'd arrived in town. They would call her worse names now, ones for a woman who didn't know the father because she'd slept with so many men. Names they called those two women singers who'd been banned for pornography even though they'd only hugged Comrade Dubček and brought him flowers. "Will my child be denied a full education?"

"That's a long way in the future, dear. We should focus on the here and now."

"If I refuse? If I want my child to have the father's name?" If she didn't want to betray Pavol the way she'd betrayed Daria in order to dance with him.

The doctor's sweet smile evaporated. "According to the police, the father committed a criminal act. They can use that to deny you housing, and your child any more than a basic education. And if we find evidence of neglect," she said as she glanced at the typed letter, "we can—"

"Take the child away," Lída finished for her. "You said *we*. Do you agree with this?"

A terrified look crossed the doctor's face. "No, not at all," she whispered while tapping the plastic basin against the sink, drowning out the possibility of a recording device picking up her words. More loudly she said, "I want you to make the best decision for your child's future."

"When do I have to decide?"

"I suggest soon, to get on the housing list. You don't want to be too far away from the factory, for the baby's sake." The doctor made some marks on the chart. "I can let the manager know there'll be a new little one at the day care starting in November. Give you six weeks to recover and get acquainted."

"Thank you," Lída said, as if she were a robot with the dial turned to "polite." It was what they'd received in exchange for their freedom—a country that took care of everything for them. Was the trade worth it, if she had to deny Pavol's name to his own child? Either way, the child would only know his father in whispers. He'd spend his whole life paying for his father's stand for freedom.

The same way she paid for her father's choices.

She crossed the hospital lobby and climbed one flight of stairs to the clinic where she'd left Ondřej. He wasn't in the waiting room. Had he gone looking for her? She'd lied to him, told him she was going to the library for the puppet show that had been announced on posters all over town, and he'd promised he'd wait for her if she hadn't returned by the time his appointment was over.

She approached a nurse with glasses and gray-streaked hair tied back in a low ponytail. Not the same nurse who'd been at the station when Lída dropped her father off, so the shift must have changed. "Excuse me, I'm here for Ondřej Pekár."

"He's still with the doctor. Are you his daughter?" The woman's expression was cool and distant.

"Yes." The nurse avoided Lída's eyes, and Lída's gaze fell to her green scrubs and her name tag. *Kuchařová*, it read. Was she related to Comrade Kuchař and his son—Pavol's friend?

"Are you over eighteen?" the nurse asked.

"October. I turn eighteen in October." By then she'd be a mother, with a huge decision to make in the meantime.

"Please take a seat out here."

"I can't see him?" Now her stomach clenched. Why was it taking so long?

"That's the rule. No minors. He'll be ready soon." The nurse turned away.

Lída picked up a wrinkled newspaper but couldn't concentrate. She'd read the same movie review over and over by the time she looked up into her father's brown eyes.

She threw her arms around him and squeezed him tight. "Are you all right? I was worried."

"A bit of nonsense. They want me back tomorrow morning for tests. I need to fill out the forms downstairs."

Lída glanced at the nurse, who frowned and said, "Remember, Comrade Pekár, no food or drink after midnight."

Lída bit her lip. That didn't sound like nonsense.

But her father shrugged and said, "It's what happens when you get old."

"You're not old, Pa."

He laid his arm across her shoulders. "I'm forty-nine. In this country, that's old."

While her father filled out forms in the office next to the hospital's main entrance, Lída crossed over to the emergency room. When she'd planned her future with Pavol, she'd dreamed of returning to school to become a nurse.

Now she'd never leave the factory floor.

She pushed through the double doors and stepped into the waiting room, deserted except for one teenage boy wearing a navy peacoat with the patches ripped off. She could tell where they'd been by the loose threads and the darker color—a ghost silhouette. He slumped in a chair next to the entrance for ambulance patients and held his bandaged head between his hands. Purple bruises ringed both eyes. Two large horizontal scabs like minus signs covered his upper lip, which sank into his mouth on one side. Behind his legs, under the chair, lay a knapsack.

"Lída? Do you remember me?" he called out softly, as if talking hurt him. Inside his mouth, on top, were swollen, fire-red gums and a gaping hole where a bunch of teeth should have been. He must've noticed her confusion, because he said, "Štěpán Jelínek."

The one who called me Gypsy and tormented Daria and her brother. She swallowed her words. He seemed too miserable, too helpless, for her to snap at him.

Besides, he'd been Pavol's friend. Pavol must've seen something in him.

Whenever Pavol came to her cottage after that night in December, he'd tell her, *I'm supposed to be at my friend Tomáš's house tonight. Or I'm supposed to be spending the night with Štěpán.*

The big bully? she'd asked the first time he mentioned Štěpán's name.

He's not like that at all. Well, he used to be, but now he's trying to change. I'm helping him change.

Lída wrapped her arms over her smock and the stretchy waistband of her skirt, the little bit of Pavol tucked away inside her. She felt a whisper. Like Pavol's voice.

Forgive him. He still wants to change.

"What happened to you?" she asked Štěpán.

"Everything." He squeezed his eyes shut and groaned.

Lída stepped toward him. He smelled of antiseptic and fresh blood. "Do you need to see the doctor?"

"I saw him. I'm done. I have no place to go."

She rubbed her eyebrows, confused. Štěpán had a home. A nice one, from what Pavol had said. And she couldn't ask more, with the emergency room staff within earshot. "Let me get my father."

"Ondřej? Is he here?" After Lída nodded, Štěpán said, "Please."

So he was on a first-name basis with her father. Had gone out drinking with him, probably, like Pavol had. At another time, Lída might've had the energy to resent both of them for that.

Ondřej was already done signing the forms. When Lída brought him over to Štěpán, the two embraced like long-lost friends. But Štěpán's voice shook when he said, "I have to get out of here."

He lifted the knapsack and dropped it right away, nearly tumbling to the floor along with it. Ondřej grabbed one shoulder strap. "What's in here? Bricks?"

Štěpán grimaced and reached for his head. "Books," he said.

Outside, Štěpán looked around nervously, and it surprised Lída that her father did the same. Indoors, it was easy to eavesdrop on conversations or record them with a microphone tucked inside a telephone or a light switch, but she'd met Pavol outside many times and never noticed anyone following them. As long as they spoke in whispers, they were safe.

They were kids, after all. Enjoying their freedom . . . when they had it. And each other . . . when she had him. She raked her hand across her eyes, burning in the too-bright sunlight.

She expected Štěpán to tell them how he ended up in the emergency room with no parents to wait for him the way she'd waited for her father. Instead, he followed them home in silence.

He'd been one of Pavol's best friends. More than a drinking buddy, though that was clearly part of it.

What could Štěpán tell her about Pavol? So many things she didn't know.

CHAPTER 11: ŠTĚPÁN AND LÍDA

Štěpán let Ondřej carry the knapsack to their house. His head throbbed with each step, and the dirt path and forest rocked before his eyes like the picture on a busted TV set. The chirps of birds returning for spring grated in his sore ears and battered skull.

Pavol had told him about this fairy-tale house in the woods. He'd said no police ever followed him there.

A short pile of wood lay neatly stacked under a tarp next to the door. Inside, Štěpán huddled against the front wall next to a bedroll and shivered in the unheated room. The smell of damp soil rose through gaps in the wood plank floor. He pressed his tongue to his scarred gums and lip, feeling the empty space.

Ondřej brought over one chair. Lída brought another.

"Would you like a drink?" asked Ondřej. "Beer? Slivovice? Vodka?"

Lída glared at her father.

Štěpán shook his head slowly. "Can't. Not with a concussion."

"Well, *I* need one. It's been a hell of a day." Ondřej pulled out a half-filled jug of amber liquid. He drank directly from the jug.

"How about a cup of tea, Štěpán?" Lída asked, already reaching toward the kettle on the wood stove.

Ondřej flipped his wooden chair around and sat with his legs spread and his arms across the backrest. Through blurred vision, Štěpán saw twin yellow smudges spilling from the brown irises of Ondřej's eyes.

"Let's hear what happened, kid," Ondřej said.

Štěpán rested his elbows on his knees and pressed his palms against his temples. "I was in prison. Didn't anyone tell you?"

"I heard rumors, but I'd rather get it from the horse's mouth."

"You know they're going to follow you too, if you have anything to do with me."

Ondřej waved his left hand. "I'm past caring."

"They arrested me at school. I'm expelled and kicked off the hockey team." Štěpán picked at the hanging threads from the patches his jailers had ripped off.

This morning his father told him that without him, the team had lost the tournament.

Thinking about the next part, a wave of nausea gripped him. "They dropped me off at home, and the first thing my parents did was throw me out of the house. My father said he lost his job, and both he and Mama were kicked out of the Party."

Ondřej cursed under his breath. Lída's eyes grew wide.

Štěpán's mouth filled with saliva. He couldn't share the rest of what his jailers had told his parents—the reason his father slammed the back of his head with Anton's hockey stick as Štěpán was walking out the door. Let Ondřej think he'd sustained the head injury in prison.

Ondřej pointed to Štěpán's face, to the scars on his lip, never stitched and nowhere close to healed five weeks later. "I see they got your teeth."

A tear dropped onto the wooden floor, and then another and another, as if the concussion had bared his emotions like raw meat. He'd lost those teeth protecting Tomáš Kuchař. So not worth it.

No one would ever see him as the hero. Not even Ondřej, a real hero, if Ondřej knew his secret.

At the Bar Šťastný in early January, Ondřej had told the stories to him and Pavol and Petr and Moučka, and the other players who stopped by but didn't stick around because they were too young to drink.

"This is my girlfriend's father," Pavol said when he introduced them at the grittiest of Rozcestí's dive bars—a crowded, humid basement with a packed-dirt floor, where amateur mandolin and guitar music and multiple conversations bounced off water-stained stone walls. Pavol said Ondřej had fought in the Czech Resistance against the Nazis. That he'd lived in the forest for years and fought with Serbs, Croats, and Bosniaks, the fiercest partisans of all. That he'd taken part in the Slovak National Uprising.

That he'd killed a man. Many men.

Ondřej had a long scar on one side of his head. "The Nazis were ruthless," he said. "We had to be equally ruthless to defeat them."

Ondřej seemed to consider it his duty to pass on these stories, to make sure no one forgot that Nazis invaded and occupied the country and the only people who fought back were ragged, out-gunned partisans. The other regulars at Bar Šťastný knew of his feats: how he'd covered a retreat from a mountain pass in Slovakia. How he'd melted back into the forest where the Nazis couldn't find him.

The regulars bought him drinks. He, in turn, bought drinks for the students.

Štěpán listened until everything in the room blurred and the cigarette smoke ceased to irritate his throat but made him feel warm and electric, a part of this world of men.

Although he weighed much less than the hockey players, Pavol drank more than any of them. He tried to keep up with Ondřej, shot after shot, beer after beer.

Sitting beside him, on the side of the table next to the wall, Štěpán cupped his hand around Pavol's ear and whispered, "You need to slow down." Touching Pavol's fine hair and soft earlobe kicked up a stirring below his belt.

"Don't worry, brácha. I can handle it."

Pavol couldn't handle it. He had no experience. He'd been the one to pass the flask along at school parties, while the rest of them got crocked and rowdy. By the time Ondřej's chronological narrative got to the Red Army's advance, Pavol leaned back in his chair, head lolling against the wall, eyes half-closed. At first slurring his questions, then unable to get more than half a sentence out.

Pavol's lips were full and wet and shiny. Štěpán wanted to kiss those lips, crush his mouth to Pavol's, share their sweet brandy-tinged breath.

But not in the tavern in front of these men.

And not unless Pavol wanted it too.

After the Nazis' surrender, after the partisans came out of the forest, Ondřej grew silent. The bright excitement of the war story faded, replaced by a haunted expression, as if a light had gone out leaving only an endless dark tunnel.

"You boys better go," Ondřej said. "We already lost one of you." He glanced toward Moučka, who'd turned pale and pressed his hand to his mouth. "Two."

Moučka dashed toward the stairs with Petr following, while Štěpán remained with Pavol and Ondřej. Ondřej jerked his thumb toward Pavol. "I'm worried about him."

"Yeah, he's not used to drinking."

Ondřej's smirk confused Štěpán, as if he knew something Štěpán didn't. "Kid, whoever puts him to bed, make sure he sleeps on his side."

Štěpán lifted Pavol's arm over his shoulders and helped him to his feet and up the narrow, uneven stairs. Outside, they passed Petr standing next to Moučka, on his hands and knees in a snowbank.

Štěpán saluted Petr with his free hand. "Good luck, guys. I'm taking Saint Pavol home."

Petr laughed. "Not a saint tonight."

Pavol yanked Štěpán's hair and slurred, "Lída. Gotta get to Lída."

Definitely not a saint. But Pavol wouldn't make it ten steps on the snow-covered road, much less all the way to the outskirts of Rozcestí where he'd said Lída lived.

"You're coming with me." Štěpán tugged Pavol's alcohol-sodden body in the opposite direction while thinking of what he'd say to Mrs. Bartošová.

He heard water running and looked down at a puddle spreading around Pavol's feet.

"Shit, Pavol. What did you do?"

"Sorry, brácha."

He couldn't take Pavol home in this condition. Not to his cramped apartment with three little sisters who worshipped him and a bathroom in the back of the building that they shared with two other families. Anyway, Pavol had probably told his mother he was spending the night at Tomáš's house, as Tomáš and Štěpán had already taken turns covering for Pavol's nights with Lída.

At the next corner, Štěpán turned toward his narrow row house, five streets uphill from the main square and the hospital.

Pavol shivered. "Can't feel my feet."

His urine-soaked socks had probably frozen by now. Štěpán picked up his pace, dragging his friend the rest of the way home.

His mother was watching TV in the living room. She glared at them coming in. "At least it's not you this time."

"Can you help me? Please?" He wanted her to take care of everything. If he pulled off Pavol's wet pants, the response of his own body would be obvious. "I'm going to run a bath for him." As he sprinted upstairs, he turned back to her. "Thanks, Mama."

While putting fresh sheets on the upper bunk where Anton had slept before he left for university, Štěpán imagined his life in Prague next year, returning to the nightclub near Wenceslas Square where the players from Holešovice had taken him.

Gay. Until the reforms brought once-illicit books to his country, he'd only known the cruel words for people like him. He hadn't known about places where men who liked men could gather and no one would bother them. And beyond Prague were other cities. His books drew him to the American ones: New York, Chicago, San Francisco. He whispered the names of these places under his breath, and their exotic syllables drowned out the harsh noises of his best friend spewing a bellyful of drink into the toilet across the hall.

"I'm going to speak to that poor boy's mother tomorrow. This isn't right," Mrs. Jelínková said after she'd helped Pavol into Štěpán's bottom bunk. Pavol wore Anton's old pajamas, the wide waistband flopped over his stomach.

"No, Mama. It was one time. It won't happen again."

His mother turned out the light. When his eyes adjusted to the darkness, Štěpán spotted Pavol on his back, snoring. Remembering Ondřej's advice, Štěpán climbed from the top bunk. He wanted to lie with Pavol's head on his lap, kiss his lips, rub his smooth flat belly to calm the upset inside. Instead, he rolled Pavol onto his side with his back against the wall and kissed him once on the top of his head.

Štěpán climbed back to the top bunk, his groin aching. He peered down at his helpless, sleeping friend, the one who'd always called him brother.

He still had his hand, his imagination, and the words of Walt Whitman.

I sing the body electric . . .

Dusk settled into the stone-and-wood cottage. After cleaning up from supper by candlelight, Lída unrolled her mattress for Štěpán. Ondřej called out from the table, "Let him take my bed tonight."

"No, Pa. You need your sleep."

"I'll have plenty of time to sleep at the hospital."

Lída's words caught in her throat. Her father had said he was going in for tests.

And what else had the nurse said? *No food or drink after midnight.* They still had hours to go, and he would drink up to the final minute.

"They don't put you under for tests," she told him.

"They said they wanted to look inside."

"That's what X-rays are for."

"They said the X-rays didn't show anything."

Lída glanced toward Štěpán, sitting across from her father at the table, as if he might know more because he played hockey and sometimes hockey players got hurt. Štěpán stared into space with deadened eyes, his scabbed and bruised face twisted in pain.

"Does your head hurt?" she asked him. He nodded.

Lída brought Štěpán aspirin and a cup of water and guided him past the curtain to Ondřej's bedroom. Helping him took her mind off what would happen to her father the next day.

Some kind of surgery. Why?

Štěpán fell asleep right away, still in his clothes. Lída covered him with the orange, green, and brown diamond-patterned quilt she'd carried years ago from the house in Znojmo.

For a long time, she sat next to Štěpán in the darkness—her former tormentor now lying helpless with bandages covering his once-spiky blond hair. Hours after leaving the hospital, he still smelled of blood.

"What did Pavol see in you?" she whispered.

She didn't expect an answer, but minutes later an anguished scream came from him.

"My teeth!" Štěpán cried, over and over. He thrashed on the mattress, kicking the quilt to the floor, and thrust out his arm. It brushed past her, and she leapt to her feet. The chair clattered onto its side.

"It's all right," she said, keeping her voice calm. "You're safe. You're having a nightmare."

She knew not to touch Štěpán like this, as she knew not to touch her father when nightmares tormented his sleep.

Stay calm. Reassure him that he's safe.

Nothing else you can do. You don't know his pain.

Štěpán grew quiet, his breathing regular. Lída righted the chair and tiptoed back into the main room. Her father sat at the table, forehead resting on his palm. The candlelight shone slick on his hands and wrists. "So fucking useless," he said. "I didn't fight to free this country from the Nazis only to have the Russians take it over."

Lída said nothing, couldn't tell him what was weighing on her mind. Everything the StB agents had done to Štěpán. Everything they could do to her. They'd never returned after that horrible day when her world broke apart. Instead, they tracked down her doctor and told her what name she could and couldn't give her baby. A reminder of the power they had.

Is this the country where I'll have to raise my child?

CHAPTER 12: ŠTĚPÁN

Dizzy, sore, bone-tired, with bandages covering his head, Štěpán trudged into town alongside Ondřej and Lída the next morning. A sunrise of pink and orange poured across the cloudless sky. Štěpán used to take the dawn for granted, thinking only of the scrape of his blades on ice, the smack of his stick against the puck, the thud when heavy rubber hit the boards. But after a month of darkness, taunts, and blows pounding his body, the sunrise was a touch of paradise: Silent. Peaceful. Majestic.

Pavol once called its beauty the proof of God's love. That was before the tanks rolled in and God abandoned them. Pavol crashed the hardest because he'd believed the most. A merciful God wouldn't have taken away his dreams and made him suffer so much. A merciful God wouldn't have locked Štěpán in a dungeon for five weeks for wanting freedom and protecting their friend.

He stopped short. He'd surprised himself, thinking of Tomáš as a friend. Tomáš had only been Pavol's friend.

"You coming, kid?" Ondřej said.

"Yeah, sorry. Lost track."

"Of how to walk?" Ondřej ran his fingers through his graying hair. He'd shaved that morning and combed his hair, but the wind had already made a mess of it. "Going to be a long day on the job for you."

Now that the school had expelled him, Štěpán had two choices: report to his work assignment at Town Hall or return to prison as a parasite.

Outside the hospital entrance Štěpán embraced Ondřej and shook Lída's hand. "Good luck. See you two tonight," he said.

"I'm staying overnight." Ondřej pointed to a worried-looking Lída. "She'll be home late. But you're sticking around, right?"

"Until you kick me out." Štěpán lowered his voice. "I really appreciate this, Ondřej."

"I've always wanted a hockey player around. And if you can kill a rabbit with a puck, all the better."

Leaving them behind, Štěpán continued to Town Hall, the pressure in his gut growing the closer he got.

In prison you cleaned toilets. Dodged guards who shoved your head inside them while they called you every slur they knew. This couldn't be worse.

He joined a long queue, so many undesirables awaiting their work assignments. In front of him stood a woman with a mismatched blouse and skirt and a bright multicolored print scarf covering her head, along with a dark-haired man he guessed was her husband. He recoiled from the smell of garlic, lemon, and sauerkraut that clung to them.

From his first days in school he'd been taught to hate these people—their strange appearance and customs, their secretive ways, the fact that they wandered instead of living and working in the places where the State assigned them.

When he first met Lída, he'd called her one. He'd believed her to be one. Dressed in thrown-together, mismatched clothing, she'd shown up at the party with Grigor Stojka and his friends and his sister. She'd only arrived in Rozcestí at the beginning of that school year.

The people in the queue, both in front and now in back of him, stepped away from him. Štěpán lifted his arm and sniffed underneath. He blew into his cupped hands and smelled his rank breath.

He'd tried to wash in the creek by Lída's house. But he had no toothbrush, no change of clothes, only the books he'd hurriedly stuffed into his knapsack so that his parents wouldn't find their hiding place and throw them out. Besides, a few minutes crouched on the muddy bank slapping freezing water on himself couldn't erase the stink of weeks in prison.

Who was he to condemn people for smelling like supper when he smelled far worse?

Finally, his turn came. The comrade at the desk flipped through a thick folder. "Counter-revolutionary. What a waste."

He was right—a waste of thirteen years of education, eleven years of elite hockey, a chance for the army team, and a spot at Charles University if he didn't make the team. But Pavol's death had been a waste too. No one had risen up to expel the occupiers as Pavol had hoped. And while people had gathered at Jan Palach's gravesite, Pavol had vanished like ash in the wind.

It was all a waste. The only thing left was complete submission.

"Yes, comrade. I'm ready to rehabilitate myself through virtuous manual labor."

"Stop shitting me."

The comrade set him up with sandpaper, a bucket of black paint, a brush, and a ladder. Winter and coal dust had been cruel to Rozcestí's lamp posts and benches, and they needed a new coat of paint. "Be careful on that ladder with your head." The man yanked the bottom edge of Štěpán's bandage and laughed.

The fresh stitches stung. *Like you people give a rat's ass.*

Štěpán started on the main square and worked through lunchtime. He had neither ration coupons nor money for food. He hadn't thought of how he would eat now. Ondřej and Lída seemed to have plenty of food—what they hunted and gathered in the woods. But he didn't know how to live off the land. Without them, he'd starve.

By four in the afternoon, his empty stomach growled. He checked off the three sides of the square that he'd finished and started on the last one. As soon as he climbed down from the corner lamppost behind Town Hall, he spied his mother coming from the elementary school where she taught. Headed his way.

He waved. She didn't wave back. In her hands was a large basket covered with the dark red cloth they used for placemats.

His heart skipped. Would they let him come home, take a hot shower, sleep in his own bed? His wages could make up part of his father's lost salary . . .

"Mama!" He extended his arms to hug her, but she kept her distance. He sagged. "I know. I'm kind of ripe."

Her cheeks were bright red, even though it hadn't been a bitter-cold day. "Do you have a place to stay?"

He nodded.

She didn't press him. Instead, she held out the basket. "I brought you food. And some clothes."

"Thank you." He lifted the cloth. A loaf of dark bread, a dried sausage, and a hunk of hard cheese rested on top of folded shirts, pants, and underwear.

A food-and-clothing delivery meant only one thing: They'd kicked him out for good.

His heart sank. His tongue worried his missing teeth. Not having them would make it hard to bite into the bread and sausage. He set the basket on the ground.

"You ruined us, Štěpán," his mother said, blinking rapidly. "Your father losing his job. And I found out today . . ."

"What, Mama?" His insides seized up like a burned-out motor.

"They canceled my assignment for the next school year. They offered me a position in the cafeteria instead." She clenched a fist. "The cafeteria? After all these years in classroom? Everything I worked for?"

He raked his arm across his face. The kids loved his mother. He'd attended a different primary school, but when they played together on the under-ten hockey team, Petr would say, *Lucky you. You get to have her all the time.*

At their secondary school orientation, Pavol figured out that Mrs. Jelínková was Štěpán's mother, and that's how they became friends. *She turned school around for me. She showed me it didn't matter that I was Slovak, that my dad was a coal miner who was sick all the time. I could do great things with my life for the country.*

A car honked at the corner. Štěpán flinched. He pulled himself together. "Mama, that's so unfair."

"You should have thought of that when you made your choices. Our whole family will pay. What's your brother going to do when they expel him?"

Štěpán shuddered. "They're expelling Anton?" If so, snitching hadn't spared him.

"Not yet. That's the next step."

The next step if he did anything else wrong, like chasing the idea that had re-formed in his bruised brain over the course of the afternoon.

Fleeing the country to live in New York City.

The center of capitalism. The enemy.

The home of Walt Whitman.

I too lived, Brooklyn of ample hills was mine,

I too walk'd the streets of Manhattan island, and bathed in the waters around it,

I too felt the curious abrupt questionings stir within me,

*In the day among crowds of people sometimes they came
upon me,*

*In my walks home late at night or as I lay in my bed they came
upon me . . .*

Štěpán pointed to the ladder and bucket, the brush lying across
its top and dripping black paint on the sidewalk. "I'm working
now. I'll stay out of trouble, I promise." That's what he'd have to do,
hunker down and behave. If he did, maybe they'd let his mother
teach next year. He didn't care that they might chuck Anton out
of school. Anton was a weasel. But his mother, the best teacher at
No. 1 Rozcestí Primary School, deserved her job back.

He reached toward her, one more attempt to hug her goodbye.
She didn't approach him. She didn't even smile. His heart twisted
in his chest.

Instead, she spat out words like ice shards under his blades:
"I should've never let you become friends with Pavol."

Heat surged through Štěpán's scalp, sweaty against the bandages. "You've known him for years. He was your *student*. He said
you changed his life."

His eyelids pricked. Damn concussion, destroying his self-
control. Tears streamed down his mother's face, but he couldn't
hear her sobs over the late afternoon traffic around the square. He
coughed out the exhaust of old Trabis like the one he once drove
so proudly.

He kept talking, trying to keep his voice even. "Remember the
night I brought him home drunk and you cleaned him up?" *Was
that the day Pavol found out he hadn't gotten into university?* "Even
then you cared about him. You wanted to talk to his mother, get
help for him."

So had Štěpán. Until Pavol came up with the idea for the letter, he was planning to say something: *Man, what are you doing*

to yourself? He'd seen Pavol stumble into class late with wrinkled clothes and fetid breath, knew his grades had dropped from second in the class to the middle of the pack.

His mother dabbed her eyes with a handkerchief and blew her nose. "Your father and I wanted you to be friends with Tomáš Kuchař. Now that's a good family. A good influence. Number one student in the class. I'm sorry you never became friends. How many times did he and his family invite you and you refused to go?"

Štěpán poked his tongue into the scar tissue of his upper lip. Every time his parents had pushed him to go to Tomáš's house, study with him, or invite him to hockey games, he'd had the same response. *Please don't make me. Tomáš is weird. Nobody likes him.*

He didn't expect Tomáš to associate with him now, to thank him for what he'd done. Even the school's biggest social loser had more sense than that.

Another honk and screech of tires startled Štěpán out of his thoughts. "I have to get back to work, Mama," he said in a resigned monotone. "Thank you for the food and clothes. And tell Papa and Anton hello for me."

Štěpán finished repainting around the square and returned his equipment to Town Hall at dusk. He signed up for the streets around the hospital the next day, hoping to visit Ondřej on his lunch break. He trudged back to the little house in the woods with his basket, enough food to share with Lída when she returned home.

When she hadn't appeared by eight thirty, he cut the sausage in half and chopped his half into pieces so he could eat it without upper incisors. He tore off a crust of bread and munched it with his back teeth.

An hour and a half later Lída plodded inside. Her shoulders sagged, and her thick hair was mussed and tangled. But her face glowed orange in the candlelight like the full moon rising. Like a painting in a museum.

"How's he doing?" Štěpán asked.

"He made it through the surgery, but they want to keep him in the hospital two weeks. Wean him from the prodigious amount of alcohol he drinks every day."

"Prodigious?"

She glared at him. "You think I'm stupid, don't you?"

"No, I . . ." Nothing he could say to Lída. She'd never believe or accept an apology.

She dropped into the chair across from him. It had been more than a year since he'd seen her, but she seemed to have gained weight. He noticed the buttons open on one side of her overalls and her stomach pressed against the fabric.

Could she be . . . ? Pavol . . . ?

Štěpán quashed the smile spreading across his face. Not a saint, but perhaps he'd left something huge behind. Something that needed protection.

Something Štěpán could help protect, if he could convince Lída to trust him.

Absorbing her glare, he said, "I was planning to visit your father tomorrow. I arranged my work schedule."

"I don't know. They said to expect a rough few days." She brushed strands of hair from her face and sighed. "He was sedated tonight."

Štěpán covered his face with his hands so she wouldn't see his disappointment. He'd only spent one day at this house and already he missed Ondřej. Without his family and without Pavol, Ondřej was the only person who half-understood him, and the only person who understood what he'd gone through.

He pushed the food toward Lída. "I saved you supper."

"Thanks. I ate at the hospital." Even so, she sliced a piece of cheese, wrapped a hunk of bread around it, and popped it into her mouth.

Štěpán rubbed his fingernail against a knot on the table. It would be the two of them for a while, and she had every reason not to like him or want him around.

He listened to the rhythm of her chewing and the chirping of crickets outside. At home, he would hear cars passing by their townhouse and muffled conversations of pedestrians. On weekends he'd lie in bed late at night, listen to drunks singing, and laugh with Anton at their lack of talent.

Here, there were no cars, no people. Only the woods.

Pavol loved these woods.

The woods are scary, Štěpán once said. *You could be eaten by a wild animal.*

And Pavol asked: *Do you know what the most dangerous animal of all is?*

Bears.

Wrong.

Wolves.

Wrong.

Sharks.

Wrong.

Snakes.

Wrong.

I give up, Pavol.

Humans, brácha. We kill more of each other than all those other animals kill us combined. It's not even close.

The flickering candle illuminated Lída's face. Štěpán broke the silence. "You probably think I'm a terrible person for the way I've treated you. And other people."

After a third bloody nose at the hands of last year's hockey team, Grigor and his family had packed up their caravan before school ended and left for Most. The half dozen other families with them had followed, which meant the school's integration program went from twelve kids to zero in the space of a week.

That was before the tanks. The tanks had nothing to do with it. Only his own cruelty toward those who were different and alone.

Lída swallowed. "Why were you such a bully?"

Štěpán scraped the bottom of the candle with his fingernail. "I was one of the oldest kids in class, always bigger and stronger than the others. It gave me power." He paused, weighing his words. "I fell in love with that power."

"Because even though you were big, someone else made you feel small." Lída drummed her fingers on the table, a quick *one-two-three* that pinged his brain.

What had Pavol told her? Pavol had it easy. Three younger sisters. A kind father, even if his father died when he was thirteen.

Cry and I'll give you something to cry about.

If your brother hits you, hit him back. Be a man.

"Yeah, my father used to reward me for winning a fight. A lot of times you have to start a fight to win a fight."

"That's so wrong."

"Most of the time, it is." Štěpán leaned forward, and the smoke from the flame tickled his neck. "But some things are worth starting a fight for. Like last spring. When we fought for our freedom. Or the right to be who we are. Even gypsies."

"It's Roma. Daria said to call people what they want to be called."

Gay.

He rubbed his eyes with his fists. "Now I know what it's like to be on the other side. To be the one with no power, and someone else in love with theirs. I apologize for being a jerk."

Lída met his gaze. "I forgive you. What happened to you was wrong. Nobody deserves to be treated like that, even reformed jerks and bullies." Her full lips curved upward. "Even non-reformed ones. You can't defeat violence with violence."

I can see why Pavol fell in love with you.

Lída tugged a lock of her hair. "Besides, I'm at fault too. I didn't say anything when you pushed Daria and Grigor around. I even made a point of telling Pavol I wasn't one of them. Not that it would have mattered to Pavol, since he believed all human beings are children of God and worthy of respect." She paused. "I didn't stand up for people the way he did. I let bad things happen."

Like my coach and teammates who didn't stand up for me. That's what happens when the State is the biggest bully of all. "Well, neither of us is as much a piece of shit as my brother. He's the one who sold me out."

"I'm sorry."

Štěpán squeezed his aching eyes shut. He had another long day tomorrow, to become a model worker so his mother could get her job back. And maybe then, his parents would let him come home. That was his only realistic option. Wasn't it?

I too lived, Brooklyn of ample hills was mine,
I too walk'd the streets of Manhattan island . . .

"Lída?"

She stared at him with those dark, impenetrable eyes. Outside was the deep woods where no human animal would hear them.

"Do you ever think of leaving?"

"I've left a lot of places."

"I mean, leaving the country. I don't think they're telling the truth about what's out there, on the other side."

Even as a hypothetical, he was taking a risk. Most people would have reacted with shock and tried to hush him. But all Lída said was, "Pavol believed that it's more important to change things where we live so all the people we love have freedom too."

"Saint Pavol," Štěpán whispered. "He tried so hard to change things here and look where it got him."

Lída was quiet for a moment, then said, "I think you're right, though, about it being different over there than what we've heard. Pavol thought so too, even if he didn't want to abandon his country."

"The books I've read—they made me want to see what's going on over there. Especially in America." Thinking of books made him think of his mother, and something deflated inside him. "Even if I could get out, though, they'd punish my family even more."

Lída pressed her hand to her stomach and flashed him a bittersweet smile. "They do that, don't they?"

"Yeah." He stood and scooped crumbs from the table to throw outside to the birds. After shutting the door, he dug *Song of Myself* from his knapsack. "I'm going to bed."

"You can sleep in my father's room."

"Thank you." Perfect. Keep everything between them separated. Still, he wanted her to know he was more than an ox—*big body, small brain*. He wanted to show her where his dreams came from. He held out the book. "May I read you a poem first?"

CHAPTER 13: TOMÁŠ

Tomáš had taken five driving lessons by the time Ondřej stopped coming in early May. While he'd learned how to shift gears without grinding the transmission, cars coming at him from all directions still rattled him. During his last lesson, he turned too sharply, his wheel hit the curb, and the hubcap tore off with a clatter and rolled down the hill. Scratches and dings marred the Škoda that his father had kept so spotless.

"No lesson today. Or tomorrow," his father told him after breakfast the next Saturday. He handed Tomáš a rag, a can of wax, and a can of touch-up paint. "You'll fix your damage instead."

"What happened to Ondřej?" Tomáš asked as innocently as he could, but he already knew the answer: He terrified everyone who got into a car with him.

"He's in the hospital."

"I didn't . . . do it?" The collision with the curb had shaken Ondřej the Sunday before, but he'd seemed jumpy from the moment he arrived at the house. His hands shook more than usual, and he cursed Tomáš when the car stalled with the tire half on the sidewalk.

He made no attempt to replace the hubcap after Tomáš chased it down the road. Instead, he quit half an hour early, leaving Comrade Kuchař to bang out the dents and hammer the hubcap back onto the wheel.

"This one's not your fault, son. He made his choices and is suffering the consequences."

To occupy his nervous fingers, Tomáš opened the can and sniffed the rich, oily smell of the wax. "Will he be back next week?"

"I don't think so. It's going to be a while before he's up and about."

"How will I learn to drive?"

"You'll wait. Get your license a few months later. If I have to drive you to summer camp instead of you driving yourself, so be it."

Tomáš's heart shriveled. He'd imagined showing up at camp behind the wheel of his own car, being cool for the first time in his life. The other kids would crowd around him the way they did whenever Štěpán drove his family's Trabi to school. Tomáš didn't have a cheap, underpowered East German sedan but a Škoda station wagon—the pinnacle of Czech engineering, his people with the best cars in the East.

"Wipe that pout off your face before I do it for you," his father snapped.

Tomáš's lip trembled. He didn't think his face had shown disappointment. The car had opened a new world for him, a world of freedom unbound by the circles and figure-eights of metal tracks. After leaving his train set at the town library, he couldn't get enough of car facts. Instead of civil engineering at the university, he'd applied to the program in automotive design.

No matter what his father said, he'd do whatever it took to get his license and drive to camp, even if it meant sneaking out to practice on his own.

After washing and waxing the Škoda, he rode his bicycle to the library. Perhaps a book could help him learn to drive better.

Behind the building, a man was repainting the lamppost. Close-cut blond hair surrounded a square bandage. The man stopped and turned.

Not a man. A kid. Tomáš squinted as he approached.

Štěpán? The hair told him yes. The face, maybe not.

He squeezed the handbrake, and with a squeal the bike coasted to a stop.

"Ahoj, Tomáš. Did you forget me?" Štěpán waved with the dripping brush. Black paint spattered his torn clothes. His once-solid face was lumpy and caved in, with bruises fading to green under both eyes. Two crumbling scabs on his upper lip left shiny white scars underneath.

"No, but you look different." Tomáš maneuvered the bike between them to avoid the curdled-milk odor of Štěpán's sweaty body. "When did you . . . get back?"

"Last Sunday." Štěpán set the brush across the top of the open paint can.

After looking around for eavesdroppers, Tomáš lowered his voice. "Thank you for not saying anything about the letter."

"Anytime, comrade. I paid a fat price, though." Štěpán curled back his lips to reveal a hideous black hole where three front teeth on top and a chunk of his canine and another incisor should have been.

Tomáš's stomach lurched. He stared at his new red-and-white Botas sneakers, another gift for his eighteenth birthday. He knew he should say more, show gratitude to his former tormentor who'd sacrificed so much to save him. He forced his gaze upward to Štěpán's stormy gray eyes. "Is this your job?"

A weak response, but better than just walking away.

"Yeah. It was this or go back to prison."

"What was it like there?"

Štěpán scowled. "Are you real?"

Tomáš lowered his gaze. "Of course I'm real."

"No, I mean why the fuck do you want to know?"

Tomáš recoiled, knowing a fist could lash out at any moment. "Let's just say you wouldn't last thirty minutes there." Štěpán thrust out his chin. "Better me than you, right?"

Right. Tomáš knew better than to say it. He owed Štěpán a debt he could never repay if their roles were reversed.

Another picture came to him: Štěpán driving his Trabi into the parking lot, honking the horn and grinning as if he ruled their school.

Forget books. Štěpán could give him the lessons Ondřej couldn't, set him free on the open road.

"I'm wondering," he began.

"Wondering what?"

"If you could teach me to drive." He clenched and unclenched the bicycle's handbrake. "I can pay you, whatever you want."

In fact, Tomáš couldn't give Štěpán whatever he wanted. He couldn't replace knocked-out teeth or return Štěpán to school and the hockey team. Even being seen with Štěpán could get him in trouble. Štěpán only asked for food, though, so at dusk Tomáš packed a chunk of leftover ham, a quarter-loaf of bread, and a block of cheese into his nylon pullover. He tied the sleeves and tiptoed past the door of his father's study with his bundle. On his way out he dropped a note onto the table by the door: *Forgot to return a book at the library. Be back at suppertime. Also moved the car to the street to practice parking.*

He would have to get the car down the hill by himself and

learn to drive in the dark, because that was when Štěpán got off work. But dark and the inside of the car meant privacy. No one could see or hear them.

Tomáš met Štěpán at the empty loading dock behind the library. Štěpán had rinsed his face, hair, and freckled arms, but his clothes still smelled of oily paint and sweat. Inside the Škoda he scooped out the food and handed the jacket back to Tomáš.

Right away the ham's smoky aroma overpowered everything else. Štěpán gnawed a piece on his uncaved-in side, next to Tomáš in the driver's seat. Bits of meat fell from Štěpán's mouth onto his pants and the leather seat. His loud smacking made Tomáš's eyelid twitch—that and the thought of someone catching them, sitting-duck outlaws in the near darkness.

"You're supposed to teach me to drive," Tomáš said.

Štěpán swallowed an oversized mouthful. "Screw you. I haven't eaten all day."

Tomáš twisted around, searching for spies. Perspiration beaded on his forehead.

"If you're scared, I'll leave." Štěpán tucked the bread under his arm.

"N-no. I'm not. I need to learn—"

Štěpán cut in, "To drive or not be a baby?"

Both. Tomáš stared at his fingernails. "You think I killed Pavol, don't you?" *I betrayed him and you. I promise I won't anymore.* A silent promise Tomáš wasn't sure he could keep.

Instead of answering, Štěpán ripped a hunk of bread and stuffed it into his mouth. As he chewed, he rolled down the window and peered outside. "Yeah, let's drive before someone gets suspicious. Do you know how to back out, or should I do it?"

"I can." Tomáš pushed down the clutch pedal and shoved the gearshift into reverse, the way Ondřej had shown him. The car jerked backward and stalled. Štěpán set the rest of the bread on the seat between them and reached for the door handle. "Let me try again."

This time the clutch engaged, and Tomáš backed the Škoda onto the now-dark street, the lamppost freshly painted but the bulb burned out.

Driving slowly so he wouldn't have to shift out of first gear, Tomáš started around the block. "Turn right at the corner," Štěpán said.

Tomáš pressed the clutch and let the car coast to a stop in the crosswalk.

"Okay. Good thing there were no pedestrians," Štěpán said. "Don't be afraid to use the brake. *After* the clutch."

The next intersection approached, faster than Tomáš anticipated.

"Straight ahead. There's no stop sign for you, but you want to slow down in case the other guy isn't paying attention."

As Štěpán explained what he called *defensive driving*, Tomáš's hands vibrated along with the steering wheel. Pedestrians jumped out in front of him. A truck sped by and honked. The sudden blaring jolted him out of his seat, well worn by his father's larger body. Unable to breathe, he turned right into a narrow, quiet lane and cut the engine.

"I suck at this," he admitted to Štěpán.

"So did I, when I started out. Flattened the same tire twice hitting the curb. I'm a slow learner."

Tomáš laughed. "That's the same thing Papa called me."

"Vůl. My second name."

No one had ever called Tomáš an ox, but he always figured that was due to his average size and above-average clumsiness. "You're smarter than you think," he told Štěpán. "Like you may not get a physics question right on a test, but when you play hockey, you understand it."

"That's what Pavol used to tell me." Štěpán bit off some cheese and gulped. "You know, I miss him every single day."

The comrades' story—*lovers' quarrel*—resurfaced in Tomáš's mind. He blinked rapidly to banish it. "Me too. I imagine him in my living room listening to records, even though he's not there and never will be."

"At least you have a living room. My parents threw me out of the house. Mama said they won't let her teach next year."

Tomáš jerked his head in Štěpán's direction. "They fired her?" He wasn't surprised that Štěpán's parents had kicked him out because that's what his own father would've done. But his father had never said Mrs. Jelínková's job was in danger.

"They're demoting her to the cafeteria. Like they wanted to humiliate her because she raised me wrong."

"She didn't raise you wrong."

Or if she did, it was because she didn't keep him from pushing smaller and weaker kids around for so many years. Not because he stopped acting like a bully and started standing up for what was right.

"What gets me," Štěpán said after swallowing the last of the bread, "is that all along my mother wanted me to spend more time with *you*." He raised his voice to a falsetto, imitating a mother. *"Now that's a good family. A good influence."* He let out a sharp laugh.

Headlights illuminated the road, with shadowy walls and houses on each side. "I would've liked that," Tomáš said.

"Why? It's not like I was so nice to you."

"I would've been popular." Tomáš breathed in the smoked ham-scented air. "I would've had friends."

Pavol had approached Tomáš about his plan at the beginning of March, their first day back at school from a week of vacation. As hard as it was to look people in the eye, Tomáš always found himself drawn to Pavol's eyes, which seemed to change color with the intensity of the light inside him. Ever since the beginning of the school year, that light had diminished bit by bit. By January, Pavol's eyes had turned the gray of ash and overcast sky. Now, those eyes were sparkling again.

"I went camping," he said. "Me and Lída and her father. Her father was a partisan, lived in the forest even in winter. He showed us how he survived." Pavol flipped his hair from his face with the back of his hand. He was the only one who still wore long hair after the *military exercise*. "Being in the woods was so peaceful. I could finally think about things with a clear head, like how I've been messing up in school."

"It's no fun doing those math problems alone." Tomáš touched his nose and straightened his glasses. "I thought maybe you didn't like me anymore."

"I like you, brácha, don't worry."

Tomáš smiled. *Brother. A true friend.*

"It's just"—now Pavol smiled too, with his whole face, not just his mouth—"being in love. I want to spend all my time with Lída." He reached toward Tomáš's shoulder but didn't touch it. "One day you're going to fall in love and want to be with someone all the time."

"I don't know. Sofie says I'm a late bloomer."

"Yeah, I've had to grow up a lot faster." Even though they were indoors, a cloud seemed to cross Pavol's face. He stepped toward Tomáš and lowered his voice. "While I was in the woods, I got this idea. Would you be willing to work on it with me and Štěpán Jelínek?"

"Štěpán? He hates me."

Pavol whispered in Tomáš's ear. "He's nicer than you think. Like you're into music . . . he's into books. We're going to get those albums and books back."

That same afternoon they went to Štěpán's house, because Štěpán's mother had a meeting at her school and he didn't have hockey practice on Mondays. The three of them rode in Štěpán's car, Tomáš huddling in the back seat while Pavol and Štěpán talked with each other in front.

Are they luring me there to torment me? Will the rest of the hockey team show up?

But Tomáš trusted Pavol, who'd never given him any reason not to, no matter what his parents and Sofie had said.

Štěpán's house was a third the size of Tomáš's, his living room narrow. Tomáš rarely visited other kids' homes—by age ten, he'd stopped receiving birthday party invitations—and he was fascinated by how different each one was inside, a window into a different life. Where the dark wood cabinet with the record player, radio, and speakers, and the neighboring cabinet with the TV dominated Tomáš's living room, Štěpán's had hockey sticks mounted on the wall above a hi-fi console and a tall bookshelf next to it. Alongside Marxist classics, accounting tomes, and guides to the Czechoslovak railway network were hockey trophies for Štěpán and his older brother, Antonín.

Štěpán had more trophies—including the biggest one, a two-shelf-high gold figurine with stick and puck.

Štěpán brought three bottles of Kofola from the kitchen and handed one each to Tomáš and Pavol. Tomáš wrapped both hands around the slick bottle and savored the faint licorice taste of the cola, a special treat even at his house. Pavol handed his bottle to Štěpán, popped into the kitchen as if he lived there, and returned with a small paring knife.

After a long drink from his bottle Pavol made a small cut on the inside of his wrist. Blood rose to his pale skin.

Tomáš's throat closed.

"Our pact," Pavol said. "We tell no one what we're doing." He passed the knife to Štěpán. Štěpán sliced his outer arm midway between his wrist and his elbow.

Tomáš shuddered. He set the bottle on the shelf and held out his trembling hand. A blood pact with Pavol? With *Štěpán*?

Štěpán slapped the handle of the knife into Tomáš's palm.

His fingers closed around it. The handle was warm, and sticky in one spot where a drop of blood had spilled. It had a faint wild-animal scent.

Tomáš's guts clenched. He used to scream at getting shots and blood tests. Once when he was six, he ran out of the doctor's office and his mother had to catch him.

The blade glinted in the sunlight through the window. He waited for Štěpán to call him a a baby or weird. Nothing but Štěpán's sloppy noises as he sucked his own blood from his forearm.

Tomáš rubbed his skin, smoothing out the goosebumps. He shut his eyes, counted slowly under his breath like an incantation—*raz, dva, tři*—and plunged the knife tip into his forearm, same place as Štěpán. His arm burned where the knife penetrated. He opened his eyes and watched his blood rush to the surface, soak his dark hairs, fill the surrounding pores.

"Ready?" Pavol said.

Tomáš raised his arm and pressed it to Pavol's slender wrist. The pain dissolved into a stickiness that seemed to close the wound as it bound Tomáš to Pavol. He shivered when he held his forearm against Štěpán's muscular arm, feeling the power and bottled-up fury beneath Štěpán's rough skin.

Blood brothers.

Pavol pulled his crimson-smeared arm away first. He dug into his satchel, took out a pen and notebook, and sat in a chair across from the sofa. Tomáš sank into the lumpy sofa that smelled of sweat. Štěpán sat between them on the rug, legs extended under the coffee table.

"All right, let's get started," Pavol said, his voice filled with purpose. "First of all, I want to apologize to you two for my behavior these past few months. Tomáš, I know math club has been lonely, and I promise I'll be back once we're done with this project. Štěpán, I'm sorry about your rug. I'll get you a new one as soon as I can."

"What did you do to his rug?" Tomáš blurted.

"Never mind," said Pavol.

"Freak," Štěpán muttered.

Heat rushed to Tomáš's face. He stared at the rectangular blue rug with pink lines and crosses woven in, trying to find any damage Pavol might have caused.

Pavol tapped the notebook with his pen. "Here's what I've been thinking. I want to put together a statement for the secondary students, the way the university students have done. We're the future of the country. If we could have our freedoms back, we'd do all kinds of great things. Think of all the books people could write, the movies people could make."

"Don't forget the newspapers." Štěpán had been one of the kids who walked around with a folded-up copy of *Literární listy* tucked into the top flap of his knapsack on the day that the uncensored newspaper came out. Tomáš had wanted his own copy because it would've made him one of the cool kids, but his father never would've allowed it.

"Music," Tomáš said over the scratching of the pen as Pavol took notes. "Because the songs were in English, we could learn another language." He ticked off in his mind the languages he already knew: Czech. The Slovak he'd learned from Pavol. Russian, required in school. German, because his parents had learned it in school before and during the war, and his father had spied on Germans in the Resistance. After he found out his trains had come from Germany, Tomáš had swiped his father's old textbooks and hid them under the table to study on his own.

"We could travel all over the world, like play tournaments in Canada," Štěpán said. "Because they wouldn't have to worry we'd defect. We'd have freedom here." With a groan, he leaned back until he was lying on the floor. "What I would give, to meet Gordie Howe."

"Tomáš, if you could travel out of the country, who would you want to meet?" Pavol asked.

Tomáš hesitated. No one had ever asked him this question.

Štěpán broke the silence. "You can't meet Albert Einstein. He's dead."

Suspecting mockery, Tomáš shot back, "I *know*."

"And so is your buddy Walt Whitman," Pavol said to Štěpán.

"But his poetry lives on. *O Captain! my Captain! our fearful trip is done, / The ship has weather'd every rack, the prize we sought is won . . .*"

Tomáš gaped. Indifferent to poetry in school—as opposed to music, languages, science, and math—he could hardly believe his long-time enemy liked it as much as hockey. *People are so different from what you think, once you get to know them*, his sister would say.

He took another swallow of cola, less tart now that it wasn't ice cold. "If I could meet anyone, anywhere—Jim Morrison."

"Good choice," Pavol and Štěpán said together.

"What about you?" Tomáš asked Pavol, expecting one of the Beatles. Mick Jagger of the Rolling Stones. Bob Dylan.

Pavol folded his hands across his notebook. "I'd want to meet the Pope." He paused. "I have some questions for him."

When they met the next Monday at Štěpán's house, Pavol had changed the plan. Instead of a statement that would be passed around in secret to sympathetic classmates and that no one else would see, they would write a letter directly to the Central Committee of the KSČ on behalf of all the students. Pavol and Štěpán assured Tomáš that thousands of others were writing similar letters, including Party members. Pavol asked Tomáš to go with them to Prague on Friday to deliver it, to get them into the castle, and he promised he would.

For the first time, Tomáš belonged. He had friends. They were blood brothers.

He believed in socialism with a human face. In making a difference for his country, for his people. And, when he thought about the music he could listen to—out loud, *with his friends*—for himself as well.

Still, what they wanted to do, what he'd offered to help them do because they were his friends, could also get him into the worst trouble ever. He had the biggest house, a place at the technical university, the predictable path to a good life if he followed the rules.

He'd stepped out of line. How hard could it be to obey from here on and keep his objections to himself? The letter was anonymous, but if he delivered it in person he'd be held responsible for it. Everything he had could be taken away.

If he backed out, maybe Pavol and Štěpán would abandon their plan. They'd all be safer that way. Pavol could spend the weekend with Lída, and Štěpán wouldn't miss hockey practice.

The question repeated in his mind: *How hard can it be to follow the rules?*

So on the day they were supposed to travel to Prague, Tomáš awoke late but instead of biking to the train station—because there was still time if he rode his bike rather than wait for his father to drive him to school—he waited. He didn't tell his parents he was staying late for math club and eating supper at Pavol's home, the carefully constructed lie he called his x^{-1} story. After his father dropped him off at school, he didn't walk the one block to the station in case the train ran late.

He didn't deserve Pavol as a friend.

He didn't deserve Štěpán either.

Now that everyone else in town had turned their backs on Štěpán, Tomáš didn't have to pretend to be cool. He only had to make amends.

The next day, Sunday, Tomáš drove to the secret meeting place he and Štěpán had agreed on—the back of the hill behind his house at the edge of woods that separated the southeastern corner of Rozcestí from a collective farm. When he was younger, his parents had warned him and Sofie to stay out of those woods because hunters from the farm roamed in search of wild game. But those woods had been hunted out for several years, and no one ever went there.

"You made it," Štěpán said after climbing into the Škoda and shutting the door. Shutting, not slamming. Not making noise. Slumping in his seat so no one would see him.

"No harder than going down the other side of the hill to the library. And it's daylight."

Štěpán poked his lip out with his tongue. "Which means we should stay away from town."

They drove to the collective farm and back. Tomáš pushed his speed up to 60 kilometers an hour and shifted into all three gears without stalling. After a break for lunch under a tree, Štěpán said, "Time to show you where I live now."

Tomáš realized he'd never asked where Štěpán was living since his parents had kicked him out, as if a place would magically appear in a town that had turned him into a pariah. "Where?"

"Lída's."

"In the woods?"

"No one spies on us there."

How did he find Lída? Had Pavol introduced them . . . before? A twinge in his heart—*Pavol always liked Štěpán more than me*—was replaced by relief. The comrades had lied. Pavol had really had a girlfriend. There'd been no lovers' quarrel with Štěpán.

Štěpán brought his knees to his chest and covered his face with his hands. When he looked up again, his palms were damp. "You should meet the other person who loved Pavol as much as we two did."

For a moment, Tomáš thought of all the other kids at school who'd been Pavol's friends. They hadn't spoken of Pavol in weeks. They hadn't offered Štěpán a place to live.

Are we the only ones left?

Tomáš's heartbeat accelerated as they skirted the center of Rozcestí to the deeper woods on the town's north side, the foothills where mines hadn't yet arrived and the rocky terrain made farming difficult. The paved road gave way to a narrow dirt path.

Tires kicked up dust as the car bumped over parched grass and roots. The path ended in front of a small cottage with a stone base, weathered siding, and a zinc roof. Štěpán reached across Tomáš and honked the horn. After a few moments a plump girl with a round face, rosy cheeks, and dark brown hair in a stubby ponytail stepped outside. She wore an ankle-length print skirt, sandals, an oversized denim shirt, and a red-and-white checked apron. She'd rolled up her shirtsleeves on this warm spring day.

Tomáš's breath caught in his throat. She looked a bit like Marta Kubišová, but rounder. What to say to this girl whom Pavol loved?

He cut the engine, got out of the car, and sniffed the pine-scented breeze. Birds chirped above him.

He straightened his glasses. Searched for her eyes. Dark brown.

"Ahoj." He rummaged through his brain for more words. "I'm Tomáš Kuchař. Nice to meet you." He held out his hand.

She shook it and introduced herself. Her hand was firm, warm, and dry. With her touch something huge stirred inside him, below his heart, below his stomach, overwhelming his senses. "Lída Pekárová."

That was Ondřej's surname. Tomáš's brain scrambled to put the pieces together. Pavol's girlfriend was also the daughter of Tomáš's's former driving teacher. "Your father—"

"Yeah," she said, cutting him off. Then she flashed a smile. "I've heard so much about you."

Tomáš fanned his steaming face. "I . . . hope they're good things."

He would understand if they weren't.

"Yes, they are." Her face turned serious. "Pavol said you were a very good friend to him."

Tomáš glanced toward Štěpán, who was wiping the car's windshield with a paint-splotched rag. Štěpán kept wiping, not at all agreeing with her. Tomáš said, "I think you two were better friends."

"Your friendship meant a lot to him." Lída pulled a loose

strand of hair forward and picked at the ends. "None of us is ever as good a friend as we want to be. This country makes us that way."

Tomáš didn't believe her. He was the one who'd broken the pact sealed with their blood. Štěpán hadn't. Not then, when he took the train to Prague with Pavol and their letter, and not later, when he paid the price for his journey.

Tomáš lowered his voice. "What's it like to live with Štěpán?"

"He's fine. Very respectful."

Tomáš focused on her neck and collarbone so she would also think of him as respectful. She must have known about Štěpán's past, but maybe he *had* changed. "That's good."

"He introduced me to this poet, Walt Whitman. Have you read anything by him?"

Tomáš nodded. "A poem about a captain whose ship survived a storm but who tragically died when it arrived at the port."

"That's a metaphor," Štěpán called out from the other side of the Škoda. "A memorial to an American president who led his country through a civil war over slavery but was assassinated right after peace came and slavery ended."

"I wish I'd had a teacher like him," Lída whispered.

Štěpán would've made a great teacher. Was it really too late? In a few years, maybe the authorities would forget or forgive. Plenty of Party members rehabilitated after Stalin died—among them Comrade Husák, Czechoslovakia's new leader. Maybe once some time had passed, Tomáš could talk to his father about letting Štěpán finish school and study at the university.

Lída and Štěpán described the poetry they read together. It sounded like a foreign language, baffling but something Tomáš thought he could understand if he studied hard enough. As daylight turned to dusk, Štěpán said, "We should go. I have a driving lesson to finish."

Štěpán turned the station wagon around, then switched places with Tomáš, who drove the rest of the way into town. Two blocks after the car bumped onto the cobblestone street, a white car cut in behind them. When Tomáš slowed, the white car stayed at his rear, not passing and honking the way most did. Through the mirror, he recognized the sharp-edged rectangular grille and fog lights on the bumper. A Russian-made Lada.

Štěpán twisted around. "Shit, we have a tail."

"Are you sure?" Tomáš's gaze froze on the road ahead. Too many pedestrians, bikes, and vehicles around to think about evading the Lada.

"Go to prison, they follow you for the rest of your life."

Tomáš caught his own panicked expression in the mirror. His father had always complained that the Party didn't have enough *support*. Not enough agents to keep tabs on all the subversives and too many slipped through the cracks. That's what Tomáš had counted on when he asked Štěpán to teach him.

"Drop me off here," Štěpán said. "Can you make it home by yourself?"

"I . . . think," Tomáš said, his voice edgy with dread. He would have to manage. He had to keep up his lessons and stand by Štěpán, who'd protected him. "Are you free next Saturday after work?"

Štěpán glanced backward again. "Yeah. Pick me up at Lída's, now that you know where."

On his way home Tomáš drove even more slowly in case the police stopped him. He only had his learner's card, and there were plenty of ways someone could end up in trouble that didn't involve politics. The Lada turned off at the square.

His father met him at the door. Pointed him to the living room sofa. Held out his hand. "Your car keys. What were you thinking?"

Tomáš dropped the Škoda's keys into his father's waiting palm.

"I'm sorry I drove without a license, but I wanted to practice so you won't have to take me to camp next month."

"I don't care about your license. Someone saw you in the car with Štěpán Jelínek."

The Lada's driver must've had enough time to phone his father while he crept home at ten kilometers an hour.

"I asked him to teach me. Since Ondřej was indisposed."

The slap caught him on the side of his head. His neck twisted with a crack.

"He was buggering you in the car!"

"No, he wasn't!"

"Look at me." Tomáš met his father's steely glare. "You're slow. You're smart in school, but you're slow everywhere else. You let people take advantage of you. This crosses a line."

"He never touched me." Tomáš swallowed the sour fear in his throat. "I don't like it when people touch me. And I don't like boys."

No. The weird stirring happened when he saw beautiful Lída for the first time, when he touched her hand.

"How do you think this makes me look, you in a car with a known degenerate and counter-revolutionary?"

Tomáš lowered his head. "I'm sorry, Papa. It won't happen again."

The side of his face burned from his father's slap—and from shame. What kind of a friend would give up so easily?

Still, Lída had said, *None of us is ever as good a friend as we want to be. This country makes us that way.*

"You bet it won't happen again. You're grounded for the week. Your bugger of a driving teacher . . . he's going on a little trip." Comrade Kuchař poked his finger hard into Tomáš's breastbone, which exploded in pain. "I guarantee he'll never set foot in Rozcestí as long as he lives."

Tomáš eyed the car keys, glinting like freedom from his father's clenched fist. He would find a way to get them back. If he had to teach himself to drive from a library book, he would do it. He would return to Lída's house in the woods where no one spied on them, and if his father had Štěpán sent away, he'd go look for him. That's what a friend would do.

He would be a friend.

CHAPTER 14: LÍDA

On Wednesday, three days after Štěpán introduced Lída to Tomáš, he didn't return from work. Lída waited for him until almost midnight, then lay on her mattress listening to the owls and crickets outside. She was accustomed to falling asleep alone, but she already missed Štěpán's solid presence, his politeness, his poetry. Now he was gone. One more person to disappear from her life.

Had he fled the country? He'd raised the possibility, but his knapsack, clothes, and books still lay in a corner of Ondřej's bedroom. He wouldn't have left them behind. Or would he, to throw everyone off his trail?

And how many times have I disappeared? One disappearance in particular troubled her that night. She thought of Alžbeta relaying Mrs. Bartošová's message so many weeks ago: *Don't become a stranger.*

Lída knew how to become a stranger. Being a true friend was so much harder.

"Have you decided about the child's last name?" the doctor asked her on Saturday, at her own appointment before she brought her father home.

"Yes, I have."

If he'd fled the country, Štěpán was far stronger than she. It was so much easier to give in, to travel the path they'd laid out. Besides, she had an innocent child to protect. They could take him away if she insisted on Bartoš for the last name. She would lose all she had of Pavol, and the child would still pay as the spawn of a criminal and a whore.

She choked on the words: "I don't know who the father is."

The doctor handed her the housing forms.

Maybe Ondřej would agree to move into town and help take care of the baby. She'd begun to imagine her future working at the factory, bringing little Michal there for day care and returning to the apartment after work to read to the baby. Ondřej would tell stories of the old days, and maybe this grandchild would give him a reason to take better care of himself.

The hospital released her father that afternoon. A taxi brought him and Lída to the edge of town, and Lída helped him the rest of the way home. It took two hours to half-carry him, weakened and hunched over, uphill on the path. From time to time they stopped for him to sit on a fallen tree limb. He wrapped his arms around his stitched-up belly, which he wouldn't let her touch. "I'll change the bandages myself," he said, as if something scary hid beneath them.

She wanted to press the matter, but if she did he might in turn ask her about her growing belly. Could he already guess? After all, she now had to unbutton both sides of her work overalls. She'd taken to wearing her father's shirts rather than her own, even though it meant doing laundry twice as often at the creek.

Now she had Štěpán's clothes. Leaving her father at home—since he was too weak to walk into town—she headed to the Bartoš family's apartment wearing one of Štěpán's plaid shirts over her skirt. The shirt was enormous, and it made her small.

Or not. "You've put on weight. You look lovely," Mrs. Bartošová told Lída after the two of them hugged.

Lída handed her the wrapped block of hard cheese that Štěpán had brought back before he disappeared. "We're doing well for food."

"Good, good," Pavol's mother said. She gestured toward the table, bare except for a pitcher of water, a loaf of black bread, and four plates. "We're having hard times. They cut the pension I had from my husband, and the mayor let me go. Said they couldn't trust me cleaning their house, after . . ." Her voice trailed off.

"Oh no," Lída said, not sure what else to say. Pavol's mother hugged her again, and she felt a dampness on her shoulder that brought liquid to her own eyes. Three girls, their faces blurred, stood behind their mother.

After the long embrace, she grabbed one of her shirtsleeves and patted her face. She tried to smile at the girls. "Ahoj," she said, voice breaking.

Dutiful Alžbeta said hello, then turned away. Eleven-year-old Nika, the boldest of the three, stared at Lída as if she were an intruder. Nika hooked her thumbs in the waistband of her skirt and tapped one sandaled toe on the linoleum floor.

"Your face looks different," Tereza said. She was the most observant, the artistic one. Over the past two months, the eight-year-old had grown thin, her delicate face pale and pinched. The other two girls had lost weight too. A pang of guilt pierced Lída's heart, and she wished that the block of cheese had been larger or that she'd brought some wild game with it.

And Tereza had noticed the change in Lída too: how her face had become rounder, her cheeks pinker, her hair thicker. Should she tell them the truth, that a part of their beloved Pavol lived inside her? In the fall the baby would appear in the world, and she would do everything in her power to help him become as gentle and kind and wise as his father.

Pavol's family said grace over their meager table, but Lída had already forgotten many of the words. When Pavol used to talk about his faith, she merely listened. Her father had been a Communist and an atheist since university, in the months before the Nazis marched from the Sudety into the rest of their country. Aunt Irina shared his disillusionment with religion and even more with politics, believing her brother a fool for joining the Resistance. *What did it ever get him?* she'd say. *Scars and a big drinking problem. And for our village . . .*

She always stopped there, before the words *collective punishment.*

Like the punishment the government had meted out to Pavol's family, to Štěpán's family, to her.

What had she done to help Pavol's family? Where did they fit into the new life she'd imagined?

"Are you sick, Lída?" Pavol's mother asked when she passed the bread and cheese along without taking her portion.

"No, just worried. My father was in the hospital for two weeks. He only came home yesterday."

Mrs. Bartošová's hand flew to her mouth, and Lída remembered that Pavol's father had died after a long illness. "I hope he's better soon."

"They won't tell me anything. They say I'm too young." At least they hadn't told her father about her pregnancy either. Her stomach growled, and she folded her hands across it to muffle the sound.

"I'm glad you came to visit. We missed you. If there's anything my daughters and I can do to help, please ask."

Lída blinked back tears. So kind to her, even though she'd

ignored them for weeks. If she asked, they would surely forgive her. That was how they were and how they'd raised Pavol.

"If my father's feeling better next Sunday, I'll bring him."

Lída stayed until late afternoon, helping Mrs. Bartošová wash the dishes and talking with the girls about school and their activities. It made her happy to hear that life was moving on for each of them. Alžbeta had joined her secondary school's dance ensemble. Little Tereza had signed up for art classes at the library. Nika, who shared her brother's love for nature, was taking an afterschool class in farming, with field trips to the collective farms outside town, and she'd applied to the agriculture program at the girls' secondary school for the fall.

"My father studied forestry at university. He worked on collective farms too," Lída told Nika. She remembered her father taking her and Pavol to see the film *All My Compatriots* last year before it was banned, pointing out what the director had gotten right and wrong about the farms. Lída had told Pavol that if she'd directed the film she would've shown women doing important jobs and she wouldn't have made fun of the villagers. *Films should treat their characters with respect,* she'd said. Pavol had agreed.

Ondřej hadn't. *Films should knock down the powerful and make us laugh at them.*

A smile crossed Nika's face. "May I interview your father for my class project?"

"Next Sunday when we return. We'll bring some meat for dinner."

As Lída said her goodbyes to Mrs. Bartošová and the other two girls, Nika grabbed a notebook with a pen clipped to its metal spiral.

"I'll walk home with you," she said.

"It's a long walk. And I'm not sure my father is up for an interview today."

"Nika." Her mother lowered her voice. "You shouldn't bother Mr. Pekár. Didn't you hear he just had surgery?"

"Please, Mama! If he's too tired, Lída can send me straight home." Nika gazed up with pleading eyes.

A fluttering in her belly startled Lída. She reached toward her side but stopped short. *Pavol?*

Lída touched her cheek, as if she could touch Pavol's cheek pressed to hers. She swallowed the lump in her throat. "That's fine, Mrs. Bartošová. Nika can come with me and leave right away if she has to. I'll walk her back to town."

"Did you finish your homework?" her mother asked.

Nika nodded, her braid bouncing up and down.

"All right. But as soon as Lída tells you to leave, you leave. Don't make a pest of yourself."

Nika skipped out the door. Outside, her face grew serious. She scanned one end of the block, then the other. Thanks to her latest growth spurt her head came to Lída's chin, and standing on tiptoe, she whispered in Lída's ear. "That's where the men in suits stood outside our building. They're gone now."

Lída clutched Nika's hand and followed her gaze up and down the street. While the StB agents had left her and her father alone, except for their visit to her doctor, she wasn't surprised that they'd tracked every move of Pavol's family and watched who came in and out of their home.

Under those circumstances, who would have anything to do with them? They were outcasts like the Roma. Like she and her father had been when his drinking caused him to lose his job or get into fights with important people who had him run out of town. Like Štěpán, who ended up at her place because he had nowhere else to go.

Lída put her arm around Nika's shoulders, all skin and bones like Pavol. "We should go so I can get you home before dark."

Nika jutted out her chin. "I can walk back on my own."

That's what I thought once too. Lída pushed away memories of herself at Nika's age, the solemn medieval buildings and narrow cobblestone streets of Znojmo, Uncle Ludvík turning up everywhere like the Big Bad Wolf to walk with her.

"Does anyone ever follow you up this path?" Nika asked once they left the paved streets of Rozcestí.

"No people. Animals, sometimes."

"That is so cool!" Nika danced ahead of Lída. "What kind of animals?"

"Deer. Foxes. Wild boars."

"The ones that kind of look like pigs? Though not as cute?" Nika swished her blond braid forward.

"Yes, but they're tasty." Lída added quickly, "Next time my father and I shoot one, we'll bring you some."

Then she bit her lip until it stung. Little kids didn't like the idea of killing animals. Pavol always bristled when she'd talk about hunting for food. But Nika slipped from the edge of the path into the woods, wiggling the fingers of her free hand as if she wanted to catch one of those wild creatures.

Lída stepped into the woods behind her. She sniffed the pine trees and the mixture of dirt and spoor.

"It's so peaceful," Nika said. "I see why my brother liked coming here."

Lída paused and leaned against a tree. Its rough bark massaged her back, tired from supporting the weight of her pregnancy. "Those were our happiest times together, inside the forest."

Nika picked up a leaf and tore it into strips, her spiral notebook wedged under her arm. "They're telling lies about Pavol.

That he was a madman and a drunkard." Another strip of leaf fluttered to the ground. "That he and another boy from school got into some kind of weird argument and that's why he killed himself."

Her heart wrung out, Lída could barely answer. "He didn't get into any argument, and he didn't *kill himself*. He died in an act of resistance against the occupation. He thought he could change people's minds. Make them fight for our freedom."

"That's not what my teachers said."

"Your teachers didn't know him. I did. He and I were in love. I'm—" She stopped. The first person to know shouldn't be an eleven-year-old child. "We talked about getting married when he went to university."

"He told me." Nika stared into the woods, as if trying to spot a wild animal. "I'm going to run away to a free country so I can tell people the truth about Pavol."

Lída covered her mouth. "No!" Surely Nika knew how drastic and dangerous it was to even talk about leaving.

"Yes," Nika said. "I can stow away on a train or in the trunk of a car. I'm small. No one would notice me."

"Dominika Bartošová, look at me."

Nika turned her face up and gazed at Lída with sky-blue eyes the same color as her brother's.

"Abandoning the country isn't as easy as you think. Years ago, my father worked as a forest ranger across the border from Austria. He was one of the people who built the fences."

They told us the fences were to keep the imperialists out. To keep the fascists from occupying us again. But now we know—they were made to keep us in. Those were Ondřej's words.

She had to convince Nika without terrifying her. "They don't want us to leave. They spend a lot of money to put us through school. They don't want us to take our education and make more money somewhere else."

Unless they make you quit school. She didn't say that, but leaving school early meant she'd have no future anywhere. In the capitalist West, she'd join the unemployed masses—not even a factory job for someone like her.

"There are three fences you have to cross. The first has a tripwire that alerts the soldiers. They'll shoot you on sight."

"I'm quick. And I'm not much of a target. They'll probably miss me." Holding the notebook, Nika rubbed her face with the back of her forearm. "Anyway, they wouldn't shoot a little girl, would they?"

Yes, they would. And there are plenty other bad things they could do to a little girl. Lída couldn't tell her that either. Instead, she said, "If they don't shoot you, the second fence is electrified. Six thousand volts. You have no idea what touching six thousand volts will do."

Nika's lower lip quivered.

Lída repeated what her father had told her. "It will kill you within seconds, just long enough for you to feel everything inside you melt." She touched her belly, Pavol's child tucked inside. "There's a third fence, barbed wire that will cut you to shreds . . . except you won't make it that far."

Nika's notebook slipped from her grasp and landed on a root with a thud. She had no more words, only tears that gathered at the corners of her eyes.

Lída wrapped her arms around Nika and drew her close.

"I'm never going to get out," Nika wailed. "No one will know about Pavol. He should have been a hero."

Lída patted Nika's back. Salty tears pooled in the back of her throat. It was all so hopeless. Pavol's death hadn't changed

160

anything. One by one, the reformers in the government had been fired and replaced, not even a figurehead remaining. Every proclamation announced *normalization*: the return to dictatorship. The censorship was tighter than ever. Nobody demonstrated anymore, not even the students in Prague whose rallies she'd heard about from Pavol.

Now Nika wanted to risk her life to tell the truth about her brother.

"Your mother needs you safe, Nika. Maybe when you're older, you can apply to leave. Maybe you won't need to. Things could get better again."

A warm head nodded against Lída's upper arm. "You can take me back now."

"Don't you want to interview my father?"

Nika picked up her notebook and reattached the pen that had rolled away. "No. I wanted to talk to you. Without anyone spying on us."

Lída rested her hands on Nika's shoulders and squeezed.

"We all loved Pavol. We want him remembered for who he was—someone who fought for freedom, for himself and all of us."

Like Pa, in the war. Aunt Irina had been right. She had gravitated to a boy like her father.

When they returned to the paved streets, Nika said, "You don't have to walk me all the way home. I'm going to the library to see the train display in the children's room."

"The library has a train display?" Lída hadn't been to the library in months, even though it was open on weekends so working people could visit it. She'd only used it as an excuse for her father, so she could get her checkups at the clinic without telling him the truth.

"Yes." Nika took a deep breath. "I like to watch the train whenever I'm sad."

"I should try that," Lída said.

"You should. The father of Pavol's friend Tomáš donated it, but I think it was really Tomáš, and his father stuck his own name on the plaque to look good because he's a big guy in the Party. My teacher said it's the best train display in the country outside Prague. She said that one day tourists will come to Rozcestí to see it, and our town will be famous." Back to her spirited self, Nika twirled on the freshly paved sidewalk ahead of Lída. The pages of her notebook fluttered in the breeze.

It didn't surprise Lída that the skinny, super-awkward boy with the glasses whom she'd met last week once played with trains. He made her think of the cute but hapless hero of a comedy film she'd seen a year ago. Pavol had said that they listened to rock 'n' roll records together and that Tomáš told weird jokes that made Pavol laugh even at his saddest moments.

Nika led them along a different route than the one Lída had always taken to Pavol's house, a route that passed through the new housing estate where she'd applied to live. The four eight-story apartment buildings, the paneláky that had recently sprung up not only in cities like Most and Ústí but in smaller towns as well, cast blocky shadows across the sidewalk and the skinny trees.

Suddenly, Nika stopped, and Lída pulled up short behind her. Black paint covered the sidewalk around a lamppost at the far corner of the estate. Nika rubbed the toe of her sandal on the thick layer of dried paint. Some of it stuck to her rubber sole.

"What happened here?" Nika asked.

Lída circled the post and peered upward. The top half had been painted a glossy black. The lower half had been scraped clean, awaiting its paint job. *Štěpán's paint job.*

She ran her fingers along the warm, smooth metal, felt the uneven line where someone or something had interrupted the painter. Beside the post where paint hadn't spilled, she made out dull, rust-colored droplets on the ground. Bloodstains. A lot of them.

"It's nothing, Nika. Go on to the library." Lída made a shooing gesture with her hand while forcing a smile in Nika's direction. "I'll see you next week."

Near the bottom of the lamppost, someone had glued a square of paper. Since it hadn't rained, the paper was dry, the ink readable:

DEGENERATES OUT!

Lída held her breath. Her stomach fluttered.

Štěpán hadn't escaped. Someone had taken him.

FIELD TRIP OF THE
CZECH RESISTANCE

JUNE 1969

CHAPTER 15: LÍDA

Ondřej recovered slowly, but by the first Monday in June he was strong enough to join Lída at work. His weeks at the hospital had weaned him from drink, and while he was gone, Lída had cleared all the bottles from the house and searched the woods for any that he might have hidden. His color and appetite improved, and he seemed to sleep better. Perhaps his weakness and fatigue after surgery helped to keep his nightmares at bay. He asked about Štěpán, but she only told him that Štěpán had moved on—nothing about the spilled paint, the blood, and the message on the lamppost. In his fragile state, she didn't want to upset him.

I've become the parent, and he the child. Who had become her parent, the one to whom she'd revealed her pregnancy but not the name of the father?

The State.

The kind doctor.

The clerks who processed her paperwork for maternity leave, infant daycare at the factory, extra ration coupons, and a spot on the apartment waiting list.

The Communist leaders who made the rules.

On that first Monday back, one of them waited for her and her father after work, leaning against a vaguely familiar green Škoda station wagon across the street from the shoe factory. He was a potbellied man of medium height dressed in a business suit, with gray hair and a bushy mustache. Crinkles around the corner of his eyes deepened when he called out, "Ahoj, Ondřej!"

"Franta!" The two men embraced and slapped each other's backs.

They separated and the man patted Ondřej's belly. Though not flat, it had shrunk a lot since his surgery. "Glad you're feeling better, Comrade Brother!"

One of Ondřej's war buddies? Because that was how they addressed each other—*kamarád* rather than *soudruh*.

"Nothing's killed off this old goat yet," Ondřej said.

"And nothing will. This your lovely daughter?"

With a shudder Lída shrank backward. War buddies had wandering hands. Too many old men did.

"Yes, that's Lída."

The man held out his hand. "František Kuchař. Your father and I go way back. He saved my life more than once."

Kuchař. Tomáš's father—who *had* taken credit for the magnificent train display in the children's room of the library, which she'd finally seen during her lunch break last week. The same Party leader who'd hired Ondřej to teach Tomáš to drive and paid with the tastiest bread and butter in Rozcestí. She missed the bread's thick, chewy crust and soft insides, the sweet butter that melted in her mouth.

He'd taken care of them. He'd also collaborated with the Soviet occupiers and spread lies about Pavol. Did he have anything to do with Štěpán's kidnapping? Her head buzzed like a hive of disturbed bees.

"Come. I'll give you a ride," the man said.

Palms sweaty, Lída opened the passenger-side door, climbed over the folded-down front seat into the back, and drew her knees to her belly. The car smelled of tobacco, sweat, and leather. She pressed her hand to the worn reddish-brown seat. Underneath, the springs squeaked.

An anxious pang pierced her. The baby twitched. With each sharp turn around the main square, she slid on the seat and the baby smacked against her ribs.

"You can drop us here. We'll walk the rest of the way," Ondřej said when they approached the end of the paved road.

"I insist." Comrade Kuchař eased slowly onto the hard dirt path. "Partisan days are over, Ondřej. It's time to live in the real world."

Ondřej's contemptuous grunt told Lída he'd heard this line before.

The car wound up the hill. The springs creaked and poked Lída at every bump. When they arrived, she eased herself out, rubbed her sore ribs, and followed the men inside.

Comrade Kuchař surveyed the dim interior, then sat at the table. Lída opened the shutters, and the late afternoon sun shone across the wooden floor, ending in a sharp point near Comrade Kuchař's feet.

Her father reached for the coffee tin. "Sorry I have nothing else, Franta." He nodded toward Lída. "She cleaned out the hard stuff."

"No worry." Comrade Kuchař lifted a silver flask from the pocket of his suit jacket, uncapped it, and took a long swig. He held the flask toward Lída's father.

No, Pa!

Her father shook his head. Lída released the breath she'd been holding. A wave of dizziness swept over her, and she steadied herself against the window frame.

She and her father sat across from each other at the table,

Comrade Kuchař between them. He drank again from his flask and cleared his throat.

"Is this where you've lived for the past two years? No plumbing or electricity?"

"You know I've lived in worse."

The man tapped the table with his flask. "It was a shame to drag this girl through your world, Ondřej, but it looks like she's turned out tough, hardworking, and productive. I hope one day she gives up her questionable associations and joins the Party, because she's a survivor. Maybe even a leader."

"She'll make her own decisions."

Never. That was the decision she'd already made.

"This, however . . ." Comrade Kuchař glanced toward the wood stove, the handmade shelves and cupboard, and the curtain screening her father's room. "It's no place for an infant."

Blood drained from Lída's head. The dizziness returned. She ground her teeth so hard that a pang shot through her jaw. Her father sat up straight, his eyes fixed on her stretched-out work overalls.

"Lída, is there something you haven't told me?" His voice was quiet, even. Not at all angry. If anything, sad.

Lída rubbed her belly. Did it matter to him, so numbed by alcohol that he hadn't noticed how she'd left him out of her life? And who was this Comrade Brother, to come into their lives and expose her secrets?

She unclenched her jaw to speak. "I'm pregnant. He's due at the end of September."

"He?" echoed Ondřej.

"Yulia at the factory said it would be a boy. She had some barley seeds . . ."

Comrade Kuchař snorted. "That's a crock. Superstition."

"You told your coworker but not me. Why . . . ?" Her father stopped, but the pain Lída detected in his one word made the rest unnecessary.

She couldn't give him her answer—that it wouldn't have changed anything if he knew. It wouldn't have turned him away from the bars into the sober, conscientious, loving father that Pavol said he once had. The images of her father living with her in the new housing estate were fantasies. Once her apartment came through, she would start her own life and leave him alone with his sickness in the wood-and-stone cottage deep in the forest.

"She wants to do the responsible thing for the baby, Ondřej."

Lída pressed her lips together. The responsible thing included claiming that she didn't know who'd gotten her pregnant despite the shame.

Her father covered his face with his hands and shook his head. "The responsible thing would have been not to bring a child into this fucked-up world."

Lída gritted her teeth again. He sounded like Aunt Irina, and he might be right. Except this wasn't for him, or her, or this *fucked-up world*.

It was for Pavol—for his kindness, his love, his faith, and his dreams that she wanted to carry forward.

Comrade Kuchař drank again from his flask and offered it to Ondřej. "Guess you need it now, Comrade Brother."

This time Ondřej took it despite Lída's silent pleas. After a single swallow he choked and coughed, then grabbed his stomach. Comrade Kuchař slapped his back.

"Just this one," Ondřej said. "I have a grandchild on the way that I might want to meet."

Leaving the flask on the table, Comrade Kuchař shifted his

heavy body in the chair and continued. "Well, we have a complication. Your daughter isn't eligible for housing. Checking her medical records against State Security files, we've discovered that the father—the *deceased* father—was a counter-revolutionary criminal."

Lída sucked in her breath, hot with rage. A fierce stabbing pierced her insides. "Wait! I said I didn't know who the father was. That was the deal. The doctor . . ."

The man's steely eyes bored into her, silencing her. Her father shot her a warning glare as well.

"We've contacted her relatives, Ludvík Červeny and Irina Červená, to take her in."

"No!" If the comrade was right . . . if the barley seeds were nothing but superstition and the baby was a girl . . . she'd never be safe. Hairy fingers like worms would crawl across her body into places they didn't belong.

"I don't think that's a good idea, Franta," Ondřej said.

Tell him, Pa! The words rose bitter in her throat and caught there.

"She can't stay here." Comrade Kuchař gestured at the cottage around them.

Lída swallowed hard. "I've lived here two years already. We hunt. We have a wood stove. The baby will be well fed and sheltered." In the silence that followed, she kept on, not caring that she had already interrupted a Party official. "In school we studied the Middle Ages, when no one had plumbing or electricity, and people still raised children. If all their babies died, none of us would be here today." These people should have let her finish school.

Too late she remembered a baby that had died, not in the Middle Ages but in the hard years after the war.

The baby, and the mother too.

"Fair point," said Comrade Kuchař. "However, the arrangements have been made. Both of you will leave Rozcestí at the end of this month. The reason you're going to your relatives in Znojmo is that we're sending your father to a sanitarium near Olomouc, up in the mountains."

Lída turned so sharply toward her father that pain shot from her neck into the back of her head. "Did you know about this, Pa?" She clenched her fists, though it was impossible to fight this man or throw him out for turning their lives upside down.

"They told me in the hospital."

"Why a sanitarium?" Decades ago people with tuberculosis went there to die, but with penicillin most came back cured after a few months. Could her father have tuberculosis? He'd lost a lot of weight but rarely coughed. The surgery had been for his abdomen, not his lungs. Even a school dropout could figure that out.

Comrade Kuchař glanced at Lída's father, then said, "Seeing as you're under eighteen, we can't disclose your father's medical condition. He needs to tell you."

Ondřej slumped over the table, his head in his hands.

Comrade Kuchař leaned toward him and touched his knee. "You can do this, Comrade Brother. It's not over yet."

"Pa, is something r-really wrong?" Lída's heartbeat stumbled along with her words. The baby kicked, and she pressed her right hand over her belly.

"It's . . . cancer. Liver cancer. They're going to try to treat it there." He didn't look up, and his hoarse syllables once again ripped a hole in her world.

She remembered what she'd told him after she'd found out about Pavol: *Everything you touch dies.* Such a horrible thing to say. Now he too was dying.

"I'm so sorry, Pa."

Because in that moment she was. She hadn't been the good daughter she'd wanted to be. She hadn't protected him the way he'd tried to protect her when he took her from Znojmo years ago. She couldn't save him. So much had already happened before she was born.

"Unless my son can manage to get his license before then," Comrade Kuchař said, freezing her thoughts, "Ondřej, you'll drive Lída to Znojmo and take Tomáš to Olomouc. He's spending his summer at the Youth Union camp nearby." He frowned behind his mustache. "I'd like you to keep an eye on him there. He's had a few difficulties lately."

"He's a good kid. Maybe needs a bit more independence."

"No, that's the problem. He's had too much independence and doesn't know what to do with it." The man tipped up his flask for a long drink and wiped his mouth on the back of his hand. He released a belch that reeked of plum brandy and onions.

He stood, swayed, grabbed the table. Lída scooted backward. It wouldn't have taken much to shove him out the door, but this sloppy-drunk, bushy-mustached official still had the power to rule every aspect of their lives. Hers. Her father's. His awkward, fidgety son's. Štěpán's.

Along with Pavol, they all had this in common.

"Let me drive you home, Franta," Ondřej said.

Comrade Kuchař laid his arm across Ondřej's shoulders. "Sure. For old times' sake. Do some of those wild moves, like you did around the Nazi roadblocks." He pressed his other hand against his head. "Or maybe not."

Ondřej twisted around to face Lída. "I'll be back soon, so start supper. I'm sure we'll have a lot to talk about."

After the men drove off, Lída crossed the path into the woods and sat on a fallen tree limb, one not too low to the ground so she could easily stand again with the weight of the baby.

How long could two people live in the same home and never really talk? And one day find out they only had three weeks left together?

She picked at the dried-out bark of the dead tree and thought of the note glued to the lamppost, left by whoever had dragged Štěpán away. She went inside, to her father's toolbox, and returned with a knife and a flathead screwdriver.

She sliced the bark from the top of the limb, next to where she sat. Then she carved into the pale wood, cutting through rings that marked the tree's lifespan:

ONDŘEJ PEKÁR LIVED HERE

LÍDA PEKÁROVÁ LIVED HERE

With each twist of the screwdriver, memories flooded through her. Here was the place where she fell in love, shared a first kiss with a boy and many more after that, dreamed of a future. She fashioned a heart.

L.P. + P.B.

Years from now someone might come upon these words, see the dreams that she and Pavol tried so hard to make real and couldn't because the tanks were stronger than they were. Farther down the limb she carved in large letters:

FREEDOM!

As she cut into the dead tree, the idea took root in her stirred-up mind.

She would not raise her child under Aunt Irina and Uncle Ludvík's roof, or under the thumb of people who could move her and her father around the country like pawns on a chessboard.

She would not give in to people who demanded she strip her child of his rightful name and treated them both like criminals because she and the boy she loved stood up for freedom and paid the price.

First Štěpán had planted the idea. Then Nika. Each time she'd dismissed it.

No more.

Znojmo lay ten kilometers from the border with Austria. She would find a way to get herself and her baby—Pavol's baby—to the freedom side.

CHAPTER 16: TOMÁŠ

Tomáš passed his driving test the first Wednesday in June, on his third try and with the help of a large smoked ham his parents sent to the clerk who scored him. "Tell me when you go out, so I can stay off the road," the clerk said as he handed Tomáš his forms for the license.

The next morning, Tomáš awoke an hour early, before his mother came downstairs to make breakfast. No longer grounded, he snatched up the car keys hanging on a hook next to the front door.

He drove the empty streets of Rozcestí to the winding dirt path into the woods. The sky turned from pink to pale blue before his eyes, and to his right the sun brightened as it claimed its place. He pulled up to the cottage, cut the engine, and rolled down the window.

Should he honk like Štěpán used to do? He didn't want to break the silence, so he waited.

He hadn't seen Štěpán in three weeks. He hoped that if his father had gotten Štěpán transferred to another town, it was to somewhere nearby. Now that Tomáš had his license, he could start searching. He'd kept telling himself that was what he'd do.

A thrashing in the woods turned to footsteps on dirt. Lída. A metal bucket dangled from one hand. She cradled a straw basket in the other. Upon seeing the car, her face crumpled as if he'd brought bad news.

Does she hate me?

But the moment her eyes caught his through the open window, she smiled and called out, "Ahoj, Tomáš!" She came closer and showed him the basket filled with strawberries. "I was gathering breakfast. Want some?"

What began as relief turned into a buzzing within him like an ungrounded electrical wire. He tried to push the strange feelings aside. "Is Štěpán there?"

Lída shook her head.

"Do you know where he went?"

She glanced toward the open door of her house and lowered her voice. "At first I thought he fled the country but now I think someone took him."

Tomáš clenched the steering wheel. "I need to find him."

Lída set down the bucket filled with water. "Tomáš, people disappear all the time. You don't go looking for them." She paused. "Maybe they don't want to be found."

"I know Štěpán wants me to find him."

Her answer came back razor-sharp. "No, you don't." She picked up her bucket. "Come inside and say hello to my father. I imagine if you drove here by yourself, you have some good news for him. He could use some good news right now."

As he followed Lída through the door, he expected the all-too-familiar stench of stale alcohol, but the strawberries' sweetness and the rich aroma of coffee filled the small room.

Ondřej perked up when he saw Tomáš holding the temporary license. He shuffled forward. Tomáš backed toward the window, tripped on a bedroll, and caught himself on the window frame.

Ondřej laughed. "That's right. You're not a hugger."

Tomáš waited until the other two sat, then chose the empty chair across from Lída.

She pushed the strawberries toward him. "I saw that huge train display you gave the library."

"How did you know it was me?" He'd seen the plaque with his father's name. It didn't surprise him, and at least he'd gotten the car in exchange for it.

"Pavol's sister Nika told me."

"Pavol used to play with it too. He'd move the people around the town and send them on trips to the mountains." While they ate, Tomáš explained how he set up the trains, and Lída didn't yawn or make fun of him.

After breakfast, he drove Lída and Ondřej to work. He thought he could get used to eating with them in their little house in the woods and driving Lída around town. Yes, she was the girlfriend of his no-longer-alive best friend. But a girl had to move on, like hawks that mated for life but found another partner when a hunter shot their mate out of the sky.

If he found Štěpán and brought him back, Lída would be proud of him. Maybe she'd even go with him to a movie. Pavol had said she liked movies.

Inside Tomáš's satchel was an irrigation permit his father needed him to deliver to the collective farm after school. He suspected his parents' eagerness for him to get his license had to do with the errands he'd run for them, but as soon as school ended, he had an errand of his own.

Once located in a confiscated church school, No. 1 Rozcestí Primary School had moved to a new building of glass, cement, and blue-painted steel panels that made Tomáš think of a panelák lying sideways on stilts, with parking and play areas on the ground level. A bell rang as soon as he stepped into the courtyard, and blue doors smacked open. Threading his way through small children rushing home, he climbed the stairs to the main office, showed his Youth Union card—youth group members often visited the primary schools to lead activities—and was pointed upstairs to a classroom on the second floor.

After touching his nose, his glasses, and his tie, he knocked softly on the glass. Mrs. Jelínková stopped wiping down student desks and raised her head. "Tomáš?"

She opened the door. Tomáš stepped into a colorful wonderland of kites hanging from the ceiling to illustrate math concepts, student work pinned to a spider web of clotheslines, and a classroom library along the wall underneath the window. He turned in a slow circle, but his smile faded when he saw the country's new hardline leader, Gustáv Husák, in a framed photo on the wall above the teacher's desk.

Mrs. Jelínková's eyes bored into him, and he quickly looked away. "Why are you here?" she asked.

His carefully rehearsed words had flown from his brain like real kites with broken strings. "I-I wanted . . ."

"Is this about Štěpán?"

Tomáš couldn't figure out what emotion was in her tone. Worry? Anger? Curiosity? And he couldn't tell from a facial expression, especially one he was avoiding. He recalled his conversation with Štěpán in the car, Štěpán telling him how much his parents wanted them to become friends.

His hands shook. His eyelid fluttered. He tried again. "I wanted you to know . . . Štěpán and I really were friends."

He glanced up, then back at his school-uniform loafers. Would she now think of him as a degenerate or a criminal? Had they bugged her classroom, meaning he'd done something else reckless and dangerous? His feet went numb and his knees wobbled.

"Thank you" was all she said.

He plucked a workbook from her desk and held it to his chest, arms crossed over it. Its pressure calmed him. The words he'd practiced in the car returned, one by one. "I have some things that belonged to him."

"You need to get rid of those *things*. They're nothing but trouble."

Tomáš nodded, because he didn't actually have the books they couldn't mention out loud in a potentially bugged classroom. Lída did, along with the clothes Štěpán had left behind when he disappeared.

Mrs. Jelínková added, "You can't let your father see them." Her voice had lost its edge, as if she wanted to protect him. As if she still cared.

"Have you heard from Štěpán?" he asked. "I want to know that he's all right."

"Yes. He's fine." She pushed a strand of blond hair from her face. She was as tall as Tomáš, and when he looked up at the papers on the clothesline, he glimpsed the bags under her eyes.

She didn't look like the mother of someone who was fine. And in September his father's people would take this lively, colorful classroom away from her.

Tomáš squeezed the workbook tighter. "Do you know where he is?"

"It's best you didn't know, Tomáš. I appreciate your *tutoring* Štěpán, but you should forget about him now. I'm sure you'll make some wonderful friends at the university. My other boy, Antonín, is there. There are a lot of solid young people there, ones in the Party like you and your father and Anton."

Despite everything they'd done to her, she remained a true believer. How could they have demoted someone like her, who'd followed all the rules? They had no right to blame her and punish her because of a kid who'd already turned eighteen and could make his own decisions.

He was eighteen now too. Old enough to make his own decisions, but also old enough to go to prison or a mental hospital if, in the eyes of the State, he made the wrong ones.

Tomáš set the workbook back on her desk and held out his right hand for her to shake. He wrapped his other fingers around his right wrist so she wouldn't see the tremor. "Thank you, Mrs. Jelínková. And tell Štěpán hello for me the next time you see him."

Mrs. Jelínková didn't shake his hand. Instead, she tore off a corner of a workbook page, wrote something in tiny letters, and pressed the triangle of paper to his palm.

In the hallway he adjusted his glasses and, squinting, made out the word *MOST*.

The next morning when Tomáš returned to the Pekárs' cottage for breakfast, he told Lída and Ondřej where Štěpán had been taken. He'd expected Lída to be pleased with him, but her dark eyes flashed, and the buzzing inside him shorted out into a smoky stillness.

"He doesn't want us to find him." Lída popped a strawberry into her mouth and waited until she'd swallowed before continuing. "If he did, he would've gotten in touch himself. Right, Pa?"

"Right," Ondřej mumbled, his head between his hands. His skin was tinged yellowish gray, and the berries and slice of bread on his plate sat untouched.

He'd started drinking again, Tomáš told himself, and it had put Lída into a mood. No reason to take it personally.

Lída followed Tomáš out to the car while her father gathered his tools for work. She stood on the other side of the station wagon and ran her fingers through her hair as if trying to comb it that way.

"Look, Tomáš, I appreciate that you've come out to breakfast with us and are giving us a ride to work." She adjusted the top of her overalls and faced him again. "But please don't come back."

Tomáš lowered his gaze. His eyelids stung.

"It's not that I don't like you. Or that I don't care what happened to Štěpán. I do." She paused, raised her voice. "I mean, I like you and I care about Štěpán. No one's in trouble with the police, if that's what you're worried about."

"I understand." She didn't like him. None of the girls did. He shouldn't have told her about his trains. She'd probably laughed at him with her coworkers after he dropped her off yesterday.

"I can't talk about it." She glanced back toward her house, at her father hobbling out the door hunched over and clutching his stomach.

If Lída didn't want him to see her father like that, she had no idea. He'd seen Ondřej in a bad state many times, and a few more wouldn't change how he thought of her.

Still, he'd do what she asked and never return, push away his dreams of driving her around Rozcestí. Unless, like a widowed hawk, she was moved by instinct and loneliness to change her mind.

Congratulations! You have been assigned to the electrical engineering program at Czech Technical University.

The letter arrived the week after Lída sent Tomáš away. He stared at it in dismay—one more disappointment. He'd wanted to design cars. He'd put automotive engineering as his top choice, with electrical engineering third.

He brought the letter to his father.

"Can't you make them change it?"

"Absolutely not, son. The country doesn't need more people to design cars. We need electrical engineers to modernize the power grid and move the country forward." Comrade Kuchař cleared his throat. Tomáš covered his twitching eyelid. "I don't want to hear any more complaints from you. You're lucky to go to university. You'll do your part there, and after you graduate."

It could've been worse, Tomáš reminded himself. They could've assigned him to become a lawyer like his father.

On a Sunday afternoon in mid-June, Tomáš graduated in an outdoor ceremony with the same cloudless sky and perfect weather they'd had all spring. Although the administration memorialized a classmate from the next town over who'd drowned in a kayaking accident the summer before, no one mentioned Pavol. It was as though he'd never attended the school at all.

Instead of going to the post-graduation parties that night, Tomáš started packing for Youth Union camp. He had five days until it started, but he wanted to make sure he didn't forget anything.

The first thing to go into his suitcase was the shortwave radio his parents had given him for his seventeenth birthday, a special reward because he'd beaten Pavol and another kid for the highest grades in his class. Last year that radio got him through eight weeks of boredom and social humiliation as he listened under the bedsheets, with headphones, to rock music and news of the reforms, all the while imagining his best friend having fun.

He carefully cushioned the radio among some clothes, which his mother had labeled with his name so they wouldn't get mixed up with anyone else's at camp. He took a break from packing and was lifting some barbells when his father's familiar knock came. He opened the door with one hand while lifting the weight with the other. The stormy notes of Schubert's *Death and the Maiden* filtered into the room.

Comrade Kuchař lowered himself into Tomáš's desk chair. "Good to see you working out, son."

"Getting ready for camp," Tomáš said, another x^{-1}. Even though she'd told him not to return to her house, he couldn't get Lída's deep brown eyes and rosy cheeks out of his mind. He didn't need Štěpán's muscles, but no muscles at all wouldn't do.

"Speaking of camp, we need to discuss some plans," said his father. "Take a seat."

Without waiting for his father to tell him where to sit, Tomáš set down the barbell and hopped onto the exercise bench. "I'm driving, right?" That was the point of getting his license.

"It's going to be a little more complicated. Come closer." His father leaned forward and patted the ribbed navy bedspread. "You need to pay attention."

With a sigh, Tomáš slid off the bench and plopped onto his bed. The springs squealed.

"First of all, you're leaving day after tomorrow, first thing in the morning, rather than the end of the week. I have to go to Prague Friday for a Party congress, so I need you to run some errands for me along your way."

"More errands?" Tomáš's voice shook. So far, he'd only driven around town, to the farms, and to Lída's house. He'd studied the route from Rozcestí to Olomouc—most of it straight, level paved roads—but he dreaded the few narrow bridges and mountain passes. Would his father's errands take him on rougher terrain? At the graduation ceremony Comrade Kuchař had joked about *Czechoslovakia's worst teenage driver.*

Still, he'd be driving on his own, freed from the boundaries that had enclosed him. What Pavol had called the walled garden of his home. Driving into the forest where Lída and Ondřej lived had given him a glimpse into another world, one without spies and rules.

"Yes, though you won't be driving alone."

"But . . ." He hesitated. He didn't want his father to hear his voice fade or crack. "You said you were busy."

"Your former driving teacher, Ondřej Pekár, will be along to keep you out of trouble."

The town drunk keeping me out of trouble? Tomáš cut off a laugh—too late.

"I would appreciate more respect from you. That man saved my life during the war."

Tomáš studied his chewed-up fingernails. He'd laughed at Lída's father. Lída hadn't wanted him to see her father hung over. If Tomáš were in Lída's place, he would've been embarrassed too.

His eyelid twitched. He touched his nose, pushed up his glasses, held his hand to his throat. "Ondřej saved your life?"

"Yes. In the Resistance."

His father didn't talk much about those years shuttling between foreign lands and safe houses within Nazi-occupied Czechoslovakia. Tomáš knew his father had something to do with the assassination of one of Hitler's top lieutenants, Reinhard Heydrich. He'd also learned in school that the Nazis retaliated by destroying two towns and murdering everyone there.

"Ondřej could evade any Nazi roadblock. It was one of his skills, along with teaching us to survive in the forest. I grew up near Prague. I didn't know how to live rough, avoid enemy patrols, gather food, or keep warm in winter."

Pavol had talked about camping over the winter with Lída and her father. It all made sense now.

Why couldn't you have gone back into the forest—instead of burning yourself to dust?

"These were difficult years that you'll never know, son. It's hard for me to talk about them, and I can't imagine how hard it must be for Ondřej. I was in London and Moscow most of the time. He spent the entire war here, underground."

"You should've told me earlier, Papa. I would've understood." *Why did his father not trust him? Because he was* slow? Antisocial?

"We fought so you children could live in a paradise. Your job is to look forward, not backward, to continue building our socialist paradise."

That had been their plan. Socialism with a human face.

"We're the old guard," his father said. "We'll be gone one day, and our beautiful country's fate will be up to you."

The mournful strains of *Death and the Maiden*'s third movement wafted into the room like the perfume of flowers at a funeral.

Comrade Kuchař spoke again. "Ondřej, my Comrade Brother, is dying of cancer. Your mother was one of the nurses who cared for him at the hospital, and we've arranged for him to spend his last days in a sanitarium in Olomouc, near your camp. The finest sanitarium in the country."

Tomáš sucked in a pained breath. *Lída's father is dying!*

"I owe him a lot, and the last thing I can give him is a death with dignity."

"I'm sorry, Papa." Tomáš surprised himself by thinking of the words so quickly, what people said in times like this. It was as if the emotions had burst from him and by magic formed themselves into syllables. "I like Ondřej. He's fun and a good driving teacher."

"That's why he's driving with you to camp."

The sad strains of the string concerto made Tomáš shudder. What was it like to have cancer? Did it hurt like the flames that consumed Pavol? What was he supposed to say to this dying man who'd been so kind to him . . . and who was Lída's father?

And what about Lída? Did she have a mother somewhere—somewhere in Rozcestí, he hoped, or maybe in Prague—with whom she could live?

"I'll make sure Ondřej gets there," Tomáš said. "If there's anything he needs . . ."

"He'll let you know, son. He's not shy." Comrade Kuchař stood and paced the length of the room. "I also need you to drop his daughter, Lída, in Znojmo on your way. That's why you're leaving early."

Lída? I'm driving her too? Tomáš clapped his hand over his mouth, so he wouldn't let it slip that he already knew her and liked her. "Does her mother live there?" He scraped his finger along the ribs of his bedspread.

"Her aunt and uncle. She's expecting a baby in September, and her relatives will take care of her and the baby."

Baby! He glanced up at his father. "She's . . . pregnant?" And he'd only thought she was plump. He'd wanted to go out with her. Heat rose to the tips of his ears.

"That degenerate former classmate of yours had quite the secret life."

Pavol? Or Štěpán? It took him less than a second to do the math. All those times he'd covered for Pavol, when Pavol was at Lída's house in the woods. He lowered his head and suppressed the urge to smile.

A part of Pavol was alive, growing inside that beautiful girl.

CHAPTER 17: LÍDA AND TOMÁŠ

The workers at the shoe factory organized a goodbye party for Lída and her father. They gave her a box of clothes for the baby, a pair of tiny blue suede shoes that Yulia had sewn, and smoked sausage and biscuits for the trip. Lída wasn't used to the gifts, the goodbye hugs, and the tears. All her other moves had occurred at night and without warning.

On their walk home, she and her father stopped at the hospital for their final checkups and to pick up medicines. Lída had nothing but a refill of vitamins waiting for her, but her father had a bag full of brown bottles of all sizes and a syringe. She collected everything at the people's pharmacy and stepped outside to wait for his appointment to finish. Her back aching, she eased herself onto a bench.

The bench's fresh paint gleamed in the early evening sunlight. She examined her father's pills, names she couldn't recognize or pronounce. She'd managed a visit to the library after Comrade Kuchař had visited her house. She'd looked up liver cancer.

It was as she'd feared. Incurable. Hopeless.

They weren't sending him to the sanitarium for treatment but to die.

"Lída?"

She looked up into a familiar face. Square jaw. Rough, pale skin. Short blond hair. But the face was whole, neither scarred nor caved in at the mouth. "Š-Štěpán?"

"Anton. His brother."

Her heart raced. "How did you find me?"

"At work. They told me you were going to the hospital next."

The top button of his blue short-sleeved shirt was already open, but he unbuttoned two more, reached inside, and took out an envelope. He handed it to Lída and spoke in a whisper.

"On my way back from university, I saw him. He told me to give this to you." Anton pointed to the back of the blank envelope. "If anyone asks, I never opened it."

Lída glanced around. People scurried around them wearing identical gray business suits or, like her, laborers' overalls. Eyes averted, they minded their own business.

"You ratted out your brother," Lída said. Her heartbeat slowed, leaving behind the dull burning that had become, in her sixth month of pregnancy, a constant companion.

Anton looked past her, somewhere over her shoulder. "What was I supposed to do?"

She swallowed the acid in her throat. "The right thing."

"What is the right thing? You tell me." He had the same hard edge as Štěpán, but that was all there was to him—hardness. Nothing beneath the thick ice on the surface except more ice. She could never imagine him reading Walt Whitman's poems and reciting his favorite passages. She could never imagine him apologizing for treating others as less than human or for calling them names they didn't want to be called.

"You're still in the Party, aren't you?"

His chiseled face tightened into a sneer. Behind him, a car honked. "Yes. I'm thinking of my future and this country's future.

I'm not a selfish degenerate like my brother." He smirked at her. "Though you can't choose your family, can you?" He pantomimed raising a bottle to his lips.

Lída clenched her fists and pressed her arms to her stomach. "No, you can't. But you can protect them. All of them, like the *teachers* of our country's future."

He didn't have a response. Lída glared at his departing back as he fast-walked into the street, dodging cars. He cut between two buildings and into the main square.

As soon as he disappeared from view, she tore off a tiny corner of the envelope and slit the letter open with her index finger. With traffic humming in the background, she read.

Dear friends,

> *I hope this letter finds you well. I have work cleaning empty freight cars when they return to the rail station. It's a job, and it keeps me fit. Maybe we'll see each other again, maybe we won't, but I'll never forget your generosity in my time of need.*

> *Thank you—*
> *Š*

A chill seized her. Štěpán was in Most. Tomáš had told her so. And then she'd sent him away—not because she didn't like Tomáš or appreciate his efforts, but because she had so little time left with her father and wanted it for herself. Now, she wished she hadn't dismissed him when he brought up Štěpán.

Did Štěpán actually want to be found? He'd hinted at his location: Most was the rail transfer point between Prague and Rozcestí where Anton must have stopped on his way home. She and her father had once lived in Most, when he'd worked in a repair shop near the station.

So much had happened since Štěpán disappeared. If he knew about her father, if he knew about her and Pavol's baby, would he come with her to Znojmo? Would he want to escape with her to the other side?

After all, he'd been the first to talk about leaving. He'd decided against it because of his mother and Anton, but Anton didn't deserve him, and if Anton wouldn't or couldn't help their mother, nothing Štěpán did would change things.

She tossed the envelope into the trash and folded the crinkly onionskin paper over and over, into a cube that she popped into her mouth, chewed, and swallowed on her way back to the hospital to meet her father.

That evening Tomáš and his father attached the roof rack to the Škoda. Afterward, they dragged the red canvas tent from the basement and lashed it to the metal rack. Despite its color-coded aluminum poles, Tomáš hadn't figured out how to set it up. The tent held six people and he'd have to help carry it on hikes. The camp leaders would never let him sleep in a one-person pup tent that he could carry and set up entirely on his own. That would be *antisocial*.

His father gave him a road map and typewritten notes with each day's journey plotted out. Tomáš stayed up late studying the itinerary.

Day 1 (Tuesday): Rozcestí to Jihlava via Prague. Pick up Comrade Pekár at the north edge of town; he will direct

you to his house, where you will pick up his daughter. Late
lunch in Prague. If you stay at the inn in Jihlava, give them
my name, and I'll take care of it. If Comrade Pekár wants
to camp in the woods, go along with him. You have the tent.
He can instruct you on how to set it up so you'll be prepared
for camp.

Day 2–3 (Wednesday–Thursday): Jihlava to Zno-
jmo. Attached are a letter allowing you into Znojmo and
the directions to the home of Ludvík Červeny and Irina
Červená, Comrade Pekár's older sister. You may stay with
them in their guest room, but keep out of their way as they
get Lída settled in and say their goodbyes.

Day 4 (Friday): Znojmo to Olomouc. Leave early!! You
must arrive by suppertime and the roads are poor. Attached
are the directions to the Youth Union camp. Someone there
will take Comrade Pekár where he needs to go.

I expect a phone call and progress report every night
between 1800 and 1900 hours.

When he awoke at six in the morning, pale light filtering through his window, Tomáš wondered if he'd slept at all. His head felt stuffed with cotton and his thoughts churned. He traced the road map with his index finger, memorizing the thick and thin lines as if they were an electrical schematic.

He shoved the brand-new textbook the university had sent him, *Power for the Socialist Future*, into his hard-shell suitcase, checked to make sure his sanity-saving radio was still there, and lugged the heavy suitcase downstairs.

His parents awaited him in the dining room with fresh coffee, a basket of rolls, and a plate of sliced ham and cheese.

"Eat a good breakfast, dear. You have a long drive and a big responsibility," his mother said, pouring hot water over the coffee grounds in the cup in front of him. He inhaled the steam rising from the cup, their nice china and not the chipped mugs they used every day.

"Where's Sofie?" Comrade Kuchař waved toward the empty place setting.

"Sleeping in. She had two exams yesterday before she took the train home."

"Wake her in half an hour. She needs to say goodbye to her brother."

Tomáš filled a roll with ham and cheese and tore a hunk off with his teeth, stuffing his mouth so he wouldn't have to talk to them. None of this was what he wanted—another lost summer at Youth Union camp after having to take away his driving teacher who was dying and the girl who'd made him feel things he'd never felt before.

His father grunted and went into the living room. "If Sofie's planning to sleep all day and you're not going to socialize with us . . ." He put on a record album and turned up the volume, loud enough that Tomáš could hear the clicks and pops before the music started.

Shostakovich's *Leningrad* Symphony, Comrade Kuchař's favorite, blasted through the French doors into the dining room. The house vibrated with each crescendo. It would've taken a miracle not to awaken Sofie.

This symphony was one of the few things Tomáš shared with his father. Listening to it, he imagined the war his father had fought, the unrelenting cold of their lands in winter, the Nazis' brutality, and what they had to do to survive. It always made him proud to be Czech, a Communist youth group member, the son of someone who resisted.

Until last year, when the Soviets invaded and took away their music and their freedom. Bullied all his life, he learned that whole countries could bully as easily as schoolmates and fathers. They saw kindness as weakness to be crushed like a beautiful snow sculpture under a giant boot.

Lída understood: *None of us is ever as good a friend as we want to be. This country makes us that way.*

Grateful for his weeks of working out, Tomáš carried his suitcase outside and lashed it to the roof rack next to the tent. He hugged his parents and Sofie goodbye and drove down the hill, his belly full and the *Leningrad* Symphony playing in his head.

CHAPTER 18: TOMÁŠ AND LÍDA

Where pavement met dirt road, Ondřej swayed on his feet, his eyes slits in the bright morning sunlight. Tomáš groaned, not ready to give up his solitude or make small talk with his dying former driving teacher who'd clearly spent the night in a bar. He pressed the brake and the clutch, and the car stopped short. Ondřej slid into the passenger seat. An odor like turpentine slid in with him.

"Your father asked me to meet you here." In mid-belch, he said, "I could use the ride."

Tomáš shrank away and rolled the driver's side window all the way down, keeping it open despite the dust that choked him as soon as he pressed the accelerator and engaged the clutch. "I guess he doesn't know I already found your place."

"No, and I didn't enlighten him."

A box and a knapsack sat in front of the small house. After Ondřej lurched inside, Lída emerged, wearing a white headscarf and an oversized work shirt over black pants. She held out her hand for Tomáš to shake. Even though he didn't like hugs and she'd told him not to come to her home again, the desire to embrace her swept through him. Instead, he shook her hand, opened the tailgate, and picked up the heavy knapsack, which he stuffed into one corner behind the back seat.

"Be careful with that. It's Štěpán's." Lída set her box beside it, and he inhaled the fresh scent of laundry soap on her skin and hair. He stepped away from her and adjusted his too-tight pants.

"Are we . . . bringing it to him?"

"I'd like to. He sent me a letter through his brother. He's working in the rail yards in Most."

Yes! Štěpán did want to be found. Tomáš wasn't even disappointed that Štěpán had written to Lída and not to him. What mattered was that he'd gotten in contact, and now Tomáš could do something for him—a small favor, but a meaningful one.

Then his joy dimmed. Most was in the opposite direction from Ústí, where they had to pick up the motorway to Prague.

"How is he?"

Lída shrugged. "Cleaning out freight cars. It sounds awful."

"Yeah, coal dust isn't the worst of it." Tomáš considered the other possibilities: toxic chemicals, animal waste, decomposed food. His fault, for asking Štěpán to teach him to drive. He ground the heel of his sneaker into the hard, dry soil.

"The whole family's ruined," Lída said, "except for Anton. He snitched, so he's fine."

Tomáš kicked the bit of dust he'd dislodged. "I bet Anton was jealous. I was at their house a couple of times, and Štěpán had more hockey trophies."

He'd always longed to be like Sofie, good at sports with lots of friends who never took advantage of her. She said she wished schoolwork and Marxist-Leninist concepts came as easily to her as they did to him. Her words had made him feel better. He would never snitch on her.

He'd tried so hard not to snitch on Pavol . . . though Pavol was already dead.

"I bet he'll be glad to get his books back," Tomáš said. "We can drop them off today."

He could figure out another route and stay on schedule. He'd make Lída happy and she'd like him. It was the least he could do, to thank Štěpán for keeping silent about his part in the letter.

Lída smiled. "You don't mind making a detour?"

"Not at all." He had to do the right thing. Veer from his father's map.

Ondřej came out with a heavy green, orange, brown, and beige quilt bunched around his shoulders and a hunting rifle in his left hand.

Tomáš gasped. His hand flew to his twitching eyelid. Carrying Štěpán's stuff to Most was dangerous enough without a weapon. At Youth Union camp he'd learned all about the vz. 24, made in Czechoslovakia between 1924 and 1942, and how to disassemble, clean, and shoot it. It had a wooden stock and a short barrel, easy for young campers to handle. He'd never seen one in the wild. Ondřej's rifle had a scope and a worn olive-green shoulder strap.

"Don't worry, kid. I have a permit." Ondřej set the rifle between the back seat and the boxes. He dropped in a box of shells and covered everything with the quilt. On his next trip he brought out his toolbox and a long-handled bolt cutter.

Did he have a permit for those too? An invisible fist tightened around Tomáš's heart. They were driving into a restricted zone near the border. His father had given him a letter allowing him, Lída, and Ondřej into Znojmo, but not with a bolt cutter that could snip barbed-wire fences.

Lída hastily tucked the quilt over the tools. Other possibilities raced through Tomáš's mind. Hopeful ones, for him and Lída, and for Ondřej who maybe wasn't so sick after all. He twisted the top button of his shirt and straightened his glasses. "Are you going to the sanitarium to work?" he asked, his voice a childish squeak.

Ondřej snapped at him, "No decent mechanic leaves tools behind."

Tomáš blinked back the pressure behind his eyelids. *What happens to a mechanic's tools when he dies?*

Lída knew she should've distracted Tomáš while her father loaded the toolbox rather than rely on a quick response from her father's alcohol-fogged brain. If Tomáš figured out her plans and told his father, her aunt and uncle's wrath would be the least of her worries. The authorities could take away her baby. She'd risk everything to keep that from happening.

When she told her father her plan that night after Comrade Kuchař's visit, he said he'd help her escape: *Whatever an old partisan on his way to the grave can do.*

That was why he'd brought the tools. Soon enough, they'd be hers. She'd hide them in her bedroom, trade them for a ride in a truck's secret compartment.

Trade them for a second rider?

"Tomáš, can we make one last stop before we leave town?" she called from the back seat.

"Sure. But I brought snacks, if that's what you need."

"No. I want to say goodbye to Pavol's mother and sisters." It would be her last chance. If she succeeded, border guards and fences would stand between them. If she failed? She forced the thought from her mind.

Tomáš waited a while before answering. "I . . . guess I should go inside too. I never went after . . ."

"Because your father would've killed you," Ondřej said.

"Yeah." Tomáš wiped sweat from his forehead with the back of his hand. His jerky motions and shallow breaths reminded Lída of the machines at the shoe factory. She couldn't tell how far she could push Tomáš before he broke down. At the factory, workers kept to a consistent speed and rhythm, but sometimes under the pressure of quotas, the bosses ordered an acceleration. The workers missed tasks, the machinery overheated, and they had to call Ondřej to fix things before the line could start up again.

Tomáš parked the car with two tires on the street and two blocking the sidewalk. Lída stepped out and checked for StB agents in the places Nika had shown her. Tomáš rocked back and forth in the driver's seat. Even with the window open, Lída couldn't touch him, the same way she couldn't touch her father or Štěpán during their nightmares.

Had something terrible also happened to Tomáš? She hardly knew him, and Pavol had told her so little about him.

Eventually he stopped rocking and pushed the door open with his slumped shoulder. He followed her to the building and huddled behind her. His hands shook, and he kept touching his throat, his nose, his glasses. Then he turned away, as if he needed to hide something. As if he were crying and didn't want her to see.

"Is your father coming in with us?" he whispered, calmer than she'd expected. They'd left Ondřej dozing, head against the rolled-up window of the front seat passenger side.

"Let him sleep." Lída buzzed the apartment. "He's not great with goodbyes."

While Lída spoke to Mrs. Bartošová, Tomáš wished he could write down her words. He needed to know how to say goodbye properly, since he'd soon be parting from Ondřej and Lída. He noted that

Lída didn't mention her pregnancy, so he wouldn't either.

When it was his turn, he couldn't find his voice. Alžbeta's glare sizzled on his bare skin.

Your fault, all of it. You didn't show up at the train station. You didn't show up after—not for three months, one week, and three days.

"One thing I don't understand," Mrs. Bartošová said, so coldly that Tomáš shivered. "Pavol said you were an honest boy, and he valued that in you. If so, why did you lie about him going to your house when he was out drinking?"

Tomáš pushed his glasses all the way up until his eyelashes touched the lenses. He deserved her anger, but not about that. He'd never seen Pavol drink. He thought he'd kept the truth and lies apart.

Lída stepped forward and held both of Mrs. Bartošová's hands in hers while looking her in the eye. "Tomáš *was* a good friend for Pavol. He never did anything like that. If anyone's to blame, it's my father. He invited all the boys to drink with him." She paused. "Except Tomáš."

Tomáš stared at his red-and-white sneakers, sure that because he didn't look her in the eye, Pavol's mother wouldn't believe him. But he'd told worse lies. He'd testified at the Party meeting that Pavol had taken his life because he'd been depressed, as if it were that simple.

"Pavol was too kind for this world," said Mrs. Bartošová. When Tomáš raised his head, he saw how her eyes glistened. His throat clenched, but inside him, a strange force rose. She'd put his thoughts into words, and he owed her the truth.

"Pavol had so much hope for this country. The Russians smashed it." Tomáš lowered his voice to a whisper, in case the StB had bugged the apartment. "If anyone's to blame, it's *my* father and everything he stands for."

They all stood open-mouthed. Saying what he believed had lifted a weight from his chest, but he still couldn't breathe.

How could he have said what he did and go to camp? It wasn't the bullies and the boredom but the twisted, inhumane ideology that had taken the life of his first true friend.

He held out his arms to hug Mrs. Bartošová, the way he had with his mother when he left that morning. Once he'd reached his teens, they only hugged when he won an award or went on a trip. It seemed like the kind thing to do for Pavol's mother, even though he barely knew her, to show he cared and meant what he said. He didn't expect her to hug him back, but she did and thanked him for coming.

Lída lingered after he turned to go. On his way to the car, Pavol's middle sister ran outside to him, blond pigtails flying.

"Wait," she said breathlessly. "I want to give back your records."

Tomáš couldn't tell Nika that they were prohibited, the last thing he should bring to Youth Union camp. If he left them in the car over the summer, hidden under clothes, they'd warp in the heat. He'd have to throw them out. Or leave them with Lída in Znojmo and hope her aunt and uncle didn't find them.

His mind whirred. If he left the records at Lída's, it would be an excuse to visit her on weekends once he moved to Prague. To see her and the baby—Pavol's baby.

Nika returned, staggering under the weight of a cardboard box. Tomáš opened the tailgate and she shoved the box beneath the quilt. In the passenger seat, Ondřej stirred and moaned. Tomáš poked his head through the driver's side window.

"Water, please," Ondřej rasped, hands covering his eyes.

Tomáš stood up straight and called, "Lída?"

"She's still inside," Nika said, leaning against the fender.

Tomáš buzzed the apartment. "A glass of water," he called

through the door. Lída handed him a full mug to bring to Ondřej. On his way, he slammed the tailgate shut.

After Ondřej slurped the water, spilling some on his faded black T-shirt, Tomáš held up the empty mug for Nika to take. He looked up and down the street for her. "Nika!" he called. No answer. *Most people have friends. She's gone off to play with them.* He returned the mug to the apartment.

In the car, he passed the roadmap to Ondřej and glanced over his shoulder at Lída.

"Next stop, Most. You two guide me."

After crossing the woods that ringed the town, they emerged into a landscape that reminded Lída of the Siberian desert in *The Elusive Avengers*—her onetime favorite Russian movie about four brave teenagers fighting a criminal gang—but with machines stirring up the earth rather than horses and wagons. Strip mines stretched to the horizon on both sides of the road, not a tree in sight. On this Tuesday morning, ant-sized miners—men who lived in Rozcestí and neighboring towns, men like Pavol's father years ago—circulated in the pits amid backhoes and bulldozers that dug and moved the ground in search of brown coal.

Some of the mines were shallow, others deep and terraced. Processing plants, six-story-high buildings of corrugated tin with belching smokestacks, broke the monotonous landscape of taupe earth and hazy blue sky. The rumble of tires, theirs and those of the other cars and trucks on the four-lane motorway, and the wind whipping through the car's open windows into Lída's face harmonized with the mining equipment in a harsh industrial symphony.

"Thank you for helping me with Pavol's mother," Tomáš called back to her.

She turned over the words he'd spoken to Mrs. Bartošová, like a backhoe tearing up the earth for coal. "Did you really mean what you said about your father?"

Tomáš's reply had an insistent, almost insulted, tone. "I don't tell lies. I only lied to Pavol's mother about him sleeping at my house because he asked me and he was my friend."

Lída gazed at her trembling hands. It wasn't just the bars. So many of those evenings Pavol had gone to her.

I'm going to Hell for this. The scariest thing is, I don't care, Pavol told her one night as he stripped off his sweater and wriggled out of the rest of his clothes. She let him lift her shirt and bra over her head and snuggled against his body, as sweet as ripe plums.

I don't believe there's a Hell. Or a Heaven, she'd replied. *There's only here and now and this one life we have.*

Every minute they drove toward Most took her farther away from Aunt Irina and Uncle Ludvík. Yet every minute brought her closer to her next decision.

Could she trust Tomáš after his words to Mrs. Bartošová? Could she convince him and her father of her new plan?

Last year, she'd stood by when Štěpán and the others bullied Daria and her brother and their friends, back when Štěpán had been the bully.

She couldn't stand by and do nothing now. She couldn't let the State keep persecuting Štěpán—the first one who'd talked about escaping. If she could get to freedom, so should he.

Besides, if he came with her, she'd have a better chance. He was strong and brave.

She hugged her belly and shouted over the wind, "Tomáš, could you wake my father?"

Tomáš gave Ondřej's shoulder a light tap. He didn't stir. With a loud sigh, Lída reached forward and shook him. He cursed and struck out with his left hand. She ducked and grabbed his arm with both hands to keep him from hitting Tomáš.

She had disturbed him in a nightmare, but they were closing in on Most. Running out of time.

She forced the words past her parched throat. "Pa, Tomáš. We need to get Štěpán out of Most."

"He'll need permission," Tomáš said. "We can return his stuff, but I don't think they'll let him take a vacation with us."

Lída shook her head. "That's not what I mean. I want to bring him with us so he can hide in the catacombs in Znojmo and then escape with me over the border." She pictured the network of cellars where she used to hide from her uncle, but this time with Štěpán alongside her.

"What?" cried Tomáš. The car swerved before Ondřej grabbed the steering wheel. "No one told me you were leaving!"

Lída held her voice steady. "Because it's none of your business. You're dropping me in Znojmo and going on to Olomouc with my father." She waited until Tomáš was driving straight again. It would do them no good if he got them all killed right at the start. "By the time I escape, you'll be so long gone you won't even remember me."

"I'll always remember you." Lída detected the hurt in his voice.

"We have another problem," her father said. "Most is full of secret police. I can guarantee they're following Štěpán to make sure he behaves." He released a gurgling burp and wiped his mouth on his sleeve.

"They'll see us and we'll all be punished," Tomáš stammered.

Lída had to think of something. The film director who'd visited Rozcestí had talked about how she set up scenes. Could Lída do the same?

Her words came slowly at first but picked up speed along with her ideas. "Maybe we should stage a kidnapping. Wear masks, grab him, and shove him in the car." She wrapped her headscarf around her face. "See this." Her father and Tomáš glanced backward at the same time, their heads almost colliding. "Let them think Party goons struck again."

"Could work," her father acknowledged with a grunt. "But it's asking a lot of young Kuchař here, to be part of it."

After a moment, Tomáš spoke. "It was my father who ordered them. I asked Štěpán to teach me to drive when your father was in the hospital, and he found out." His voice trembled. "I need to make this right."

If he were a hugger and not driving, Lída would've hugged him, the way she'd hugged Pavol when he was sad. Everything Tomáš had done, from trying to find Štěpán to what he'd said to Mrs. Bartošová, told her that Pavol had guessed right about him. He was a good friend, and she could trust him.

"You're not your father, you know," she said.

"No, I'm not."

"You're not responsible for what happened to Štěpán, or what they're doing to me."

"Like sending you to live with your aunt and uncle? Is that . . . bad . . . or something?"

Ondřej groaned. A chill rippled through Lída. How much to tell Tomáš, who knew so little about the world? "I couldn't get an apartment because of Pavol. Our child will never go to university, even if he turns out as smart as you."

"You're having a baby?" The high-pitched cry came from behind Lída. A body thumped onto the seat next to her, all legs and arms and pigtails. *Nika!*

The car swerved again. A truck honked. Tomáš yelled and

wrestled the car back into the correct lane.

"Nika!" Lída screamed, shaking all over. "What are you doing here?"

"I was hiding. I told you I would."

The wind battered Lída's face. A truck roared past them on the left. "Tomáš, turn the car around. Nika, we're taking you home."

"I can't!" Tomáš shouted. "The traffic!" His arms and hands trembled. If Lída pushed him harder, he *would* get them killed.

She glimpsed a row of boarded-up houses and on the other side a pile of rubble taller than the car. They'd arrived at the outskirts of Most with her plans already falling apart.

"See how easy it was for me to stow away?" said Nika. "I'm going with you. Then I'll hide in someone else's car and sneak across the border and tell people the truth about Pavol, so they'll make the Russians leave and give us our freedom back." Nika gasped for breath.

"No, you're going home and staying out of trouble until you're old enough to make decisions," Lída said. "When Tomáš can turn around safely, he's taking you back to your mother and sisters—I'm sure they're worried to death right now."

"They know where I am. I left a note."

Lída gripped Nika's upper arm, fingers stretching all the way around it. "What did the note say?"

"I told Mama not to tell anyone." Nika blinked rapidly, as if she'd suddenly realized the hugeness of what she'd done. "She won't go to the police. She'll pray for me. That's it."

Lída let go of Nika's arm and pressed her palms together. The only thing Nika's mother *could* do was pray.

The baby turned and kicked inside Lída. If they drove Nika to Znojmo, they'd have to flee immediately. Lída couldn't hide a child or protect her. She had her own baby to protect. "I told you last month. This is dangerous, and you can get into a lot of trouble. You can get your family into even more trouble than they're already in. And you're too young."

"No, I'm not! I can help you with the baby. I'll play with it and take care of it . . ."

Lída bit her lip until she tasted blood. She couldn't bring Nika into her uncle's house. Her father's tools might pay for smuggling two people out, but not three. Even if he promised to help, she couldn't ask Tomáš to drop a runaway child on the other side of the country and drive off like he'd had nothing to do with this.

Suddenly, the car jerked onto a dirt road and stopped short. Lída slammed against Nika, pinning her against the door. Nika's elbow poked Lída's ribcage from one side while the baby punched the other, and the pain snatched the breath from her.

"I can't take this!" Tomáš cried. "Out! Everyone out!" He pressed his hands to the side of his head and banged his forehead on the steering wheel.

Cursing, Ondřej threw the door open, and Nika squeezed past him. Lída's right side throbbed as she maneuvered herself out of the car.

Tears streamed down Nika's face. "I can't go back! They're making Alžbeta quit school to work in the factory, and they'll make me quit next. Nobody talks to us, except to call us names."

Lída squeezed Nika's shoulder. "They did the same to me. Because of my father's drinking."

Nika sniffled and wiped her face. "Pavol came home smelling like him. I guess that means he drank too." She looked up at Lída with mournful blue eyes. "He said he smelled bad because it was winter and it wasn't good for your skin to bathe in winter. I stopped taking baths because Pavol was always right."

Lída hugged Nika tight while stroking her soft pigtails.

She couldn't take Nika home to say the wrong things to the wrong people—or else try to escape again, with people even less able to protect her.

She had directed them into this mess, and she would have to live with the consequences. She might not get Nika over the border alive. She might not get herself and Pavol's baby over the border alive. But she had to try, for Pavol and for herself. The baby that had kicked her ribs minutes ago now rolled inside her, the gentle motion like a whisper from Pavol telling her: *Look out for my sisters when I'm gone.*

CHAPTER 19: ŠTĚPÁN

To Štěpán, the Czechoslovak Socialist Republic was an octopus with eight arms and eight armpits, and the city of Most was the filthiest and smelliest armpit of them all. Several years earlier, a giant lignite deposit had been discovered underneath, and since then, bulldozers and dynamite had leveled the old city center block by block, replacing it with concrete paneláky several kilometers away where the ground contained no such value.

As an undesirable, Štěpán had been assigned to a closet-sized efficiency in the basement of a gray-and-white eight-story prefab building, surrounded by the larger apartments where families of police officers lived.

Every morning he took a smoke-spewing bus to the rail station for his job cleaning freight cars. Half of them carried coal to plants across the country, and he had to dislodge dust from the floors and walls to keep it from building up and exploding. It was hard work, and painful in the first weeks when he was still recovering from prison and from the beating his masked kidnappers gave him in Rozcestí. The relentless sun burned his skin, which peeled in long, translucent strips. His hair grew out, and his muscles hardened, making him the lean, mean unthinking machine that the Communists wanted him to be.

He worked alone, lest he contaminate the other workers with

his *counter-revolutionary ideology* and his *deviant sexual behavior.* He'd pledged to stay out of trouble for his mother's sake, though solitude ran against his nature. All his life, he'd played for teams and run in packs—with the exception of the Party. *No different from the hockey team,* his mother used to say.

But it was. Everyone on the hockey team worked together for the same goal—to win. Štěpán saw with his parents that Party members pretended to work together but looked out only for themselves. A bigger house, a better job, a car, and they'd turn against each other to get it. Their common opponent was fear, and fear won every time.

In sending the message to Lída, he'd reverted to his nature, his desire for one more chance to see friends who'd stood by him. And while he no longer had his book of Walt Whitman's verses, he'd learned them by heart:

Failing to fetch me at first, keep encouraged;
Missing me one place, search another;
I stop somewhere, waiting for you.

When the midday whistle sounded on that last Tuesday in June, he ate his lunch as usual at the end of the platform with his feet dangling over a little-used spur. Farther up the platform where passengers awaited their trains, his minder stood, at times staring at his pocket watch or speaking into a hidden microphone.

The 12:35 train from Prague came and went behind him. After the last of the debarking passengers filed into the station, Štěpán tossed his empty lunch bag into the trash, jumped from the end of the platform onto the tracks, and crossed to the freight yard. As he passed an abandoned car, someone threw a burlap sack over his head.

He yelled. A shoulder in his ribcage sent him crashing into the railcar.

"Make noise, get hurt." It was a man's voice, muffled but familiar. A sharp blade pressed against his throat, which stung as if he'd cut himself shaving.

Rough hands taped his wrists together with alarming speed.

He knew from experience to submit.

The attackers dragged him across the tracks, bouncing him among them until his head spun. His heart pounded so hard he thought it would explode. He couldn't breathe. The sack smelled like fertilizer, pure poison. His lunch roiled in his stomach. His knees turned to rubber.

"Help!" He could scarcely push the words out.

"Shhh, Štěpán, it's us. Don't fight." He recognized Lída's voice. Were she and Ondřej the kidnappers? What the . . . ?

Hands pushed him into the back of a car. He bumped his head on the doorframe, but the sack cushioned the impact—a relief. In the past few months he'd taken a lot of blows to the head that had left him with headaches and dizzy spells.

They covered him with a heavy blanket, and the car jerked forward with a screech of tires. His shoulder hit metal with a crack and a burst of pain. As the car bounced and weaved, someone tried to cut the tape around his wrists but pierced his skin instead. Warm liquid tickled the inside of his wrists and his palms.

"Got it." The clumsy tape-cutter ripped the rest of the tape from his forearms.

"Yow!" Hair and skin went with it. Štěpán reached up and yanked off the hood and blanket.

"Sorry." The speaker had glasses. Dark hair. A twitchy eyelid. Shirt buttoned to the top even though he wasn't wearing a tie.

"Tomáš! What are you doing here?"

Štěpán blinked and glanced around. He lay next to a quilt behind the back seat of the station wagon where he'd taught Tomáš to drive. But Tomáš wasn't driving. Ondřej was, and Lída sat beside him holding a map. In the back seat with Tomáš were boxes and knapsacks with his in the middle. On the other side of the boxes sat a girl with straw-colored braids—Pavol's sister Nika.

Something hard pushed against his leg. A rifle with scope attached. He shrank back. The edge of a toolbox dug into his shoulder. Bolt cutters poked his thigh.

"We rescued you. It was Lída's idea." Tomáš twisted in the back seat. "You're going to cross the border with her."

"And then go to America, like you want to do," Lída said without turning around.

Nika knelt on the seat and faced Štěpán, her face as pale and earnest as Pavol's. "I'm going with you!"

The burning spread up Štěpán's neck to the tips of his ears. "Did you ask me if this was what I wanted?"

Tomáš's face fell. He lowered his gaze. "We just thought . . ."

Štěpán rubbed his throbbing shoulder. "Did you think about what would happen if they caught me? I've been to prison. Once, for five weeks, and look what they did to me. It's not going to be five weeks if I'm arrested for abandoning the country. More like five *years*."

"Maybe they won't care. Maybe they'll just let you go," Nika said. "I was watching that strange man when Tomáš and Lída and Mr. Pekár grabbed you. He just smiled and did this." She held up her hand, making a circle with her thumb and index finger. She inserted and withdrew the index finger of her other hand, then drew that finger across her throat.

Štěpán shuddered. Lída whipped around and grabbed Nika's hand. "Don't you ever do that!"

"Why not? What is it?"

"It's very rude," Lída said.

"It means homosexual," Ondřej said. "Men who sleep with men. And his minder thinks we plan to kill him because he did the deed."

Lída flopped in her seat. "Pa, that's enough. She's a little girl."

Ondřej waved his right hand in the air. "Welcome to the world, little girl! Did anyone invite you here?"

Trembling, Nika reached into her backpack and pulled out a worn brown stuffed bear.

Ondřej slapped the side of his face. "Oh, no. She needs her toy."

Nika sniffled and hugged the bear.

Štěpán pressed his toothless gum with his tongue, wondering how they'd all ended up in the Party boss's car and whether Tomáš possessed the balls to have stolen it.

Tomáš now untied the string at the top of his own pack and took out a dark red train car, which he rolled on top of the boxes. "I also brought a toy, Nika. It's from my old train set."

Nika ran her finger along the metal side of the train and smiled wanly.

Štěpán leaned back and pulled his knees to his chest. No way Tomáš could've done this on his own. All through school, kids used him. He'd give them candy, toys, the answers to tests if they said they'd be his friend. Could Ondřej and Lída have done the same?

Štěpán took a deep breath and released it, trying to release his tension along with it. "Tomáš, you're not crossing over, are you?"

"No. I'm driving to Youth Union camp with Ondřej."

Of course. Whatever his father the Party leader ordered. "Are you aware that if we're caught, they're going to torture us and make us say you knew about this?"

Tomáš looked up from his fingernails but didn't face Štěpán. "I'm supposed to drive Lída to her aunt and uncle's in Znojmo.

After that, it's her decision what she does." He twisted around and their gaze connected before he looked away. "And you. You didn't snitch last time."

Beginner's luck, Štěpán thought. He wouldn't give the authorities an excuse to test his willpower again.

Bypassing Prague, they took the motorway heading east. Ondřej pulled into a rest area to switch drivers and for Lída to use the bathroom. "She always has to pee," he said after she went inside. Nika giggled. Tomáš's face flushed.

Do you have any special reason to embarrass your daughter? Štěpán wanted to ask, but he suspected a wicked hangover as Ondřej's only reason.

As soon as Tomáš climbed over Lída's seat and out the passenger side door to switch with Ondřej, Štěpán leapt over both seats and bolted outside—colliding with Lída on her way back to the car.

"Where are you going?" She stood with both hands on her hips blocking him, a brick wall with fire-shooting eyes. A lot wider around the middle than she was two months ago. *She's pregnant, and that's Pavol's kid in there.*

"I'm t-taking a piss. Like you."

"Use a bottle." She shoved him into the car with all her weight, then knelt on the seat and glared at him.

Sprawled on the dirty rubber mat behind the back seat, he blurted out, "My mother. If I get in trouble, they won't let her teach again."

"They already won't let her teach next fall. Your brother could've gotten her job back, but he didn't. The only person you can hurt now by leaving is him."

In front, Tomáš turned around and folded his arms across the top of the seat. "Your brother was jealous. You had more trophies."

Despite his general cluelessness, Tomáš had a point. With those trophies came love. After his arrest, that love went away, if it ever existed in the first place. His family threw him out of the pack to save themselves.

Lída shook her head, as if she understood. "Your family, Štěpán . . . the government destroyed it. We're your family now."

No you're not. But the words stuck in his throat. Lída and Ondřej had taken him in when no one else would. And maybe this plan Lída had concocted would give him another chance for a future. He rubbed his sweaty, sunburned forearm smeared with coal dust like a clumsy tattoo. Did she know what it was like on the other side? Would it be any different for him in a place where everything revolved around money and nobody knew or cared about their neighbors?

A glance through the rear window made him realize how futile it would be to return to Most from here, an isolated rest stop with a Soviet tank parked at one end and a police car at the other. He shouldn't have emerged from the cover of the quilt, much less the car. He'd already risked his life and theirs.

He crawled under the quilt. When he peeked through the window again, the police car and tank hadn't moved.

Next time, he'd be more careful.

"Don't go all the way to Jihlava, Tomáš." In the front passenger seat, Ondřej took a long pull from a bottle of vodka. "We'll camp near Humpolec where no one will see us."

Humpolec. From there he could catch a bus to Most. It was still midafternoon. He'd be back in time to work the next morning. *Some hoodlums jumped me,* he'd tell his boss. *I got away from them. Came back to do my part for world socialism.*

They left the car at the end of a narrow dirt path and hiked through the forest carrying their tent and supplies. Ten minutes later they came upon a lake. The water was brackish around the edges, the lake bed visible. Štěpán inhaled the verdant air, so different from Rozcestí and Most with their coal mines and factories.

"I'm going to clean the car. Anyone want me to bring back something?" Tomáš asked after he and Ondřej set up the tent in the woods nearby.

"The quilt." Lída kicked the dirt. "Be more comfortable to sleep on tonight."

"I'll walk with you," Štěpán said.

At the car he dug Yevgeny Yevtushenko's *Babi Yar* from his knapsack and stretched out on the back seat, keeping the door open for ventilation. The bright sunlight made it hard to read outside, and he needed quiet to figure out how he'd get into town and back to Most. Tomáš stood at the open tailgate, folding the quilt.

Try to get rid of him, or find out more?

"Do you have a plan"—Štěpán paused, swallowed—"for how to get over the border?"

"You see this toolbox?" Tomáš tapped the metal box that had banged Štěpán's shoulder multiple times. "Ondřej is leaving it with Lída."

"Doesn't he need it? For when he's at Youth Union camp with you?" Štěpán wondered which of his ex-friends' parents had complained about Ondřej getting their kid drunk and had him run out of town. *Moučka for sure.*

Tomáš hesitated. Cleared his throat a bunch of times and did that weird ritual that ended with straightening his glasses. "We're going to Olomouc together, but he's not going to camp. He's going to a sanitarium to die. He has liver cancer."

You're kidding me. Štěpán pressed his head between his knees.

He locked his fingers over the back of his head and focused on his itching scar to banish the memory of that morning Tomáš told him Pavol was dead—then as now bearing bad news.

He squeezed harder. Poor Lída. She'd said her father had only gone to the hospital for tests and to dry out. He raised his head. "And Lída's pregnant, isn't she?"

Tomáš nodded.

"Ondřej's never going to see his grandchild."

"No." Tomáš's eyes were dry, not like when Pavol had died.

Štěpán shut his eyes against the sudden pressure. He'd had a grandfather he loved, who told him stories of hiding from the Nazis. At least he had ten years with him. Lída's child would have zero.

"I have a question," Tomáš said after a few moments.

"What?"

"Are you really a homosexual?"

Štěpán rubbed his eyes and blinked. "The word is *gay*." He said it in English and repeated it for Tomáš. "You should always call people what they want to be called."

"Gay," Tomáš said. "You're right." He pushed his glasses back on his nose. "I don't like people calling me slow or antisocial. But I don't know what I am. Except different."

"Maybe there's a test you can take. It would be good to find out."

"Since you like guys . . . do you like me? In that way?"

Štěpán forced a laugh. "Hell no." Tomáš flinched. "I mean, *you're* not gay, are you?"

Tomáš shook his head, so hard he had to grab his glasses to keep them from flying off. "No. And I get this funny feeling inside when I stand next to Lída or touch her. I don't like touching people normally, so it's weird. But she was Pavol's girlfriend, and she's having his kid, so I don't think it's right for me to—I don't know. Ask her out? I mean, that wouldn't work anyway because she wants to leave the country."

Štěpán took a deep breath to pull himself together. To avoid hurting Tomáš, the only one from school who recognized his existence. "I've never gone out with a girl—or a boy, for that matter—but here's what I think. Lída's going through a lot right now, with losing Pavol and being pregnant and her father dying. She needs you to be a friend. That's all. Just a friend."

"Thank you." Tomáš lifted the neatly-folded quilt. "I'm going to take this to Lída now. I'll leave you alone to read."

"Better yet . . ." Štěpán checked his watch. Twenty minutes to five. "Could you give me a ride into town?"

CHAPTER 20: TOMÁŠ AND LÍDA

Like Pavol, Štěpán explained the world to Tomáš. He would be a true friend to Lída. Whatever she needed to get over the border with her child—Pavol's child—he would do it for her. His father had given him a wallet full of koruny to last the summer. He would spend it all on her.

"I have to go into town to call my father," he told Lída after handing her the quilt. He could walk around before then, maybe buy a gift for her and her baby.

Ondřej waved the empty vodka bottle. "I'm going with you."

"Great," Tomáš said, perhaps too enthusiastically because Lída frowned at him. Ondřej was in no condition to drive, but he could give directions. "Do you two have enough food?" He guessed she'd stay at the camp with Nika to rest. Her face was pale, and she kept rubbing her lower back.

"Bread, cheese, sausage. Enough to manage. But try to get something into my father besides alcohol while you're in town."

Tomáš nodded even though he had no idea how to accomplish that. Lída had needed to beg her father to eat a bowl of cabbage soup in Most before they kidnapped Štěpán. Ondřej had been drinking steadily since Tomáš started driving again, and now he tripped on a root as he started toward the car.

"Tomáš, where's Štěpán?" Lída called out.

Tomáš turned around. "I'm taking him into town too."

"I don't think that's a good idea."

"I don't like bars, and I have to find a phone. My father will be suspicious if I don't call. Štěpán can keep an eye on your father while I'm talking to mine." The response came to him so quickly it made him proud.

After circling the small main square and counting eight Ladas, Tomáš parked several long blocks away from it, on a tree-lined street of two-story attached houses. Ondřej led the way back to the square on foot. Štěpán followed at a distance, and Tomáš trailed even farther behind, gaze fixed on Štěpán's back. If they were lucky, no one would guess the three of them were connected. Štěpán would look out for Ondřej while Tomáš called his father, and then Tomáš had agreed to switch places with Štěpán.

Closer to the square, the streets became narrower, the buildings closer together. As if he had a radar for them, Ondřej found a tavern in the middle of a street one block past the town square, with red metal tables and chairs outside and large open windows to take advantage of the warm summer day.

Štěpán lingered for a moment at the bus station near the tavern. *Does he really want to return to Most? After he agreed to watch Ondřej so I could make my call?* Tomáš dismissed the thought as soon as Štěpán followed Ondřej inside.

Making himself useful before he had to check in with his father, Tomáš filled up the empty water jug from the car at a gas station so they wouldn't have to waste fuel boiling lake water on the camp stove. At six he returned to the tavern. A couple stood next to the outdoor tables conversing in Russian. Tomáš's chest tightened, and he turned in the opposite direction.

He spotted a short queue at a wooden phone booth under an archway in the square. He waited for the others to finish, dropped his coin into the slot, and dialed his home number.

His father answered. "You didn't go where you were supposed to go."

Tomáš sucked in his breath so hard his throat burned. "We're camping. You said we could camp if Comrade Pekár wanted. He taught me how to pitch the tent."

"That's not what I mean, fool. Someone saw your car in Most. Most is west of Rozcestí. You were supposed to go east, to Ústí, and pick up the highway from there."

"I took a wrong turn. I'm sorry." Tomáš tugged at the top button of his shirt. His eyelid twitched out of control, his father's power over him even at a distance. "We made up the time."

"You had no business in Most."

With a sinking in his chest Tomáš acknowledged that Ondřej had been right. Secret police like Štěpán's minder swarmed through Most. They'd assigned Štěpán a job there because the whole city was a dumping ground for undesirables and those who watched them.

"I'm now discovering that I can't trust you."

"When have I given you any reason not to trust me?" Tomáš's voice wavered, and he couldn't hide it. On top of being a coward, he was a lousy liar. Telling himself it was a different reality—x^{-1} instead of x—had its limits, especially when he was standing at a public phone in a strange town and not at all where he was supposed to be.

"Pavol Bartoš. Štěpán Jelínek. Need I say more? Difficulty making friends is no excuse for making the wrong friends." His father's voice hardened. "Let me explain. From when you were very young, you never played with the other children the way a good socialist child learns to do. You were slow. You didn't cooperate."

Strange. Slow. Antisocial. He'd heard it all before.

"When you were six, your mother and I took you to a doctor in Prague."

"A doctor?" He filed through the note cards of his memory. There was a nice woman in Prague who played games with him. She showed him how to take turns, and she was sweet and patient about it, unlike his parents. His father always snapped at him whenever he did something wrong. His mother worked all the time, at the hospital and at home. She said she had two full-time jobs and no time for play.

"She wanted to send you to another doctor in Moscow named Grunya Efimovna Sukhareva. Doctor Sukhareva studied children who couldn't talk or refused to talk, who rocked themselves, who were antisocial. I said no. You could talk about your trains. Your scores in school were superior. I told her that one day you'd make a fine scientist or engineer."

Tomáš's hand shook so hard the receiver knocked against his jaw.

"We had you tested, and we sent the results to Doctor Sukhareva."

"Tested?" Štěpán had mentioned getting tested. *It would be good to find out.*

"She wanted to examine you in person. Your mother and I made sure your results fell within the normal range so you wouldn't have to go."

Tomáš's knees wobbled. He grabbed the stone arch for support.

His father kept going. "I covered for you when your teachers marked you for not fitting in. I made excuses for years. I've come to believe that was a mistake."

"That's not fair!"

The two people waiting in line gaped at Tomáš. Were they secret police, following him everywhere he went?

He lowered his voice. "I'm going to camp like you asked me to."

"You're eighteen, no longer a child. Those who still can't integrate into society by age eighteen belong in special hospitals, not disrupting our socialist order."

"Are you going to lock me away because I took a wrong turn and went to Most?" His voice squeaked like a child's.

"You had responsibility for two other people. And you could've turned around long before then." A terrifying pause. "You went there to see someone."

Tomáš's heart stuttered. How much did his father know? How much was he guessing?

"You were lucky," his father went on. "Some masked men grabbed that degenerate criminal before you got to him. I hope they dispose of him properly this time."

Tomáš clenched his jaw shut. To show relief implied agreement. To fake disappointment would reaffirm his antisocialness. To say nothing . . . could they know he'd been one of the masked men?

Behind him, the line had grown. People frowned, grumbled, tapped their feet.

"Papa, I have to go. There are people waiting to use the phone. I promise, I'll keep to the plan from now on."

"I need to think about this." His father paused. "I expect you to call me tomorrow morning at the office before you leave for Znojmo. From now until you arrive at camp, I want to hear from you twice a day."

Tomáš hung up the receiver. His father had guaranteed nothing—could ship him off to a mental hospital after the summer or send police to collect him in the middle of camp.

His heart pounded against the prison of his ribs. He would never satisfy his father or escape his reach. The car that had brought him a taste of freedom had been used to track him down. One more step out of line, and he'd lose everything.

He'd promised to take Štěpán's place in the tavern. Instead, he returned to the Škoda, dug his electrical engineering textbook from his suitcase, hugged it as he rocked himself, and waited.

Lída waited.

She had so little time before Tomáš dropped her in Znojmo. She'd have to stay there now, accept the future others had mapped for her and her baby. If Nika had wrecked the escape plan, the blame lay not with her but with the people who spread lies about her brother. She was a child, one who didn't understand the danger no matter how hard Lída had tried to explain to her.

On the other hand, Štěpán's situation was Lída's responsibility. She'd directed his kidnapping, and even worse things would happen to him if he didn't flee the country.

Both of them needed her father's tools more than she did.

"I messed everything up, didn't I?" Nika said as they strung a fishing line around the perimeter of the camp and attached a small tin with rocks to signal predators—the kinds with four legs and the kinds with two. After tomorrow, Lída would need the same in her bedroom.

Yes, you did. Saying those words aloud, though, wouldn't make a difference, nor would Nika seeing the tears streaming down her face.

How would she take care of a baby under her aunt and uncle's rule? Animal mothers did it by instinct, biting off and eating the umbilical cords of their offspring, licking them clean as they gave them life, feeding them, and cleaning their waste. Protecting them.

Did she have those same instincts? Nika would be her test.

While Ondřej, Štěpán, and Tomáš went into town, she and Nika ate supper and washed in the lake. Afterward, she brushed out Nika's soft hair and sang her a lullaby, one of the few she recalled in her mother's voice. Lying on her patch of quilt in the tent, Nika closed her eyes and wrapped one arm around her stuffed bear. "Thank you for letting me come with you. I love you, Lída."

"I love you too." Lída rubbed her sore back. Maybe one day she and Nika would meet again on the other side. She'd find another way to escape . . . unless Štěpán returned to Most, and alone she could lead Pavol's sister to freedom.

CHAPTER 21: ŠTĚPÁN

The next bus left at six thirty. Štěpán figured Tomáš would be done before then. The bus at eight would still get him home around midnight. Meanwhile, he had the near-impossible task of pretending he didn't know Ondřej while looking out for him.

He sat at the bar, ordered a beer, and stared at his coal-stained fingers. Could people tell he didn't belong? His friends had pulled him out of the straight line, what he needed to do to help his mother. *We're your family now,* Lída had said—Lída, who'd have to raise a child on her own, on the other side where she had no family and knew no one except useless Nika. Assuming she and Nika didn't die crossing the border.

If anybody could make it, Lída could. Would her child inherit her fierceness, or Pavol's big, tender heart?

Would Pavol have had a better chance over there?

Would I have a better chance?

At school they taught him that *over there* people had to fight for jobs. The losers ended up unemployed, hungry, addicted to drugs, all alone in the world. Those without education had the worst jobs of all, worse than cleaning coal dust and animal waste from freight cars.

"You look down in the dumps," said the bartender when he dropped off the beer.

Štěpán mumbled his thanks.

"Girl trouble?"

He nodded.

"Never seen you before. I hope you didn't come all the way out here to visit her and she stood you up."

He shrugged. Let the guy make up a life story for him. Safer than anything he could come up with.

"Lot of heartbreakers in this town. They find a young man who'll take them to the city, use him until the next one comes along. One with more connections. Better looking." His eyes froze on Štěpán's mangled mouth. "Sorry. Beer's on me."

Two men in their early twenties pushed through the door and waved to the bartender. One was short and skinny with a shaved head and a light brown goatee. The other was taller and meatier, with brown hair that clung to his head like a skullcap. The bartender didn't wave back. They sat at the table next to Ondřej, who'd ordered a basket of bread, a bowl of potato soup, and fried cheese. He'd finished the soup along with a shot of slivovice and a beer.

The men signaled to the bartender, who brought them each a beer. "Anything to eat?"

The man with the shaved head pointed to the untouched plate on Ondřej's table. "Fried cheese. Like what he has."

The next time Štěpán checked, the two men were sitting next to Ondřej, one on each side of the square table, empty glasses and plates in front of them. The hair on Štěpán's neck rose along with memories of nights at Bar Šťastný.

"You with the fucked-up face," called the larger guy. "Come join us."

His shaved-head companion called out, "Hockey player, right? No teeth."

"Leave him alone, Vlado. He's having a bad day." The bartender filled three shot glasses, brought them to the table on a small tray, and took the cash Ondřej handed him.

"Nice guy," the bartender remarked to Štěpán. Štěpán nodded, unable to tell him how Ondřej would buy rounds of drinks for the kids in Rozcestí and tell stories of the war.

The bartender went to take the order of a young couple sitting at an outside table. Štěpán checked his watch. Twenty minutes until seven. Tomáš should've finished his call already. He'd have to take the late bus to Most.

"Slow night," the bartender said when he returned.

The man named Vlado snapped his fingers. "Another round. On me, but just us. Not the loser with no teeth."

Štěpán groaned under his breath. Ondřej had challenged them to a drinking contest, not caring that he'd had surgery two months ago and had been drinking all afternoon on a dying liver.

Outside, shadows lengthened across the plaza. Štěpán watched the man and woman holding hands and laughing together. *Could I fake that if I had to?*

Ondřej's voice rose, too loud. "I tell you thish sho you know your history . . ."

A chair scraped. Štěpán's skin tingled. A current zipped through him. He still had that hockey player's sixth sense, tuned to the shift in the game. The blind-side body slam. The enemy's coordinated offensive strike.

"Old man, we don't give a rat's ass," Vlado said.

"This is a bar, not a schoolroom." The other man downed his sliv and slammed the glass on the metal table.

Štěpán spun on his stool to face them while the bartender slipped outside with the couple's food order.

Ondřej glared at the two men and quoted Marx, slurring:

"*Hegel remarked somewhere that all great world-historic facts and personages appear, so to speak, twice. He forgot to add: the first time as tragedy, the second time as farce.*"

"Are you calling us farce?" The larger man poked Ondřej's breastbone. Without waiting for an answer, he lifted Ondřej from his chair. Ondřej fought to free himself, but the man was stronger and not nearly as impaired.

Vlado kicked the chair aside and drove his fist deep into Ondřej's stomach.

Ondřej's breath escaped with a harsh bark. He crumpled in the larger man's arms. Vlado reached toward Ondřej's back pocket.

Until this moment, Štěpán had watched, frozen, but now fury exploded inside him. He leapt from the stool and grabbed Vlado's wrist, twisted it upward like the neck of a chicken until it snapped.

The man screamed in pain. "You broke my wrist!"

"And you hit an old man and tried to rob him." As his anger boiled over, so did memories. The interrogation that knocked out his teeth. His father smacking the back of his head with a hockey stick. The goons who beat him in broad daylight while calling him a pervert.

The other man let go of Ondřej and came at him. Štěpán dropped him with a single punch to the jaw.

The bartender stood at the door, eyes and mouth wide open. One hand dangling, Vlado started to run, but Štěpán grabbed his good arm, pulled him back, lifted him up. Adrenaline gave him superhuman strength. "This is for not showing an appreciation for your history."

Vlado's feet kicked in midair. Štěpán stepped forward and flung him through the open window. Vlado skidded across an outdoor table on his back and crashed into two chairs, knocking them over. He jumped up and ran off, leaving his partner sprawled on the floor inside.

"He's going to the police," Štěpán said. So much for not calling attention to himself.

"No, he's not," said the bartender. "Those two have a reputation for rolling drunks. About time someone taught them a lesson." The second man was stirring, and the bartender grabbed his hair and jerked his head back. "Don't come here again robbing my customers."

The second guy climbed to his feet with the help of a chair and staggered out of the tavern. The bartender snapped his towel at the guy's departing rear. Ondřej groaned and writhed, arms pressed against his midsection.

"He needs to go to the hospital," Štěpán said, though he had no intention of taking him there. He had one goal: to get to the bus station.

"He'll be fine. A hangover and a sore stomach. I'll get you some ice for your hand."

Štěpán wiggled the fingers on his right hand, which had begun to stiffen. The bartender returned with a dishtowel filled with ice cubes and went outside to speak to the couple. Probably assuring them that bar fights and people thrown out of windows were not the norm in this town.

Štěpán crouched next to Ondřej. His eyes were closed, as if he'd passed out from drink or pain. *Tell him goodbye before I go?*

Ondřej's lips moved. Drool spilled from the corners. "Did they get my wallet?"

"No." Štěpán ran his fingers through Ondřej's disheveled hair. An aching tugged at his heart.

Ondřej took him in when his father put him out. *We're your family now.*

If he helped Ondřej, he'd miss his bus. He'd have no choice but to flee.

Štěpán lifted Ondřej's T-shirt and saw the curved scar that ran from Ondřej's breastbone to below the waistband of his pants. On his pale, heavily veined skin were smaller, older scars, some jagged and circular like bullet holes. Ondřej moaned.

He was a hero once. He defied bullets and tanks to free his country. And now . . .

Štěpán blinked back salty liquid. *This country is killing him— like it will kill me if I stay.*

He slipped his hand under Ondřej's shoulders. "I've got you. Put your arms around my neck."

Despite his paunch, Ondřej was surprisingly light. Štěpán lifted him onto his back, collected the ice-filled towel, and stopped next to the bartender and the couple outside.

"He's pretty bad off. I'm taking him to the hospital. Can you point me in the right direction?" Štěpán turned his head from Ondřej's toxic breath.

"Cross the square, go left at the next street and you'll see it. I hope that girl who dumped you sees what a good person you are." The bartender slapped his chest. "Beauty. It's on the inside." The man and woman murmured their agreement.

In Russian.

Štěpán's insides turned to ice. How long had they been watching him? Would they follow him?

Štěpán turned left and then right, avoiding the likely-to-be-crowded main square in favor of a cobblestone back street too narrow for cars, with stairs at the far end. Near sundown, the solid orange and tan buildings cast the street in dark shadows. As he climbed the steps, perspiration streamed down his face and stung his eyes. His knees ached. The dishtowel dripped cold water on his legs and feet.

At the top of the stairs, Ondřej gagged. His body convulsed against Štěpán's back and shoulders and a hot, putrid sludge poured out. For a few moments, Štěpán held his breath against the stench, but he couldn't stop breathing, not with this burden.

He emerged at a tree-lined road with cars speeding past— where people could see and ask questions. Perhaps the Russians had run to their Lada and were already looking for him.

"Do you know where we are?" Štěpán gasped. Breathing through his mouth.

The words burbled from Ondřej's mouth. "Straight ahead. Left at the light."

In the car, Tomáš sat hunched with his head on the steering wheel and a book clutched to his chest. Štěpán yanked open the passenger-side door and dropped Ondřej into the back seat.

Tomáš turned. His eyes bulged behind his glasses. "What happened?"

"I'll tell you later. We have to get out of here. Ivan's all over this town."

In the back seat next to Ondřej, Štěpán ducked and stripped off his puke-sodden shirt. Tomáš rolled open his window, started the car, popped the clutch.

"Count to five," Štěpán told him. He wiped Ondřej's face and his own neck with the shirt's clean tail and dropped the shirt on the floor. "You can do it."

This time the clutch engaged.

As Tomáš drove twenty kilometers under the speed limit, Štěpán peered out the hatchback window to make sure the Russians he saw at the tavern weren't among the drivers in the long line of trucks and cars following them. He shoved his tongue into the space between his gritted teeth and whispered verses from memory to calm himself.

Do I contradict myself?
Very well then I contradict myself.
(I am large. I contain multitudes.)

For years he'd made life shitty for others. He'd bullied weaker kids for sport. To make himself feel powerful. To take what they had and he wanted.

Now the universe had taken a giant shit on him.

Resist much, obey little. In America, where Walt Whitman had lived, people could do that.

He wouldn't stop at his own freedom. He would help Lída and Nika escape Czechoslovakia and look out for them afterward. Maybe he could convince them to go to America too.

He would resist by being as brave and good as Pavol.

He would have a heart as large and strong as his body.

CHAPTER 22: TOMÁŠ

The orange sun dropped below the tree line. Tomáš drove the Škoda to its hidden parking place and helped Štěpán carry a snoring Ondřej to a patch of soft ground underneath a pine tree.

"Lída shouldn't have to see her father like this." Štěpán lifted Ondřej's head to his lap and pushed the hair from his face. "Let him wake up and walk back with us. If he needs to go to the hospital, the car's here."

"And we're all going to be in a pile of trouble."

"A man's life is worth the trouble." Štěpán slapped his arm and raised his hand to reveal a mosquito carcass and a dark streak.

Tomáš leaned against another pine and picked at its bark, a heaviness in his chest. *A man's life is worth the trouble . . . We are created in the image of God, and life is precious.* Štěpán and Pavol were telling him things he needed to know.

He should have shown up. "What happened?"

"Ondřej was telling his war stories. These two jokers tried to roll him, and one punched him in the stomach. I defenestrated the guy to teach him his history."

Tomáš raised his fist. After everything, Štěpán still hadn't lost his coolness. The moment of exhilaration passed quickly, though. He lowered his arm and sniffed at the airing-out Škoda. "I'll never get the smell out of the car."

"Sure, you will. Moučka puked in my Trabi, and one scrubbing with a bleach solution took it away."

"Because your Trabi's nothing but plastic. My Škoda has leather seats."

"Don't think it hasn't happened before. Your father, my father, him..." Štěpán tapped passed-out Ondřej's shoulder, then scanned the woods as if Russians and secret police lurked even here. "All those old Communists are serious lushes. You and me, if we stuck around and toed the Party line, we'd have guts out to here"—he stretched his arm all the way out—"and rotting livers, and our days would be split between benders and hangovers. We'd have to drink with Russians, and those guys are real pros."

"I don't even drink. I hate the taste, and my mother always told me how dangerous it is." Tomáš wiped his forehead with the back of his hand. His mother may have worked all the time, but she was the only one in the family who ever understood him. "She's a nurse. She knows."

He realized too late that Štěpán would call him a mama's boy. This time Štěpán didn't. "You should always listen to your mother."

More mosquitoes landed on Štěpán's stinking, shirtless body, and flies buzzed around his head. Tomáš ached for him.

"I'll get the jug from the car so you can wash off," he said.

"No. We're going to need drinking water." Štěpán squeezed the water from the dishtowel over his hair and shook his head like a dog drying off. Droplets sprayed in all directions.

Tomáš shifted from one foot to the other. The drama with Ondřej had distracted him from his phone conversation with his father. While he'd been hiding in the car crying like a little kid, plans to run away had raced through his mind along with his father's harsh words. He thought of the lyrics to "The End," and for the first time he could imagine what it might feel like to want to kill your father. He wanted to smash things, break the entire country.

He could do it. The textbook showed him how.

He slid his forearm across his nose and pushed up his glasses with the back of his hand, trying to sort his tangled thoughts.

"I didn't show up to watch Ondřej. I'm sorry," he said.

"Want to talk about it?"

Tomáš's jaw went slack. "You mean it?"

"We're in this together. *One for all, all for one.*"

The Three Musketeers, one of the books the cool kids read during the reforms, one of Pavol's favorites. Tomáš's heart twisted. He dropped to the ground and wrapped his arms around his legs, knees to his chin.

"Remember you told me I should get a test? I found out my parents already got me one. It didn't turn out so well." Rocking back and forth, he pressed his face to his knees so Štěpán couldn't see. "Papa said they fixed the results so I wouldn't have to go to a mental hospital in Moscow, but he's not going to cover for me anymore. All because I didn't take his route and drove to Most."

"Shit. You think he meant it?"

"He said he'll make up his mind when I get back from camp. I guess he wants to make sure I behave there." He gulped the sultry air. "I'm scared."

"Look at me, Tomáš."

Tomáš raised his head.

Štěpán ran his fingers backward through his wet hair, standing it on end. "It's all right to be scared. We're different. They don't want us to be different here. They want us to be the same."

"They want us to be the same," Tomáš repeated. Štěpán had put his thoughts into words. "I thought it would work out for me, because I always got the best grades. When Papa sent me to the

236

political classes, I got the top scores there too. But one step over the line, and . . ." He raked his index finger across his throat. "I never could find the lines, to keep from stepping over them."

"I didn't help," Štěpán said. "I set traps for you. Remember when I told you that they extended recess for an hour, and we all sneaked inside and left you alone on the playground?"

Tomáš's chest throbbed at the memory, but he had to keep talking, as if that would help him understand things in the future. "Or when you told me I'd get a prize if I collected all that nasty chewed-up gum you put under the desks and stuck it to my new coat. All I got was a spanking from my father."

"I was such a jerk then."

"You were."

"I appreciate your honesty." Štěpán must've interpreted his shocked expression as disbelief because he said, "I mean it. Everyone else lies, and when someone can't help but tell the truth, that's a person you can trust."

Unless they convinced themselves that x^{-1} was x to survive. Tomáš nodded anyway.

One for all, all for one.

If he escaped with Štěpán and Lída and Nika, he'd never have to worry about his father sending him to a mental hospital. He'd never see his father again.

He'd never see his mother and Sofie again, but they'd never once saved him from his father's rage.

"Štěpán, do you think it would be any different for me . . . over there? Or do you think I'd be weird wherever I went?"

Štěpán flexed his right hand, and Tomáš made out a dark stain across the back like a bruise. "I think it could be better for both of us. Here, the government can take everything from you if you don't fit in. Over there, you can find more people who are like you.

In America, Walt Whitman was gay, and he was still a famous poet. People respected him. That wouldn't happen in this country."

Tomáš pictured Štěpán's hero in the same place his father had reserved for him. It wasn't funny, but he forced a smile anyway. "Yeah, but capitalism is cutthroat. A war of all against all. If you don't steal from them, they'll steal from you. And what about the unemployed people? That could be us." Tomáš hugged himself into a tight ball while he waited for Štěpán's answer, as if Štěpán knew more about the world outside because he'd read books from the West before the government banned them.

Štěpán swatted a mosquito on the back of his neck and winced. "I don't want to tell you what to do. But if you're in a place where you're trapped with no decent future, you have to go. Try something else. Because you don't want to end up like Pavol."

Tomáš squeezed his eyes shut. "No. I don't want to end up like Pavol."

"That's good."

After a moment Tomáš opened his eyes and swallowed the lump in his throat. "Do you think I killed Pavol because I didn't go to Prague?" It had been months ago, and Štěpán still hadn't answered his question.

"If you did, so did I. I left him alone there."

"You didn't know what he'd planned. At least you did what he asked of you. I was just a coward."

Tomáš couldn't tell why Štěpán frowned at what he said. Fear had kept him from going to Prague, and fear made him want to run now. No doubt Štěpán could see it on his face.

He blinked and wiped his nose. If he escaped, he'd have to give up his car like his train set. His father's tracking the Škoda to Most had contaminated it, made it another tool of oppression rather than a means of freedom.

Unless he used it as a weapon—one strong enough to smash an electrical tower and cut the current to the fences. Ondřej had brought a large bolt cutter, and he'd found more in the toolbox.

"Štěpán . . ." Tomáš's eyes met Štěpán's, dark beneath the rising moon. "I want to cross over with you. Tomorrow." Holding his breath, he strode to the car, plucked *Power for the Socialist Future* from the front seat, and squeezed it to his chest. He fast-walked back, able to breathe again. "Here's the way we should do it."

CHAPTER 23: LÍDA AND TOMÁŠ

Lída awoke to morning sun glowing red inside the tent. She opened the flap to let out the stale air and heat of sleeping bodies. She counted only two besides herself—Nika and Tomáš.

Had Štěpán returned to Most? And where had her father gone?

Nika stirred. "I'm hungry."

Panic rose to Lída's throat. "I'll make us some porridge," she said stiffly, keeping her voice even to avoid frightening the child. She gathered Tomáš's camp stove kit, powdered mix, and a water jug and crawled outside, the baby heavy in her belly.

Nika followed her. "Let me help."

Hands shaking, she set a pot of water on the stove, left Nika to watch it, and returned to the tent. "Tomáš?"

He rolled onto his back and stretched, cat-like.

"Where are Štěpán and my father?" She whispered the words so Nika wouldn't hear. They'd have to leave as soon as Tomáš dropped them in Znojmo, and without her father or Štěpán she had no idea how to find a smuggler.

"At the lake. Doing laundry."

"Really?" Lída chewed the inside of her mouth. Her father only washed his own clothes when he had something to hide. "Help Nika with breakfast. I need to find them." She drew shallow breaths into her compressed lungs, a mix of baby-taking-up-room and dread.

"I promise they're fine." Tomáš sat up with his knees to his chest and pulled a slender book from under his sneaker. "Štěpán read us poems last night while you were sleeping."

"In the tent?" She must've been fast asleep. Yesterday had exhausted her.

"Outside, so we wouldn't wake you. We three were talking, and now I need to show you something." Tomáš reached for another book tucked into a corner of the tent, a textbook like the ones Pavol used to show her, but thicker with smaller print. He gave her a faint smile. "I decided I'm coming with you."

"No, you're not. You're going to camp. Your father . . ."

Tomáš's smile faded. "When I called him last night, he threatened to have me locked up. Because we went to Most."

Which was my idea. Lída stretched her hands on her belly to feel the baby bouncing inside. She would hear Tomáš out, then explain why it wouldn't be possible to smuggle yet another person with one box of tools as payment.

"If we do it my way," he went on, "all five of us can escape together. Your father too, so he can get medical care in the West."

Her instinct was to say that it wouldn't make a difference, but she didn't know that for sure.

He held the book against his chest like a shield. "We can cross this evening, skip your aunt and uncle's."

Lída swallowed the burning in her throat. *Give him a chance, even if it's not your plan.* She lifted the book from Tomáš's hands, flipped to the table of contents. *Basic Electric Circuits. Introduction to Power Systems. Transformers. Power Flow.* While she skimmed the strange words, Tomáš explained how he'd push his car off a cliff into an electrical pylon and knock out the current to the border fences and floodlights. Under cover of darkness, they'd use Ondřej's tools to cut their way through, then swim across the river.

As he spoke, a pall lifted from her, like morning sun burning off the fog. Like Pavol's smile, soft skin, and sandy hair that she imagined combing with her fingers while she read his textbooks over his shoulder in their little apartment in Prague.

"Is something wrong? Do you think my plan is bad?"

The hurt in Tomáš's voice reverberated inside her. She ran her finger along the wavy water-stained edges of the chapter on transformers.

"It's brilliant, Tomáš. Like you." She blinked and gulped the stuffy air of the tent, filled with the warmth of people who connected her to Pavol. If only they could have been in Prague together, with her holding Pavol's book.

When Ondřej and Štěpán returned from the river, Ondřej praised Tomáš's plan. He said he'd helped to build the towers and fences and thought one car hitting one pylon could knock out power to the entire region. "We had to do everything cheap after the war. Besides, we didn't have the brightest people designing the grid. They'd already been executed for conspiring against the State."

He refused breakfast and crawled into the tent to sleep off whatever he'd done to himself in town the night before. Both Nika and Tomáš wrinkled their noses at the odor of paint thinner that clung to him, his failing liver no longer able to process the alcohol he'd consumed.

Tomáš might be right about medical care in the West, though. Lída wanted to believe it. She needed any shred of hope.

Along with her identity papers, Lída had brought black-and-white photographs of her father at university and in the Resistance. If she escaped by swimming the Dyje River rather than in a truck over a bridge, she'd have to wrap them all in plastic and tape them to her body. When Tomáš told her after breakfast that he needed to go into town to fill up the car and buy food, she asked to go with him.

"I want to go too," Nika said.

"You can't. You're a runaway. You'll get us all in trouble," Lída said.

Štěpán stopped hanging wet laundry on tree branches and glanced over his shoulder. "You can stay with Mr. Pekár and me, Nika."

Nika's lower lip quivered. Yesterday, Ondřej had scared her, and his stumbling up from the lake doubled over and half-carried by Štěpán this morning hadn't improved the little girl's impression of him.

"I already told you. No one's going to know I ran away."

Lída rubbed her belly. Maybe they could pretend to be a family, her and Tomáš and Nika. The police would be less likely to bother them.

As they approached the town, Tomáš's heart raced and his thoughts jumbled. He would have to call his father for the last time. By the hour of his check-in at the Červenys', he'd be long gone, and soon after, the police would be chasing all of them.

His father had contaminated the phone booth at the square, so after waiting nearly an hour for gas at a station at the edge of town, Tomáš waited in another line for the phone next to the toilets. He checked the snaking queue of cars for Ladas, Russians perhaps hunting for Štěpán. None, and Štěpán had stayed back anyway. His hand shook, and the receiver slid from his grasp. He gave the operator his father's office number. Lída popped out of the bathroom and stood next to him—too close, but instead of scaring him more, it calmed him down. A few steps away, Nika licked an ice cream bar that he'd bought her from a kiosk.

"I'm filling up the car and leaving for the Červenys' soon," he said when his father answered.

"Very good, son, very good." Comade Kuchař's voice boomed. The line clicked, a sign that it was tapped. "Look, I want to apologize for yesterday. I said some things I shouldn't have."

The pulse in Tomáš's neck quickened, blood rushing to his brain. His eyelid twitched. He pushed up his glasses and focused on Nika's little pink tongue circling the bar, leaving ridges. "You mean about the doctor?"

"I overreacted. Anyone can make a wrong turn. You've done exactly what I asked today."

Tomáš leaned against the wall, knees still shaky and pulse throbbing. "Yes, I'm here. On time."

"Can you forgive your old man for speaking before thinking?"

Tomáš's throat unclenched. His father rarely asked forgiveness or engaged in the kind of *self-criticism* he required of everyone else. "Yes, Papa. I forgive you."

"I'm planning a nice surprise once you get to camp. Can't tell you what, or it wouldn't be a surprise."

A cake? His parents had done it before, sent cake for him and the rest of his barracks, hoping to encourage new friendships. "Thank you. I'm sure your present will be perfect. I'll . . . let you know when it arrives."

"You should find camp a different experience this year, now that you're in the senior group." Comrade Kuchař's tone was friendly, as if speaking to a junior comrade, not a child. Because he'd obeyed orders, or so his father believed.

"Think like a leader, son. It's time for you to step up. Reach your potential. And when you do, remember me at home urging you forward."

"I-I will."

"Good things come to those who play by the rules—and who make sure everyone else follows the rules."

"Yes, Papa." Tomáš's mouth twisted into a grimace, his father's words like an unexpected knife between his shoulder blades. Could his father read his mind, figure out their plans? Would he ever escape this?

"Excellent. I look forward to our call this evening. Be sure to stay out of everyone's way at the Červenys'. Study your books and your camp guide." His father paused. "I love you, son."

For a moment Tomáš's heart seized up. *I love you?* Years ago, his father would say it, but he stopped around the time he said Tomáš had outgrown the trains.

What do you say back? Even though you aren't sure you mean it? "I love you too, Papa."

He hung up the phone and turned to Lída, who leaned against the cinderblock building, watching Nika. "I can't believe it. He actually apologized."

"He doesn't want your forgiveness." Her voice was cold, hard.

Tomáš counted the cars waiting to fill their tanks. Thanks to his father, he had what he needed, things no one else had. Did he really need freedom? Would it be so hard to follow the road his father had already paved for him?

"I'm not sure what you mean," he said.

Lída had heard it before.

The apologies.

I'm sorry, but you're so beautiful and pure. You make me lose my head.

The promises.

This is the last time. It will never happen again.

The bribes.

I brought you a present. Something you've always wanted.

The *I love you* at the end.

And she couldn't blame Tomáš for falling for it, for saying *I love you* back. He didn't understand people. Pavol said everyone took advantage of Tomáš and it hurt Pavol's heart to watch it happen.

She wanted to warn him, but as they ran their errands he lagged behind her and Nika, too far away for a safe conversation in a public place. He stopped outside a department store with faded dresses and scarves in the window and called her name.

She grasped Nika's hand. "Yes?"

"I-I wanted to get you something last night but didn't know what you liked." He reached into his back pocket, pulled out his leather wallet. "Buy something for yourself and the baby."

Nika pointed to a stuffed giraffe in another window. "How about me?"

"Sure. You too." He waved some koruny. To the passersby, he looked like an exasperated father, Lída thought, but something had changed since the phone call. He'd become tentative, jerky, a puppet pulled by invisible strings. His offer made no sense; clothes and toys would weigh them down during the escape. For all five of them to cross the border according to his plan, they only needed three things.

Her father's bolt cutter.

A radio so they would know the power had gone out. Tomáš said he'd brought one, a shortwave that could get the stations from Austria too.

The car.

They also needed Ondřej to lead them through the forest, but wide-open windows and the lingering stench of the Škoda confirmed what she'd feared all morning.

From deep inside her, desperation pushed through every pore. *We can't afford to wait.*

CHAPTER 24: ŠTĚPÁN

Ondřej moaned inside the tent. Štěpán laid *Babi Yar* facedown on pine needles and hurried to him. Sweat beaded on the older man's face and plastered his graying hair to his head.

"Morphine. In the box, in a paper bag," he murmured between rapid, shallow breaths.

Good thing Nika went into town with Lída and Tomáš. Štěpán found the vial and syringe and, with shaky hands, drew out the amount on the label. How much alcohol remained in Ondřej's system, and would the standard dose finish him off? Tomáš could've figured it out in seconds, but Štěpán had never paid attention in math class and what he'd learned each year seemed to vanish by the beginning of the next.

If I kill him . . .

Ondřej motioned for the syringe. Štěpán handed it over, relieved that someone would be checking his work. Ondřej pushed the plunger, and half the liquid spilled onto his fresh T-shirt. He pointed to a spot on his hip. "If I'm going to lead you to the border, I need my wits about me."

Štěpán took a deep, whistling breath through his missing teeth.

Ondřej hooked his thumb into his olive-green fatigues and yanked them down. "Do it, kid, so I can rest."

Štěpán exhaled slowly, jabbed the needle into the yellowed

paper-thin skin of Ondřej's hip, and wiped a drop of blood with his finger when he finished.

"Good job." Ondřej lifted the syringe from Štěpán's hand and held it up as if toasting him. "Na zdraví."

Štěpán raised the water jug without answering and propped Ondřej against his shoulder to drink. Blood dripped from the needle stick. He pressed the edge of his undershirt against Ondřej's skin until it stopped.

Ondřej trembled, teeth clenched. "Talk to me, kid. Take my mind off the pain."

What should I say? If they hadn't shipped him to Most, he would've had more time in the house in the woods. He could have asked about Pavol—when he'd started drinking and if any of them could have kept him alive. He didn't want his words to cause Ondřej more pain, but he needed the truth.

"Why did you challenge us to drink with you?" he began, because another senseless challenge had wrecked Ondřej when they all needed him to guide them.

"I'm a drunk. I like company. Some of you kept up with me. Some of you didn't."

"Pavol shouldn't have tried. It messed him up." The hole left by his absence ached inside Štěpán, a pain so strong that, instinctively, he closed his fingers around the handle of the water jug as if it were stronger stuff.

"Pavol, Pavol, Pavol," Ondřej said, his eyes losing focus as he spoke. "That boy would cry over dead birds."

With his free hand Štěpán scratched his cheek, rough with stubble after a day and a half of not shaving. He'd never seen Pavol cry—one more thing Pavol had concealed from him.

Ondřej reached for the water and drank. "There's a lot I regret in my life, kid. In the history of the Resistance, we Czechs were widely known as the most ineffectual. We couldn't even kill Heydrich right, though as consolation he suffered greatly before he croaked." Ondřej lowered his gaze to a damp spot on the tent's canvas floor. "But getting Pavol started, then finding out he was the father of my grandchild—that's my biggest regret."

Štěpán picked at the edge of the quilt where Lída and Nika had slept. "Because he started drinking, or because he got Lída pregnant?"

"Both. I should've paid more attention. I was too caught up in my own sickness." Ondřej drew his forearm across his face.

"He said you and Lída took him on a camping trip in February to snap him out of it."

"He seemed to get better," Ondřej said. "So did I, though it was harder for me because I'd get really sick, like hallucinating, if I quit altogether. I told him, however hopeless you feel, drinking yourself into a stupor every night isn't going to cure it."

"How'd he respond to that?" Talking about Pavol diminished the aching, as it brought into the stillness Pavol's voice, his earnest face, his warm, smooth skin against Štěpán's.

"He said he couldn't live like this, in a world without God, in a world where men who'd turned from God made all the rules."

"What did you say to him? It's not like you believe."

"I know, Štěpán, but you have to listen to where people come from and respect that. Like you listen to and respect Tomáš even though he's different from you." Ondřej coughed and kneaded his side. "I told Pavol to take some sort of action rather than beating himself up."

"Is that where he got the idea for the letter?"

"I didn't tell him what to do. I certainly didn't encourage him to follow in Jan Palach's footsteps. The only reason any of us killed ourselves during the war was if we were captured or about to be, to avoid revealing names under torture."

Štěpán ran his tongue along his ripped-up gum. "I didn't reveal any names when they tortured me."

"Then you're stronger than ninety-five percent of us partisans. You would've made an outstanding soldier for the Resistance—and gotten your ass killed."

Ondřej's eyelids drooped. He belched stale air and relaxed in Štěpán's arms.

Štěpán closed his eyes. He imagined Ondřej in the war, his body not yet destroyed by alcohol and despair—the same despair that had engulfed Pavol. Then he imagined himself twenty-five years earlier, a partisan in this forest seven years before the real Štěpán Jelínek was born.

"I loved Pavol, but he could never love me back. Not in that way."

"Pavol did love you, like a brother," Ondřej said.

Štěpán opened his eyes. Ondřej's lips were wet, and the scar on the side of his head glowed red inside the tent. When Ondřej tilted his head back, huge pupils framed by watery eyelids reflected Štěpán's face.

Štěpán had never talked about it with an adult, at least not one who hadn't accused him of degeneracy and delinquency. "Were there any people like me in the Resistance? Would you have accepted me as a comrade and brother if you knew I was gay?"

Ondřej tapped Štěpán's forearm with his fist. "Absolutely. Let me tell you a few things about the Resistance they didn't teach you in school."

Ondřej described a gay Dutch fighter, a painter who blew up the police headquarters in Amsterdam to destroy the files of people targeted by the Nazis. And a gay Yugoslav partisan who killed hundreds of Nazis before he died in combat. "I knew his commander. He said the guy was one of the fiercest fighters he'd ever seen. Besides, nothing Marx and Engels wrote said anything about homosexuality. Not like the Bible."

Then why the hatred now?

Before Štěpán could ask, Ondřej spoke again. "Lída said that while I was in the hospital you read her verses every night by an American poet."

"Walt Whitman."

"Do you want to go to America because of him?"

"Yes."

"And you think they're going to treat you differently from people here. But the Brits and Americans were some of the cruelest. After the war, they arrested and castrated their best codebreaker by injecting him with poison. For being . . ."

Štěpán finished his sentence. "Gay." He scraped his tongue against the sharp tip of a broken tooth. "I can't win either way. They get me for being a tool of decadent Western imperialism here, and a sexual deviant there."

Ondřej sucked in a halting breath. His head lolled against Štěpán's chest. "I'm not saying that. When you get wherever you're going, you simply need to be careful. You know as well as I do that freedom can be given, and freedom can be taken away."

Štěpán knew. He would be careful to hide that part of himself. At least until he figured out which people he could trust.

But he wouldn't let Ondřej poison his hope.

While Ondřej slept, an idea came to Štěpán.

After Tomáš, Lída, and Nika returned from town, after Ondřej woke from his drugged sleep, Štěpán gathered his possessions by the folded tent.

Into the pile went his clothes, books, and canvas knapsack. Beside them he set his wallet and identity papers.

"What are you doing?" Lída asked.

"Disappearing."

"I thought you were coming with us." Lída pushed a strand of hair from her wan, sweaty face.

"I am." Štěpán stripped off the undershirt streaked with Ondřej's blood and put on a fresh one. "But when I escape to the other side, I don't want them to punish my mother anymore. So everything I own there"—he pointed to the pile—"I'm scattering it on the trail and in the lake. If the police find it, maybe they'll think the people who grabbed me in Most brought me here to kill me and dump my body."

Nika hugged the giraffe Tomáš had bought her in town. "It won't work. They didn't stop punishing us after Pavol died."

Tomáš kicked at the dirt. "Yeah, but he died protesting *them*."

Štěpán poked his lip with his tongue. He'd kept Pavol's last words to him a secret. None of the others knew that Pavol had lost everything long before his desperate final act. Tell them? It would accomplish nothing, not when they needed to focus on the future rather than the past. "At least it'll buy us more time to escape if the police think I'm dead. They won't come looking for me."

"Maybe it's something we all ought to do," said Lída. "Thanks to you two not paying attention last night, we'll need the extra time." She turned toward Ondřej, who leaned against a tree, shading morphine-dilated pupils against the early afternoon sunlight.

"Definitely do," Tomáš said, and Štěpán visualized the gears turning in his strange and intricate mind.

After packing the car, Štěpán shook out his clothes on the muddy lake bed. He placed the wallet and identity papers on the grass underneath the knapsack and dropped the bloodstained shirt next to it. Then he picked up his stack of books and hurled them one by one into the lake. *Babi Yar* hit the water first with a splash that sent larger ripples toward him. The pages of *The Iliad* and *The Odyssey*, both fat books, riffled in the wind before smacking the surface. A collection of Kafka's stories, legal until a few months ago, skittered across the water before sinking beneath it. Some books floated, their backs broken and their pages swaying, while others vanished underneath. The last one in his aching right hand was the collection of Walt Whitman's poems.

"Are you sure you want to throw that one away?" Lída asked. When he'd read *Song of Myself* for her by candlelight, she'd always ask him for *just one more poem* like a little kid at bedtime.

"I'm sure."

Winding up until his tendons stretched to their limits, Štěpán hurled the book toward the middle of the lake. The book that came from the farthest away—all the way from America—would travel the farthest when he cast it out.

"Either I'll get to buy a new one where I'm going . . ." He swallowed the clog in his throat, glanced up at the pale blue sky and all around him, as if Pavol lived in that fathomless space. "Or else I won't need it at all."

CHAPTER 25: TOMÁŠ AND LÍDA

Police cars, a green jeep with a red star, and a brown military truck lined the side of the blocked road. Holding his breath, Tomáš handed his identity papers to a pair of police officers. After wiping his palms on his pants, he handed over Lída's and Ondřej's identity papers and his father's letter authorizing him to bring them into a restricted zone. He sat erect, playing the role of his father. Important. Trusted. Able to go where others could not.

If I obey him, this could be my life.

Both men frowned, as if they saw through his act. One riffled through the papers. The other counted heads. Tomáš's knees tapped the bottom of the steering wheel. Underneath the quilt behind the back seat lay Štěpán, Nika, a rifle, and bolt cutters. *If the police search the car . . .* He saw himself returning home in the red-starred Soviet jeep for his father to beat him and send him to the hospital in Moscow.

The officer handed back the papers and waved the car forward.

As the roadblock receded to dots in the rearview mirror, his father's words that morning rose inside him. *Good things come to those who play by the rules—and who make sure everyone else follows the rules.*

Would it be enough if he alone played by the rules, and none of the others got caught? If Štěpán and Nika could cross the border by trading Ondřej's tools, he could drop Lída at her aunt and uncle's house and call his father from there. Before leaving with Ondřej, he'd give her the rest of his money and the radio. He had no idea how much a smuggler cost, but his father had bought him the most expensive black market model last year. Between that and the koruny, Lída could leave with the others, or join them later.

He'd survive camp without the radio and money for snacks. It was the smallest price to pay for not stepping up when his friends counted on him. He would never see Lída again either, but he didn't deserve her. She deserved someone brave, like Pavol, not a coward like him.

The red and gray roofs of Znojmo approached, in their midst a pale green tower. He turned to Lída beside him. "Do you have the map?"

"What map?" She hugged herself. Blood streaked her lip.

"The one my father gave me." He glanced at Ondřej dozing in the back seat. Another reason they couldn't cross over. Ondřej was in no shape to lead them on such a dangerous journey.

"I tore it up and flushed it down the toilet. The directions too," she said.

"Why?" Tomáš's heart thudded. His eyelids stung. How would he explain to his father? He'd lost control, the way his father said the Party lost control and had to call the Soviets to restore order.

"So that you can't find my aunt and uncle's place, even if you change your mind about getting us out of here. We have a plan. *Your* plan. You're not crapping out on it." She jerked her thumb backward. "You're the one who said it was my father's last chance."

Tomáš's face burned, and liquid leaked into his eyes, shrouding his vision. A convoy of jeeps honked and passed them.

Tomáš couldn't ask Štěpán for advice. Too many police on the road. He'd never find the house on his own, and he'd likely drive into another roadblock if he tried. His hands slipped on the steering wheel. The car drifted into the oncoming lane.

Hoo-onnnk!

He yanked the Škoda back onto the two-lane asphalt road, heading downhill toward a bridge. A tank with a red star squatted in front of the right-side parapet.

Behind him, Ondřej rasped, "Take a left at the gravel road. Go uphill to the end."

Seeing no one in the oncoming lane, Tomáš wrenched the car to the left and fishtailed as soon as he hit the loose gravel. He downshifted and let the engine and the elevation slow him.

Concentrate.

The narrow, rutted road took him along the knife's edge of a cliff overlooking the river. Tomáš's stomach squeezed past his heart, into his throat.

One foot on the clutch. One foot on the accelerator, lest the Škoda roll backward on the uphill road and drop into nothingness.

With one last push on the accelerator, he reached the top of the hill. A ruined church overlooked the river. He stepped out of the car on wobbly legs.

The church had no roof and only three walls, with scorch marks all the way up. Grass and a single tree pushed through the stone floor. A stiff breeze blew his hair into his face. It carried an old scent, of dust and life plowed under.

There were no guards or checkpoints here. Both banks of the Dyje lay inside the border at this spot east of Znojmo. A place to regroup. Tomáš threw a stone toward the river and watched it fall below the bank, too far away to make a noise whether it hit water or land. His back to the others, he dared a half-smile.

At least he hadn't killed anyone with his driving.

Tomáš was wasting time, throwing rocks and fiddling with the radio he'd dug from his suitcase. The four o'clock news had come and gone, and he sat on the church's stone steps listening to Dvorak's Symphony no. 8 in G Minor performed by the Bratislava Symphony Orchestra.

Bile rose to Lída's throat. Aunt Irina played that recording constantly, humming along while she cooked.

They should've left by four, her father said, so they could get to the border at dusk and see the path to the river. They couldn't count on the full moon. The weather report predicted clouds at sundown and thunderstorms overnight, the first storms in weeks.

By then, they'd be in Austria.

Lída didn't know what magic Štěpán had performed while she'd gone into town with Nika and Tomáš, but her father had eaten and kept down the bread and sausage they brought back. After resting in the car, he seemed stronger, his mind clearer.

Lída pushed aside a clump of weeds and eased herself onto the step next to Tomáš. "We have to go," she said.

Tomáš snapped the radio off. In the stillness that followed, she could make out her father talking with Štěpán and Nika, explaining the route through the forest.

"Here. Take this." Tomáš emptied his wallet and handed her a thick pile of cash.

She flipped through the bills, some of them large. All of them worthless on the other side of the border. "What's this for?"

Instead of answering, he held out the radio. "A gift, since you wouldn't let me buy you anything."

"We're using the radio to . . ." She mouthed the word, *escape*.

"It's black market, not bugged. You can trade it in Zjnomo."

Lída jumped to her feet. The baby flipped inside her. "You *were* going to bring me to their house." Her words came out as a ragged cry. "And take my father to that place to die."

"No, I—" He squeezed his eyes shut. "You can still get across the border—all of you. With the money and the radio. That'll probably work better than my plan anyway."

"Better for you. Since you won't have to be involved. Do you think you can just go to summer camp as if nothing's changed for you?"

She'd wanted to believe Tomáš could be counted on. Ever since the phone call that morning, though, he'd started tossing his money around, as if he could decide things for everyone the way his father decided where they'd all go.

If Tomáš was right about what had happened last night, he'd never be able to satisfy his father. He'd end up in a mental institution . . . or Comrade Kuchař would turn him into a monster.

She had to tell Tomáš the truth. For herself. For him.

She swallowed the liquid that burned her throat. "You're falling for their tricks and you don't even know it. Remember when you called your father this morning? I heard everything he said."

Tomáš recoiled. "W-what did you hear?"

"Apologies. Promises never to do it again." She ticked each of the points on her fingers, all the shit Uncle Ludvík had pulled on her. "Blaming you for setting him off. Gifts to show you he means he's sorry, but in reality he's not. Telling you that he loves you, but to him love means you do whatever he wants. What he wants is wrong, Tomáš."

"He's taken care of me." Tomáš pulled his knees to his chest. Lída sat next to him. He scooted away from her.

"I believed that too. My aunt and uncle have a nice house. But . . ." She pressed her hand to her mouth, the smell of tobacco on her uncle's breath filling her nostrils and turning her stomach. *Make him understand.* "When I was twelve, my uncle came to me at night. He molested me while my aunt was out playing cards with her friends. He made me keep it a secret, but I told my father and that's why we left."

She tried to catch Tomáš's firefly gaze, but it was hopeless. He was too afraid. Or shocked. Or like everyone else, he thought she was trash and deserved every punishment she'd received.

Tomáš unbuttoned the top button of his shirt and buttoned it again, over and over. *I'm too young . . . too slow . . . to handle this.* In the walled garden where he grew up, he'd never heard of a man coming to a little girl—for *sex.*

Could he take Lída into Znojmo, even with a stack of money and a radio, now that he knew? Could he go there himself?

"Anything I can help with?" Štěpán crossed the rocky terrain in front of the church, his hair wind-blown and bits of blond stubble sticking out on his cheeks and chin.

"Tomáš plans to ditch us. He wants to give us money to pay a smuggler instead of going through with our plan."

Tomáš covered his face with his hands and waited for Štěpán to say something about his missing the train back in March.

"Come on, Tomáš. Let's talk. We're going to work this out."

What was the point? He *had* decided to abandon them. *Be honest, because Štěpán said that's what he liked about you.*

You're scared. Scared to take a dangerous trip. Scared to leave a country you once took pride in to live in another—even though you're the only one here who knows its language.

For a moment, Tomáš's pounding heart shifted to a different

beat, excitement at getting to try out a language he'd studied but rarely had a chance to use.

Scared you won't find your people there. They'll think you're as weird and slow and defective as everyone else does. Your teachers and books were right: capitalism is cruel and exploitative and unfair, especially to people like you.

Scared to tell your friends you're scared. Because they may not really be your friends.

Pavol was your only friend. The one you trusted.

The one you abandoned.

"I don't know what to do," Tomáš said after a moment. His right sneaker had come unlaced. Leaving it untied, he followed Štěpán to the edge of the bluff.

"There's something I need to tell you before you decide," Štěpán said. "It's about Pavol."

"Was he . . . gay too?"

Štěpán shook his head, and Tomáš caught what might have been a wistful expression. "I didn't tell you earlier because . . ." His voice cracked. "It's hard to explain with Lída and the plans they'd made to be together in Prague, but I think you should know. They denied him admission to the university. They were going to send him to work in the mines after he graduated."

Tomáš gulped and sputtered. "The mines? The ones that killed his father?"

"Yeah. Those mines. I think he feared losing Lída and that's why he kept it a secret. Even though it's obvious that she loved him and wouldn't have left him if he had to be a coal miner rather than an engineer."

Comrade Kuchař would've rid himself of a family member who'd become a burden and no longer served his goals. No loyalty to anyone or anything but the Party.

Štěpán continued. "We can't tell her. She shouldn't think Pavol didn't trust her to stay with him."

"I won't say anything." Nor would he tell Štěpán what Lída had just told him; it was her story to tell.

"But why didn't he tell me? A friend would've told me." Tomáš's eyelids prickled. Maybe Pavol didn't like him either and was only using him.

"He didn't tell *me* until I was about to get back on the train so I could make hockey practice. And even then he kept his plan secret."

Tomáš's lower lip trembled. "It was my fault. I could've saved him."

"It was all our faults," Štěpán said. "But we didn't have any good choices. We couldn't have fixed things for him." He stared at his blackened fingers. "The point is, here we are, and we can control our own lives if we make it across that river."

Tomáš shaded his eyes and peered up the hill at the church's broken walls. Maybe they had come to this place for a reason. Maybe Pavol's God inhabited this rocky patch of ground overlooking the river, and He had answers.

All those times he and Pavol talked about how they had to act according to their conscience to make their country a better place. What if conscience no longer mattered and they couldn't change their country?

You don't want to end up like Pavol.

"I'm thinking," Tomáš said. "I want to help the rest of you, and I know it's getting late, but before before we do anything else . . . can we talk about Pavol and what he meant to us? Even before we met each other, or"—his eyes met Štěpán's—"liked each other, he was our best friend. But we never got to say goodbye."

CHAPTER 26: ŠTĚPÁN, LÍDA, AND TOMÁŠ

They stood in a small circle on the windswept cliff above the riverbank. Štěpán between Ondřej and Tomáš. Lída between Ondřej and Nika. Tomáš between Nika and Štěpán. Nika recited a prayer from memory the way Štěpán recited Walt Whitman's poems. At the end, he joined her and Lída as they said, "Amen."

"I'll go first." Štěpán stepped away from the group and picked up a stone. "My grandfather, before he died, used to take me to the Labe River one day a year in early fall." He paused, and the wind stilled as if the universe recognized an ancient religious ceremony that no one dared teach him. "He'd tell me to think about something that was bothering me, or something I was sorry for."

Now he smiled at Tomáš.

"Even then, I was sorry for a lot of things. Like beating up other kids. He said I should transfer it to the stone, along with whatever it was that made me angry, because most of the time when I did something wrong, I did it out of anger."

Štěpán tossed the stone into the air and caught it. His palm was damp and slimy.

"You changed the direction of my life, Pavol, but I'm sorry I wasn't a better friend to you when you needed me. I didn't try to stop you when I saw you hurting yourself with your drinking, and I didn't try to talk to you sooner about what was eating you from the inside. I thought it was all one big party, and I wanted to have a good time." His eyelids stung. So much more to the good time than he wanted to talk about here. This was about Pavol, not him. "I'm going to move forward with my life now, and it's not the way you would've wanted because you wanted to change things here rather than leaving. Wherever you are, I hope you understand and forgive me."

Štěpán hurled the stone over the riverbank to the center of the Dyje. The current would carry it downstream, west to east, until it reached the Danube and the Slovak lands that gave birth to the boy he loved.

Lída picked up her stone. Two weeks ago would've been Pavol's eighteenth birthday. He would never celebrate becoming an adult. So many other things he'd never get to do.

The baby flipped somersaults inside her. Lída pressed her palm to her belly, feeling his tiny limbs growing bigger and stronger by the day. *Michal. Michal Bartoš.* She knew the barley seeds were right, it would be a boy, and *over there*, he would have his rightful name.

She gazed up at the sky, clear blue in this place without factory smoke or coal dust. Her mouth was so parched she could hardly speak.

"Pavol, if you hear me . . . know that I love you and I will always love you. I will raise your child to be as principled and kind as you were."

"Yes," Štěpán said.

"Your sister Nika is here with me. I'll take care of her too. Together we'll tell the world about you and how you gave your life for your country and for freedom."

But Pavol was more than a freedom fighter. He was a real boy she'd held in her arms while they cried over their lost land. And she couldn't shake the feeling that she hadn't done enough to save him so they could live to fight another day.

What had Štěpán said? One thing you're sorry for. One thing you'll let go of when you throw the stone.

She tightened her fist around it.

"I fell in love with you, but I also fell in love with everything around you. Your family, your faith, the fact that you had a home. I wanted to comfort you in your despair." She squeezed Nika's shoulder. She didn't want to remind the child that the brother she adored had strayed from his faith by having sex before marriage. But it was hard *not* to remind her with six months of pregnant belly.

Besides, Nika would become a woman soon. She needed to know her body didn't exist to make men happy.

"Maybe I chose the wrong way to console you, with my body instead of my heart, and it only added to your guilt. I'm sorry. But I know I have to stop blaming myself. Like Štěpán, I'm going to move forward. I'll go back to school like you encouraged me to do, even if it means learning a new language. I know I'm smart enough to do it. And I'm going to make my own home and my own life, for me and our child."

The stone flashed in the sunlight before it disappeared beyond the cliff and into the water. She imagined the ripples, circles flowing outward, breaking the water's smooth surface. A single person, like Pavol, changing the course of all their lives. Setting all of them free.

Tomáš tapped his nose and straightened his glasses. Unlike the others, he'd participated in self-criticism sessions before. Young

Pioneer and Youth Union camps required them once a week for all campers and staff, but this was different. Not petty confession theater. The real thing.

No *I failed socialist praxis by faking a headache and not covering my latrine shift.* Or *I deviated from Marxist principles by thinking about new sneakers during political theory class.* Or *I was greedy and took two cookies for dessert, so my comrade at the end of the table didn't get any.*

He grimaced, stamped his feet, shook out his hands.

"The stone," Štěpán said. "You forgot the stone." He picked one up and held it out to Tomáš.

Tomáš wrapped both hands around the rough gray object, and without taking his eyes from it, he said, "Pavol, I deserted you that morning. You and Štěpán counted on me, and I didn't show up because of my father. I was a coward." He lifted his gaze to the four people standing around him. "I'm still a coward."

He waited for someone to agree with him, but the only sound he heard was the wind whistling through the collapsed walls of the church. A few seconds later, Lída said softly, "You have a lot more to lose than we do."

In the corner of Tomáš's eye, he saw Štěpán nod. Tomáš smiled weakly, not sure he deserved their kindness and understanding. Especially not Lída's.

"All my life, Pavol, I wanted to have friends and belong to something. I used to believe communism meant everybody belongs, shares, and does their share. But then I saw things, like why did my family live in a huge house and I had nice clothes and enough to eat and a big train set while you were going hungry? Maybe my parents didn't think I noticed when Mama wrapped up food for you to bring to your family, but I did. I made a list in my mind of ways real life didn't match what it was supposed to be.

When you talked about the reforms, and socialism with a human face, I began to understand."

It had taken him so long. Štěpán and Lída spoke of failing Pavol, but he bore the most responsibility of all.

He scraped the stone with his fingernail. How much had it really mattered when he failed to appear at the train station that morning? Štěpán said Pavol's drinking had gotten out of control. Lída said he'd lost his faith. And what had his father said?

Sometimes we don't know people as well as we think. They have secret lives. Problems they don't share with us.

He hadn't known Pavol the same way Štěpán and Lída had. Pavol had taught Tomáš about the world but he'd left some things out.

He hadn't taught Tomáš about hopelessness, about having dreams snatched away on the whim of cruel and heartless people. He'd kept it a secret until the end, only telling Štěpán when it was already too late.

He hadn't taught Tomáš about despair, the kind of despair that would lead someone to set himself on fire on the remote chance it would help those he left behind.

Why? If they shared everything under socialism, why couldn't they share their sadness? Would it show that the revolution hadn't brought happiness or peace or a perfect world—and that people weren't machines with no feelings?

Tomáš touched his throat, willing his voice to rise. "There were so many things I didn't understand. I grew up with my life mapped out for me. If I followed the rules, good things came to me. I didn't know what it was like to have nothing and no hope that things would get better."

The final lyrics of "The End" came back to him. No choices left in a place where there'd been only two choices to begin with: obey or have everything taken away.

On this journey Tomáš had become a part of the world—a wild, confusing world where anything could happen. Not his walled-off home, bound by bricks and barbed-wire fences and rules. A world where people could get into a car or board an airplane and travel anywhere. Where they could study and read and hear and say anything they wanted.

Where they could be anything they chose.

I want to choose.

He stepped toward the river with his rock, away from the others. "Pavol, you didn't think you had any choices except to give up your life. We're your friends, and we're making a different choice. We've decided to give up our home. Me . . . I'm giving up the home you called a walled garden . . . to live in the world."

He ground the toe of his sneaker into the dirt, hard and dry as the stone in his hands.

"I may not make it over the border, and I may not belong in the new world any more than the place I'm leaving. But I'm going to take that chance. Watch over me, Pavol. Watch over all of us."

With both hands, he flung the stone toward the river. It splashed into the Dyje and sank quickly, taking his fear with it.

Lída's voice came from behind him. "So you're coming with us?"

"I'm coming with you." Tomáš filled his lungs to bursting with the fresh air of forest and water, steeling himself for what would come next. He returned to the circle. His friends squeezed his fingers. He hadn't abandoned them. His decision made him one of them. For real.

Ondřej held out his hand. "Give me the car keys, kid. You're about to take the ride of your life."

CHAPTER 27: TOMÁŠ

Štěpán and Nika hid in the rear while Tomáš sat with Lída in the back seat, Nika's pink backpack on Lída's lap cushioning her belly. The floor still reeked, but in an hour it wouldn't matter. Tomáš would shed the car the way he'd shed his trains, and he had no idea what would come next. He rolled down the window, leaned his head out, and gazed into the blue sky, wishing he had wings to fly freely across the border like birds with no nationality, obeying only the laws of nature.

Ondřej drove them down the gravel road, along the dirt path between abandoned homes and barns, and into town. He told them the national forest had roadblocks even tighter than the ones into Znojmo. "When I worked there, people from the area used to camp in the forest. Nowadays, you have to be one of the Party elite to enter. Only people they trust absolutely."

At Znojmo's southern edge along the river they picked up a tail. "Green car with lights on the roof, not flashing—yet," Tomáš called out to Ondřej, a hitch in his voice.

"Park police. I'll lose them in town and take another route."

With a screech of tires, Ondřej turned onto a narrow cobble-stone street and accelerated. Nothing behind them for one, two, three seconds. Then the familiar grille of the police car peeked out at the end of the street.

"He's coming for us." The words caught in Tomáš sandpaper throat.

A quick turn left, and they slipped the first tail. Tires rattled on cobblestone. Would they pass the Červeny house during their escape? All the houses looked alike, and Lída said nothing as she clutched Nika's backpack and chewed her lip. With another hairpin turn to avoid a roadblock, Tomáš's record albums tumbled from their box and clattered to the floor.

Tomáš turned his head back and forth until his neck popped. Would they end up trapped, squeezed into the ever-smaller space between the roadblocks and the tail?

Breathing rapidly, he rubbed the back of his neck. Spots appeared before his eyes. The pain dissipated as they slipped past a clump of tanks and out of town. Beyond was deserted, paved country road with the forest to the left and a farm to the right where people stood in fields among yellow rapeseed blossoms.

Ondřej revved the engine. The speedometer ticked up to 150 kilometers an hour. They were headed toward a tractor crossing the road. Sour sweat filled Tomáš's nostrils. He braced himself against the front seat.

Ondřej swerved. The car fishtailed, then slowed. Tomáš adjusted his glasses and made out the shape of a tank in the distance, on a straightaway with forest all around. Ondřej jerked sharply to the right. The tires bounced on tree roots and dirt. A dust cloud enveloped them, and Tomáš coughed. A U-turn threw him against the doorframe. A split second of pavement, then more roots and dirt.

"Welcome to the fire road," Ondřej said.

For once Tomáš found comfort in his father's words: *Ondřej could evade any Nazi roadblock. It was one of his skills.*

The car sped up. Tires thumped. Springs groaned. The wind

battered his face. Behind them a jeep crossed the dirt path but didn't turn to follow them.

Did the guy know where they were going, plan to cut them off somewhere else?

Lída moaned and pressed the backpack to her stomach. "If my baby survives this . . ."

A huge jolt sent Tomáš flying into the air, then bouncing on the seat. Nika yelped, and Štěpán shushed her. Trees and brush whipped by in shades of greens and browns like paint thrown from a centrifuge.

After minutes that seemed like hours, the tires bumped onto a smooth one-lane road. No other vehicle in sight. Ondřej slammed the brakes. Tires squealed, and the car stopped.

"Everyone out. Leave your stuff inside," Ondřej said.

They stood at the edge of the road while Ondřej sped up, rounded a curve, and slammed the Škoda into a low stone wall with a crash and high-pitched grinding. The front of the car tilted upward.

"Pa!" Lída screamed.

The front tires were still spinning when they ran up to the car. The front end overhung the wall that separated the curved single-lane road from a deep ravine. The grille of the Škoda had been smashed in and all the headlights and fog lamps shattered, leaving metal and glass shards on the ground. Between the road and the bottom of the ravine, high-voltage electrical towers rose from a ter-raced strip of land.

Ondřej climbed out of the car and stood on the wall. "Pretty good driving?"

"Perfect." Tomáš stayed on solid ground next to him. All they had to do was tilt the car over the wall and hope for a direct hit. The odds were excellent.

The rear bumper lay on the ground. The back glass was shattered, the tailgate wedged in gravel. Štěpán knelt and examined the skid marks.

"All right, troops," said Ondřej. "Identity papers, driver's licenses, everything goes in the car."

Tomáš threw his wallet onto the front seat, making it look as if he'd been behind the wheel. *Czechoslovakia's worst teenage driver.*

Ondřej threw his documents onto the floor of the back seat.

"I left mine at home." Nika puffed out her lower lip. "I want my bear and giraffe."

"You, little girl, are not bringing stuffed animals on this trip." Ondřej poked his head inside and came out with a pair of water jugs that he handed to Tomáš and a bag of food that Štěpán took. He handed the radio to Lída. Tomáš set down the water jugs and raised the antenna so they could get a signal in this dense and remote forest. Finally, Ondřej brought out the rifle, ammunition, two bolt cutters, and a pile of work gloves. Nika sniffled. Tomáš patted her shoulder, and she quieted. Lída smiled at him, and it was as if his whole body smiled back.

Ondřej shoved the gloves into one leg pocket and dropped the small bolt cutter and loose bullets into the other. He clipped the long-handled bolt cutter to his rifle strap and slung the rifle over his shoulder. "Drop your gear. Let me see your hands empty."

Tomáš extended his arms, palms out. In a few minutes he'd possess nothing. He'd be like Štěpán—missing, presumed dead. They would call it a tragic accident. It would make his family sad, but his parents would keep their jobs and Sofie her place at the university.

Ondřej pushed down on the hood of the dented car, and it tilted on its stone-wall fulcrum. "Time to toss this thing."

Tomáš stood behind the car, his suitcase and detested camp

tent lashed to the top. He shoved his hands under the left rear wheel well, and together the five of them tipped the Škoda like a seesaw. Down, up, down, up, picking up energy and force. On the fourth upswing, the car flipped over the sheared-off wall, rolled down the embankment, flew into the air, and slammed the concrete tower support straight on.

Smash!

Boom!

An orange-and-black fireball rose to the sky and sent bits of glass tinkling back onto the road. The metal tower buckled. A line of sparks zipped toward them, and with the others Tomáš ran.

CHAPTER 28: LÍDA

Sirens howled from all directions. Helicopters and planes buzzed overhead, dumping what looked from a distance like trickles of water on the burning forest.

They hiked single file beneath the canopy upwind from the fire, hiding from border police and firefighters. Lída poked her head out and stared into the smoky sky until her father pulled her back. In her sweaty right hand, she clutched the radio. With her left hand, she tucked Nika close to her, felt Nika's scared-rabbit heartbeat against her side.

How long would it take for police to tell Mrs. Bartošová that she'd lost another child to fire? They wouldn't tell her the truth, give her hope, inspire her to make her own run for the border by revealing that Nika and the rest of them had escaped.

If they escaped.

Lída's empty stomach grumbled, reminding her she had someone else to nourish. She handed Štěpán the radio, picked through the bag of food he carried, and chewed bread, cheese, and sausage while walking. The baby pressed on her bladder.

"No time to stop. Piss fast and catch up," her father said.

Out of sight of the others, she lifted her blouse and opened the plastic envelope that she'd taped to her right side. On top was the photo of her father in fatigues with his rifle over his shoulder and a few days' stubble. Dark hair fell into his then-unscarred face. His eyes were bright and defiant.

She slipped her identity card in with the photos and retaped the envelope. Her father had told them to leave everything behind, but having papers would make it easier to get help for him and to start over with her baby. She had no other family in Czechoslovakia that she cared to protect.

While she squatted over a patch of dirt surrounded by bushes, the wind shifted with a thunderous roar. A hot gust shoved her forward. Sparks flew at her. She yanked up her pants and lumbered back to the trail toward the others.

Wood smoke choked off her breath. The warm, rich aroma like her cabin in winter had become a thick soot that filled her lungs and turned everything dim. She couldn't see anyone else on the trail. Had she gone in the wrong direction? Helicopter blades whipped overhead, then faded.

She held her arm in front of her. Her fingers vanished. Sparks glowed in the crackling semidarkness.

A hand closed over her wrist. She screamed.

Through the smoke, her father's face appeared.

"My fault," she rasped, ashamed that he'd had to rescue her, that she'd wasted so much time.

"We're on the ridge, above the fire line." A coughing fit doubled him over. Using the rifle for balance, he led her up a narrow rock trail. The others waited, wet cloths pressed to their faces. Both Štěpán and Tomáš had stripped off their shirts to tear into rags. Sweat streamed down their bare chests and backs.

Lída used to hike this ridge with her father when he worked there, but living things changed and she no longer recognized the trail. Below them, fire consumed their forest—a fire they'd started. They'd have to cross it to get to the three fences, the river, and the border.

She grew accustomed to the smoky smell that clung to her, the din of sirens and aircraft. In the distance hikers shouted to each other on the trails, but Lída's group ducked into the trees whenever helicopters neared or voices came closer.

When the sun fell below the tree line, the forest turned from dim and smoky to black. Birds screamed above them. Rabbits hopped across their path on their way downhill. Deer bounded past on the uneven trail, their four feet swift and stable. Nika screamed when a deer came close to her, then clapped her hand over her mouth.

Below them flames shot up from the gorge, between their trail and the river. "Where do we cross?" Lída asked her father, her voice wavering.

"I'll find the best spot."

Tomáš pointed to the sky. "That's the best spot. Hijacking one of those planes."

"Too late for that, kid."

Her father led them downhill, following the rabbits and deer. A hot breeze blew through a small clearing. To Lída's left, sparks descended like confetti. A terrified rabbit dashed toward the flames.

"Guess it doesn't know any more than we do," Štěpán muttered under his breath.

Lída pressed the wet rag of Tomáš's shirt against her trembling lower lip. Like the rabbit, Pavol had run toward the flames. He didn't know what else to do.

A hot breeze dried her face.

This was where she'd have to cross fire. Feel the heat Pavol felt. Risk the same end. She squeezed her eyes shut, as if she could erase the StB photo from her memory.

Yellow brush burned on both sides of the trail, throwing off a harsh, acrid smoke that made her chest tighten and her eyeballs sting. "One at a time. Stay close and to the center," her father shouted. It was safe to speak loudly now that they were surely alone, cut off from everything but their own quick footsteps and the thundering, crackling fire. As they walked, Ondřej shook water from the jug over his hair and passed it back for the rest of them to soak themselves. Lída let go of the contents of her bladder, calculating that any liquid would slow down the flames. Heat licked at her damp calves. Each step on charred ground burned through the leather top of her hiking boots to her feet.

She pressed herself against her father, his rifle and bolt cutter hard against her right shoulder, Nika's small hands on her back. A wall of fire sizzled all around them. The forest roared. Trees thudded to the earth.

Slowly, the heat dissipated, and they returned to the near-darkness of the woods below the fire line. Lída wiped her palms on her pants and took the radio from Štěpán. She clicked the on-off dial and held the speaker to her ear.

Static. She thumbed the tuning dial for another station. She couldn't understand the one broadcasting in German but finally found a station with emergency bulletins in Czech.

Power out in all towns to the south and west of Znojmo . . . expected to be restored shortly . . . downed electrical wire touched off a fire in the national forest . . . forest under immediate evacuation order . . .

"What's going on?" Tomáš asked. She gave him the radio. He turned the dial and listened while walking, stumbling over roots. "Electricity out in Austria too."

"How do you know?" she asked him.

Tomáš grinned. *"Ich spreche Deutsch."*

Her father gasped for breath. "Doubt the fences will have power, then." He spat onto the forest floor. "But we need to move fast because they could restore it at any time. It will be the first thing they restore."

"I burned my feet," Nika moaned.

"We're all hurting, kid." Ondřej's face was drawn and his jaw taut. He kneaded his side with his right hand. Inside Lída, the baby did a backflip.

Štěpán slowed in front of Nika. "Hop up. I'll give you a ride." Nika climbed onto his bare back and wrapped her arms around his neck. She wrinkled her nose, but Lída figured she knew better than to complain about how ripe Štěpán smelled.

She was glad she'd kidnapped Štěpán and knew she was lucky he chose to come with them. He had a strong back and a big, generous heart.

Glancing backward toward the burning brush, Lída saw that the sky had turned orange. Sirens grew louder and more insistent, and from the distance came voices on megaphones.

"*Attention! All visitors to the national forest are ordered to assemble at a police checkpoint in the security zone. Hunters carrying weapons must leave those behind before approaching the security zone.*"

In the distance, vehicles passed an opening at the trailhead. Lída wrapped her hands around her belly. Her father took the radio from Tomáš and hurled it back into the forest.

He left the rifle with Lída and walked up to the trailhead. Lída could just make out his silhouette at the edge of the cleared strip, five hundred meters of razed land all the way to the horizon. To the right, military vehicles drove back and forth, headlights shining. Staying low to the ground, Ondřej slipped onto the strip and cut a hole in the trip-wire fence.

When he came back to where the rest of the group waited at the forest's edge, he waved them into a tight circle. "That zone is a lot wider than I remember it," he said in a near-whisper. "I'd say it's about a half kilometer, starting at the first fence with the tripwire. Good news is that it's near dark and the power *is* out. More good news: The cleared land is a perfect firebreak. Bad news: You'll have a lot of time in the open where border guards can see you."

"Can we pretend we're evacuating?" Tomáš asked.

"If you can convince them that you have no identification because it burned up at your campsite."

"What about this?" Lída held up the rifle. "Should we leave it behind?"

"I'll keep it." Her father took it from her and loaded the chamber with the shells from his pocket. "I'm not coming." He snapped back the bolt.

Yes, you are! But now Lída registered that her father had never once said he'd go all the way to Austria with them. "Pa, you can get medical care in the West." *Please, Pa . . . don't leave us.*

"They're going to pump me full of chemicals and radiation and watch what happens." He patted his swollen belly with his free hand. *Mine swollen with life. His swollen with death.* "I've put my body on the line for the greater good for thirty years. This body is tired and going back to where it came from."

One more chance to convince him. "But we need you to lead us."

"I'll slow you down."

He squeezed her hand, and she didn't bother to wipe away the tears that slicked her cheeks. For years, she'd been losing him bit by bit, but the vital parts of him had resurfaced at times when she needed him. Now she'd lose him all at once, completely and forever.

She crunched her quivering lip between her teeth. Bloody and chapped, it stung where her teeth touched it, leaving a metallic taste in her mouth.

Ondřej handed each of them a pair of gloves. "Hide these until you get to the second fence, so they don't know what you're doing." Lída stuffed hers inside the elastic band of her pants.

He gave the short-handled bolt cutter to Tomáš and the larger one to Štěpán. Whispered words to each boy and then to Nika. Lída couldn't hear what he said with the fire crackling behind and inside her.

At last Ondřej stepped toward her, and she hugged him tight. In between them, the baby moved, as if it too wanted to be a part of this. "Your mother loved you." His face was damp, and his body as hot as the fire behind them. "I love you. Nothing in this life has given me greater happiness than being your father."

He hadn't had much happiness in his life, but for Lída it still mattered.

"I love you, Pa. You've been a good father." Not by society's standards, not even always by her own. But there was good deep inside him. Strength. A will to survive. The fact that she wouldn't exist if not for that strength and will. She wouldn't have arrived at this point if he hadn't agreed to help her find a new home, a home of safety and freedom for her and her baby and her friends. "You made me brave, and I thank you." She touched her belly. *May this child have his courage.*

Ondřej shuffled backward toward the deep woods, the burning woods. He waved them onward. "Fly, my little fledglings."

She had said her farewell. Now she had to be the last one through the fences, making sure nothing caught on Nika's hair or clothing.

As soon as they were past the tripwire fence, they ran. Smoke and dusk had turned the sky almost pitch black, and the floodlights had gone out with the rest of the power. Sirens alternated with announcements to gather at the checkpoint, in the distance to their right. In the brief quiet moments, Lída heard her own panting breaths and those of the others, running at full speed, except for Štěpán, who paced himself at an effortless lope.

Rabbits, wild boars, and foxes fled along with them.

They'd made it halfway across the grassy strip when headlights closed in.

A stag with a giant rack of antlers dashed into the vehicle's path. Brakes screeched.

Lída glanced toward Štěpán, running parallel to the animal fifty meters away. Luck—or fate or magic, since Štěpán's surname meant *stag*.

The animal moved on. The vehicle sped toward them. The order blasted through a megaphone atop the jeep. "Stop with your hands up!"

Štěpán slowed first. He dropped his bolt cutter and raised his hands.

Tomáš stammered, "Tell them we had to cut the first fence to escape the fire."

Lída's heart seized. *What do I do now, Pa?* But he was gone, back in the woods, and she and the others had to face the border guards alone.

She raised her hands, her heart thudding so hard it threatened to explode through her chest. An echoing thud rose from deep inside her belly. Beyond the first fence, the fire had eaten its way to the trailhead where they'd left Ondřej.

A shot rang out from behind the jeep. Lída heard a pop, and with a squeal, the jeep spun out thirty meters from them. One of the tires went flat. The vehicle tilted and sank in the dirt, its headlights pointing toward the trailhead.

Another shot came from the first fence, followed by a clank and a hiss. Steam rose from the jeep's radiator. Soldiers jumped from the vehicle and hid behind it, machine guns blasting toward the woods, their backs to the four kids. Tomáš and Nika sprinted toward the end of the security zone.

"Come on!" Štěpán tugged Lída's arm. He scooped up his bolt cutter. Tomáš and Nika were closing in on the second fence. The electrified one.

But she couldn't will her feet to move. A hundred meters from the trailhead to her left, a shadowed Ondřej leapt to the ground from an embankment at the edge of the woods. The border guards gave chase, rifles ablaze, *rat-tat-tat-tat-tat*. The shadow quivered and jerked.

Without another glance backward, Lída ran.

CHAPTER 29: ŠTĚPÁN AND TOMÁŠ

A head of Štěpán, animals hurled themselves into the fence and scratched under it to escape. Tomáš cut the wire mesh from the level of his head all the way down. It surprised Štěpán how calmly and efficiently he worked, creating a neat opening like a door.

A door to freedom.

Far behind them, border guards hovered over Ondřej's body. More sets of headlights dislodged from the checkpoint and approached the disabled jeep.

They slipped through the second fence. "Gloves, everyone," Tomáš said.

A headlight flashed across them. Štěpán ripped and sliced at the snaking barbed wires of the third fence. A bullet whizzed overhead.

A megaphone blared. "Stop with your hands up!"

Tomáš stepped around Štěpán. "Cut to the left. I'll cut to the right and we'll meet in the middle."

Working together, as if they were forwards passing the puck back and forth toward the goal, the two of them snipped the barbed wire, dragged the pieces of the third fence away, and stepped through. A loose barb tore through Štěpán's pants. His ankle stung. Another ripped his bare skin under his ribs. Hot blood ran down his side. A flash of light illuminated the trail ahead of them and the river below.

With a whoosh, a pair of rabbits passed them. Their little paws crunched on the gravel trail.

Štěpán took the lead. "Slowly. We don't know if this trail leads to the river or if it drops off a cliff."

Despite stabs of pain in his leg and side, he lowered himself down the bank. Lída pointed to the rabbits, the top of their fur golden in the light from the flames behind them. They zigzagged along the gravel lip of the bank and into a line of trees just as another volley of bullets flew overhead. "Do what they do. Zigzag down. The footing is better." Her voice was calm and sure, as if her father's death hadn't yet sunk in. But she'd seen Ondřej die as surely as Štěpán had. He had no time to say anything with the rough trail and the shooting behind them.

They skidded into the trees. Štěpán grabbed the trunk of a skinny pine and helped the others onto the steep dirt path toward the water. They stumbled from tree trunk to tree trunk, catching themselves and each other all the way down.

Another flash lit up the pines, cutting through the smoke overhead. Could guards with flashlights and machine guns be coming down the bank for them?

Seconds later, a crack of thunder jolted Štěpán. It rumbled across the sky and faded. Lightning pierced the twilight, followed by a boom eight seconds later. The breeze slapped his face.

They reached the riverbank. Štěpán's ankle burned, and his foot squished inside his shoe. He wiped his slick body above his waist. His hand came away dark. The smell of blood reached his nostrils.

"Would be the cruelest of ironies if lightning hits the water while we're swimming across," he mumbled.

"Not likely. We're in a gorge," Tomáš said—way too calmly for the situation.

"But they could shoot us from the high ground." Lída pointed to the top of the gorge. "We're in range."

Tomáš pushed his glasses up his nose. "If we let the current carry us downstream, we can get out of range. But not too far downstream because we don't want to end up back in Czechoslovakia."

"Hell no," Štěpán said. Worse than getting struck by lightning.

Tomáš traced the flow of the river with his index finger while counting under his breath. "Current's picking up with this storm. Let's go."

"Wait! I can't swim!" Nika folded her arms across her chest. Her jaw trembled.

"I thought everyone knew how." Štěpán raised his pitch to a mocking falsetto: *Swim for the worldwide socialist revolution.*"

"Ear infections. Doctor's note."

Štěpán flexed his muscles. It would be tough to take her across. He had no shirt, nothing for her to hold on to except burning, bleeding skin. She was gangly and scared. She could panic and drag him down. "How's this, Nika? Pretend I'm a dolphin and ride on my back."

"Are you sure?"

Another bolt of lightning. Štěpán counted three seconds before the thunder. A dull ache settled into his head, the change of weather and his exhaustion overtaking him. He breathed in and out a few times. His ribs throbbed. "I'm sure," he said, though his voice shook.

Nika climbed onto Štěpán's back and he jumped into the river, followed by Lída and Tomáš. Pain shot up his leg. His feet sank into the mud near the riverbank—polluted river mud in an open wound. No time to worry about that.

Bullets pelted the water.

"Keep together," Lída said.

"And if we stay close to this side at first, the angles don't favor the bullets," Tomáš said.

Štěpán breast-stroked beyond the mud. "Glad someone paid attention in physics class."

Lída eased onto her back, and Tomáš dogpaddled next to her. Such a skinny thing on land, Nika weighed heavily on Štěpán in the water. His back ached where she lay against him, arms wrapped around his neck, pushing him down and making it impossible for him to kick. The current was carrying them downstream toward Znojmo, the dam, and the part of the river where both sides were on Czechoslovak soil. Bullets slapped the water behind them, followed by ever-louder orders to halt.

Had border guards made it all the way to the shore?

Daylight flashed with a simultaneous crack of lightning and thunder. The zigzagging bolt seemed to break the smoky sky open, all its water dumped on them. After the flash was only darkness, save for the flaming wall of the forest on the Czechoslovak side. Štěpán knew they couldn't stop swimming.

There were no more helicopters or planes. Only what Pavol once called the tears of God.

And bullets. The guards were firing into the water, near them and farther upstream, unable to see but willing to shoot up the entire river to keep them from crossing.

The rain came harder, and the bullets stopped. As he fought the current to get to the opposite shore, Štěpán sucked air. His head hammered. Lída and Tomáš passed him on each side. He twisted to peer behind him. The armed men were gone. The fire had begun to recede.

Štěpán wheezed. Nika's breaths chilled his neck. His arms

could no longer move, much less paddle. He saw himself sliding under the water, Nika with him.

I . . . can't . . . do . . . this. He called weakly for help.

"Hold on." Tomáš paddled toward him and stretched out an arm. "Give you a tow."

"I can make it if you take Nika," Štěpán gasped.

Nika slid from his back into Tomáš's arms. Her weight no longer on him, Štěpán could breathe again.

"Try to float on your back," Tomáš told Nika. Swimming on his side, Tomáš hauled her to shore as rain pelted and lightning flashed high above them. Tomáš lifted Nika onto the rocks where Lída waited, then clambered up.

Štěpán stayed in the water, clinging to a pockmarked rock. His headache had turned vicious, and the shadowy forest spun around him. The others' voices seemed to be coming from the bottom of a well. Muffled. Not quite real.

"Float on your back, Štěpán. Like Nika did."

He kicked his legs out. Hands dragged him from the water, one holding his arm, the other his leg.

"He's bleeding."

Someone ripped his pant leg and tied it around his calf. His brain felt as if it were squeezing through his ears. He crawled onto his hands and knees and vomited river water. Hot liquid bubbled on his lips, but the rest of him was ice cold.

Tomáš helped him stand. "I saw a place where we can rest. It's under a rock shelf, not far from here."

They climbed a muddy path to a hollowed-out berm under a large, flat rock. Across the river, only a few pockets of fire remained, the rest extinguished by the storm. Water dripped from the rock above them, but the dirt and roots they sat on remained dry. Lída scrambled to the far edge, her back turned to them. She stripped off her top and wrung out the water. Nika followed her like a fuzzy duckling waddling after its mother. Lída wrapped her arm around the child's shoulders.

Knees raised to conserve body heat, Štěpán pointed toward the other shore. "That fire will be done by morning," he said to Tomáš.

"Yeah, nothing but charred forest and burned-out electrical lines. They can switch some of it to other circuits, but it's going to take weeks to fix." Tomáš pushed up his glasses. "It's like Pavol lit the torch, and together we carried it to freedom."

Štěpán squinted at the firelight on a riverbank he would have never seen from this angle without Pavol, without Lída, without Tomáš. Whatever happened next, wherever on this *other side* they ended up, Tomáš would be all right.

I will be all right.

And Lída? She would become the director she'd dreamed of becoming, maybe not of movies but of life. The kind of person people could trust with their lives.

Štěpán's headache and chills receded, replaced by a ponderous fatigue. He stretched out on the ground next to Tomáš and laced his fingers behind his head. "Remember how I used to kick your ass?"

"Yeah. I've been working out."

"I bet you could totally kick my ass right now." Štěpán swallowed the bilge taste of the river. "Thanks for saving it."

Tomáš helped Lída drag branches to cover their refuge so border guards wouldn't see them from across the river, and they took turns standing watch, in case the rain-swollen river rose too high.

They said little to each other when they switched shifts.

Nothing about the gunfire Tomáš had heard as he ran with Nika toward the disabled electrified fence. He hadn't seen it, but he could pull information together and draw conclusions from it. Ondřej carried a small hunting rifle. The border guards had AK-47s.

Ondřej never had a chance.

Dull daylight awakened Tomáš. Outside, a light rain continued to fall. Mist hovered over the water. The white smoke still rising from the scorched forest across the river shrouded his former home and spoke, silently, of the impossibility of return. The river rushed with whitecapped waves that licked at the ground meters from where they lay.

His stomach rumbled. Except for a bite of bread and sausage, he hadn't eaten for twenty-four hours.

Nika picked her way to their shelter from the nearby stand of trees. Lída lay on her side, her hands curled around her belly. Štěpán slept on his back. Sometime in the night, he'd taken off the tourniquet. His ankle no longer bled, but clear liquid oozed from both wounds.

When the rain stopped, they broke camp. The gorge on the Austrian side of the Dyje was steep and rocky. Tomáš guided them along the climbable rocks to a part of the trail where they could use the trees and roots as ladders, taking care not to slip on the still-damp surfaces.

"Youth Union camp taught me some useful things," Tomáš said when Štěpán asked him how he knew where to go.

Where the gaps in the tree-root ladder were too great for Nika to climb, Štěpán gave her a boost. He seemed stronger, but Tomáš knew he hid things from them. Carrying Nika across the river had almost killed him.

The moment they reached the top of the gorge, the rain began again. Tomáš caught the water in his cupped hands and slurped it up. They followed a dirt road past fields on each side. Štěpán's limp grew more pronounced. His face was flushed, and he shivered long after the rain stopped.

Nika stopped to pet a cow that stood behind a woven wire fence. Her small hand slipped through the mesh, but when Tomáš tried, his got stuck. He wriggled it free, disappointed that he couldn't touch the gentle creature that reminded him of the ones in his train set so far away.

Štěpán shuffled up to Lída and whispered something in her ear. They hugged, though her arm dangled where blood and pus caked the skin over Štěpán's ribs.

After Lída led Nika away from the fence, Tomáš slowed next to Štěpán, timing his steps to his friend's. "Was that about Ondřej?"

"Yeah." Štěpán pressed his palms to his bloodshot eyes.

"I need to . . . what should I tell Lída?"

"How about *I'm sorry for your loss?* And maybe share something about Ondřej that you remember. Something good, like how he taught you to drive."

"Thank you." The tightness in Tomáš's throat vanished. He would tell her in his own time. Now he needed to get Štěpán to safety.

He gestured for Štěpán to put an arm around his shoulders, to lean on him if he needed help walking. Štěpán's arm was burning hot against Tomáš's neck. "What did you say?"

Štěpán ran his other hand through his wet hair, spraying drops onto Tomáš's glasses. "Walt Whitman said it for me: *I bequeath myself to the dirt to grow from the grass I love. If you want me again, look for me under your boot-soles.*"

Tomáš gazed at his mud-caked sneakers, no longer able to tell the red parts from the white. "I like that. It's perfect for Ondřej."

"You should read poetry. I think it would help you figure out a lot of things."

A few minutes later, Štěpán spoke again.

"Should we knock on a door?"

Tomáš shuddered in his half-nakedness. He'd always worn his shirts buttoned all the way to the top, but now he wore no shirt at all. He wondered what these Austrian farmers would do if they saw a group of ragged, soaked, muddy Czechoslovak kids on this Thursday morning. Would they welcome them in . . . or shoot at them? They were, after all, the enemy. That's what his textbooks, his teachers, and his father had said.

He would have to be the one to talk to them, and he was the weird one. The one who was different.

But he had his friends, and with them he could do anything. Be brave. Be there for them.

"Let's pick out a farmhouse that looks like it has nice people."

They chose a stucco house with a white stone basement and dark wood trim. While Lída knocked, Tomáš rehearsed the German words.

A round woman wearing an apron with her gray hair in a bun opened the door. Her eyes widened, and her mouth became a black oval. "*Wer bist du?*"

Tomáš repeated the words he'd practiced in his mind. "We are refugees from the other side. Can you please call someone to help us?"

An army truck arrived ten minutes later. Two soldiers hopped out. Despite the kindness of the woman, who'd served them warm bread and jam and hot coffee and loaned him a shirt, Tomáš's insides froze at the sight of the uniformed men. "*Vier mehr,*" one spoke into his crackling radio.

"Four more?" Tomáš stammered in German.

"*Ja.* A dozen people took advantage of the fire and power outage to cross over. You bring the number to sixteen." The man extended his hand. His wide smile made Tomáš's entire body relax. "Welcome to Austria."

Who were the others—the ones he and his friends had also helped to freedom, whose lives they'd changed forever? Were they the Party elite, the only people allowed into the park? He could never imagine his own father going to the other side, but maybe his father was right, not only about Pavol but about every other person in this big, chaotic, amazing world.

Sometimes we don't know people as well as we think. Not even a State that claimed to know everything could control everyone.

We all have secret lives. Including me.

A FORK IN THE ROAD,
A PARTING OF THE WAYS

SUMMER 1969

CHAPTER 30: ŠTĚPÁN, LÍDA, AND TOMÁŠ

For three nights Štěpán stayed in the hospital while doctors stitched up his wounds and shot him full of antibiotics. The rest of them crowded into his room, and his roommate complained about a bunch of rowdy Czechoslovak teenagers disturbing his rest.

Don't blame them. I'm the rowdy one, Štěpán wanted to tell the old man, but he didn't have the words.

He wouldn't be here long enough to learn German either. With Tomáš translating, Štěpán told the man and woman from the United Nations High Commission on Refugees that he wanted to go to America to finish school and play hockey.

He didn't want to offend the Austrians by asking to leave, but they seemed as happy for him to move on as he was. They gave him papers to fill out. He asked for a Czech-English dictionary. The land of Walt Whitman would be his land. On the inside of the manila folder with his asylum application, he wrote the verses from memory:

I too am not a bit tamed, I too am untranslatable.

I sound my barbaric yawp over the roofs of the world.

He would leave those words with Tomáš. He'd noticed Tomáš staring up at the airplanes when they'd made their way through the woods. Even though Tomáš didn't read poetry, he would understand.

The people from the United Nations said Štěpán had a clear case for asylum because he'd gone to prison and still bore its scars on his face. They told him he could Americanize his name on the immigration papers. He could be anybody.

He thought about it. He would always be a Czech boy. And he knew the man he wanted to be.

He picked up the pen.

SURNAME: Jelinek

GIVEN NAME, FIRST AND MIDDLE:

He flipped through the dictionary.

Steven Whitman

"You can call me Steve now," he told the commissioners and his friends, and his roommate at the hospital who only grumbled.

It didn't help foreign relations with his Austrian roommate that he kept singing "Break on Through" while snapping his fingers whenever his friends showed up. Tomáš and Pavol liked "The End" from that album best of all, but Štěpán found the seven-minute song morose and creepy and a laughably oversimplified rendering of *Oedipus Rex*.

When the hospital let him go with a bottle of pills, he went to the refugee center for unaccompanied minors next to the Vienna airport, the place where Tomáš and Lída and Nika were already staying. Nika had made him a huge thank-you card out of construction paper, and when he walked into the communal dining room, a banner in a kid's uneven block lettering read VÍTEJTE, STEVE! NÁŠ HRDINA!

Welcome, Steve! Our hero!

Not a bad way to begin his life as Steven Whitman Jelinek.

He shared a room and a bunk bed with Tomáš, who'd already settled onto the bottom bunk but offered to switch.

"Thanks, Tomáš." It would be a relief not to have to climb

up and down the ladder. "Maybe I don't need to be the hero all the time."

Tomáš glanced up from his German textbook. "Good. Because I kind of like it."

The UN people came to the center the following week with more manila folders and a bag of books. "Good news, Štěpán."

"Steve."

"Right-o, Steve." The man grinned. "A preparatory school in upstate New York has invited you to play hockey and redo your senior year on a full scholarship, with room and board." He handed Štěpán a brochure from the school. Štěpán flipped to the page for the hockey team.

Along with the incomprehensible English text, he saw the coach's name: *William Nedved*. His mouth dropped open in shock before a smile crossed his face. He traced his finger over the coach's face in the black-and-white photo. A dominating forward, Vilém Nedvěd had disappeared suddenly, and no one had talked about him since.

"Yes, he defected about five years ago," the man said.

That will be me. Everyone and no one will know who I am.

"Is this near Brooklyn?" Štěpán asked next, heart racing. In this new life, he could visit the places in the poems and the offices of the *Brooklyn Eagle*.

"It's in the northern part of the state, closer to Canada. I'm sure the school organizes field trips to New York City." The man handed Štěpán a map. "We've arranged for you to leave at the end of the week, so you can have six weeks of intensive English-language instruction before the semester begins. We don't want you to fall behind in your studies."

Štěpán examined the other pages in the brochure. It was an all-boys' school, like his old one, but with ivy-covered buildings and no murals of smiling students and workers on the walls. The last page had a list of universities where the graduating students went. Perhaps he could also go to university and play hockey there. He would have to study hard and play hard and, if Ondřej was right, keep his secret to himself for much of the time. At some point, though, he would find people like him; he'd managed to find them in Czechoslovakia. *Because we are everywhere.*

In America he wouldn't have to sneak around to replace *Song of Myself* or the other books he threw into the lake. He could read any book he wanted in freedom.

In Austria Lída saw Pavol everywhere. When the staff drove her into the city to pick out new maternity clothes, her gaze fixed on a thin boy with sandy shoulder-length hair who loped along the Ring Road with his backpack hanging off his right shoulder. He turned; she saw his beard and looked away. Another one passed on a bicycle a few minutes later, wearing a colorful headband and matching vest over his T-shirt. She waved instinctively, but he didn't respond.

Still, it was as if Pavol had escaped before her, and skinny boys with long dark-blond hair brought him back to life. In this land of freedom, he *was* alive, and the Pavol of the StB photo with charred face and hollowed-out eyes no longer existed.

By now, he would've been eighteen. In her mind, he would always be seventeen. Kind, earnest, handsome, and in love with her.

In the room she shared with Nika she placed the photos of her father inside plain wooden frames and set them on their dresser. Nika picked up the one with Ondřej wearing combat fatigues and holding his rifle.

"Is that what he looked like when he was your age?"

Lída hugged her. "He was twenty when they took the picture. In 1940, at the beginning of the war."

"He was so different then."

"The war changed him."

"Do you think we went through a war, kind of? That we'll be changed?" Nika asked. For someone who'd wanted to escape to tell the truth about her brother, she'd become strangely quiet since arriving at the camp. At night her crying kept Lída awake. She refused to buy a new stuffed animal with the allowance the refugee center gave them. Only the ones that had burned up in the car would do.

"Yes, we're changed. But we need to make it a better change."

The next morning, Lída met with the director and, with Tomáš translating, asked, "What do I need to do to get Nika's mother and sisters out of Czechoslovakia?"

There'd been talk of sending both Lída and Nika to a children's village in Austria, where the baby would live too. But a children's village wasn't a family—not even the chaotic, wandering kind of family that Lída once had and lost. To Lída, it sounded cold, collective, and impersonal, like the place they'd just fled.

Nika deserved a better future. So did the baby.

It was up to Lída to cobble one together.

"It's going to be complicated," the director said. "We'll have to call in the Red Cross. But given that Mrs. Bartošová is this child's mother and the grandmother of your child, I think we have a chance." He paused and gave her a rare smile. "The fact that you brought documents helps."

It took Lída most of a week to fill out the paperwork and another week to meet with the people from the Red Cross, but ten days after Štěpán left for America, the shelter director and the woman from the Red Cross called her, Nika, and Tomáš into her office. Already seated inside were the same UN people who'd worked with Štěpán.

"The country of Canada has offered to take the Bartoš family, as well as you and your child," said the woman from the Red Cross. "The others will fly to Toronto first, and you and Dominika will meet them there a few days later. We've arranged for this by the middle of August because you aren't allowed to fly within a month of your due date and it'll be easier if your child is born on Canadian soil."

Tomáš repeated the words in Czech. Even before he said them, she knew from the grin that split his face.

"My baby will have a real home." Tears flooded Lída's eyes, carrying both the greatest joy and the deepest sorrow.

"We're so impressed with your courage and initiative, and the way you've faced and overcome adversity. We know you'll make a good life in your new country."

After translating, Tomáš added, "Not just your baby. *You're* going to have a real home now, Lída."

She wiped her face with the back of her hand. No one would call her kráva again. No one could make her believe she was a cow. She hugged Tomáš, then Nika. And each of the kind strangers in turn.

After the meeting, she and Tomáš walked across a field toward the airport, where he'd been going every afternoon, taking a break from studying and volunteering as a translator. She wore sandals on this warm summer day, and the dry grass and weeds tickled her toes.

She thought of Štěpán's words. And her father and Pavol who loved nature.

I bequeath myself to the dirt to grow from the grass I love,
If you want me again look for me under your boot-soles.

She shook out her hair in the breeze and breathed in air tinged with jet fuel. Now that she had a moment to herself, she wondered what it would be like to live in a giant city of brick and concrete, after she'd navigated forests, gathered firewood, and killed and skinned her own food.

Her father would never have survived that life, but she'd once dreamed of joining Pavol in Prague. She could make a home wherever she landed. Because, more than anything else, people made a place a home.

"Thank you for helping me," she said.

Tomáš stopped and grasped both her hands in his. "I'm going to miss you."

"I'm going to miss you too."

His gaze faltered before he met her eyes again. "I mean, I'm *really* going to miss you." His eyelid twitched behind his glasses. "I think I've fallen in love with you."

She squeezed his hands. Tried to find the right words because the wrong ones would cut him as surely as the barbed-wire fence had sliced Štěpán. Above and behind her, a buzzing pushed into her consciousness. "Tomáš, wherever you go, you will find someone right for you. She'll be smart and kind, and the same things that fascinate you will fascinate her. You'll want to spend your whole life with each other. Raise your kids together." She pictured Nika walking to the children's room of the Rozcestí library whenever she felt sad. "Maybe you two will build the world's largest train set together."

Tomáš let his hands drop to his sides. His head drooped.

He was a strange boy, innocent and kind. That's what Pavol had said about him. And she wanted to help him and be his friend the way Pavol had been, even if an ocean would now separate them.

"If you need any advice, like how to talk to her, write me and

I'll answer. I'll always be there for you. So will Štěpán."

"Okay," he said. He walked toward the fence. She couldn't tell if she'd consoled him or if he believed her, but she'd show him. She'd write him a letter the moment she arrived in Toronto and every week after that.

The buzzing in the distance turned into a steady drone that grew louder until the roar of jet engines filled her ears.

Tomáš clung to the chain-link fence and stared up at the sky. A giant plane-shaped shadow screamed past, and its fleeting wake whipped Lída's face and hair. The plane's wheels touched down with a shriek and a tiny puff of smoke. The smell of burned rubber hitched a ride on the breeze.

Tomáš whirled around. His eyes sparkled. "That's an Austrian Airlines, Sud Aviation Super Caravelle, with twin rear-mounted engines. The plane's made in France. Engines are British, Rolls Royce."

He returned to his viewing spot, where a propeller plane lined up on the runway to take off. Lída's heart ached at the thought of leaving him.

Because she did love him, just not in the way she'd loved Pavol. She didn't think she'd ever love another boy that way.

Between when Štěpán flew to New York and when Lída and Nika received their plane tickets to Toronto, the first astronauts landed on the moon. Tomáš stayed up with the night-shift staff to watch Neil Armstrong proclaim, *That's one small step for man, one giant leap for mankind*, at 4:56 in the morning Central European Time. Lída tried to stay up with them, but seven months pregnant, she gave out soon after Nika.

"It's the world beyond the world," Tomáš said in both Czech and German to anyone who'd listen.

He'd started applying to programs in aerospace engineering at universities in Austria and Germany. That meant language tests and exams in science and mathematics.

"We'll need your secondary school transcript," the director told him.

"That's going to be hard. I'm not supposed to be alive. I faked my death so they wouldn't go after my family."

"We'll have to figure something out."

Tomáš recalled the math competitions he and Pavol used to enter, how they'd send away for problems from Moscow and elsewhere hoping to win prizes, though they never did win. "I have an idea. Send a telegram to Dr. Navrátil, the head of the school, and tell him I won a prize but you need my transcript to claim it." He picked up the director's snow globe. Inside were a train and a mountain lodge, miniature versions of the ones in his old train set.

He shook it, and as the white flakes descended, he imagined his family the moment the police told them they'd found the charred Škoda at the bottom of a gorge with all his stuff inside. Did his mother and sister cry? Did his father feel guilty for sending him to a camp he detested, for filling their final conversations with threats?

He couldn't tell them he was still alive. He couldn't contact them at all. Even if the police identified Ondřej and put the pieces together, they'd pretend the five of them had died in a car crash because the government—his father's government—didn't want to admit that people ran to the other side for freedom.

Tomáš returned the globe to the desk. "If you talk to Dr. Navrátil . . . If he says I died in an accident maybe you can say you want to send the prize to my family. Maybe there's something I can put in, some kind of code to let them know I'm alive."

The plan worked. Sort of. The transcript arrived. But there were more forms, and the director told Tomáš he couldn't start classes in the fall. His life was now off track. Uncertain.

An invisible vise squeezed his chest. He reached for his throat, his nose, his glasses. He couldn't speak.

Would this be his future on the other side?

If he didn't look the man in the eye, if he stared at his new sneakers instead—not Botas but blue and white Adidas from West Germany—he could listen better.

" . . . stay and translate . . . so helpful . . . time to adjust . . . Dr. Navrátil said . . ."

"You spoke to him?" Tomáš quickly glanced upward, then back at his feet.

"At length."

"Was he sad? Because of what happened?" The sneakers were bright blue, with three white stripes. Comfortable and made to last a long time.

"He said you were one of the best math students he ever had, but you needed time to grow up. He wished you'd had the time."

Tomáš's lip quivered, and he hid his face with his forearm. He had the time. Pavol was the one who would never have it, and Dr. Navrátil had refused even to name Pavol at graduation. Having to wait until spring or the following fall to start university wasn't the same as not getting to go at all.

I will translate. I will be a good helper. When I start university, I will be ready.

When Štěpán, Lída, and Nika left, it was as if his limbs were torn off one by one. But in the next weeks, more refugees arrived from Czechoslovakia, and Tomáš translated for them. In his free time, he watched airplanes take off and land from behind the airport fence or studied alone in his room. Realizing that the more he read, the better he'd understand German, he started books by Hermann Hesse, Thomas Mann, and Günter Grass, banned in his old country. The kind of books Štěpán liked.

He wrote letters to his friends, and they wrote him back. Lída sent him a poem she'd written—inspired, she said, by the poetry she and Štěpán had read every night when he lived with her. At the end of September, a photo of a newborn baby tumbled from her letter.

His name: Michael Andrew Bartos. Pavol's son. Ondřej's grandson.

Unlike the baby and Štěpán, Tomáš needed to add only one letter to his name to make it work in his new language. Tomáš was Thomas in both German and English, and it reassured him that he could fit in wherever he ended up, even if he had to wait a while to get there.

When the fake math trophy was ready, he and the director went to the shop in Vienna to mail it to his family. He dropped a cloth into the box.

The shop owner lifted it out, examined it. Tomáš had cut part of the waistband of the pants he'd worn during the escape. His mother had written his name in permanent marker so he wouldn't lose track of his clothes at camp.

"What's this? For cleaning?" the man asked.

"It's for my mother. She'll understand."

They taped up the box. The man addressed it. Before he left, Tomáš hugged it tight, as if he could fill it with his love for her and that love could cross barbed-wire and electrified fences, border guards and censors.

He'd come to realize, though, that not everything about his

old home was bad. It was where he'd made a friend in Pavol and learned of socialism with a human face, where he became *one for all, all for one* with Štěpán and Lída, who called people what they wanted to be called, taught him to be brave, took him from his walled garden into the world.

It was his turn to fly.

QUESTIONS FOR DISCUSSION

1. Why does Pavol believe that his life is over and that he's out of choices? What options might he have had that, in his despair, he didn't see?

2. What does Tomáš like about Communist philosophy? How does this philosophy contrast with his reality? How do you deal with contrasts between the values you've been taught and the way people act in real life?

3. Why was Štěpán a bully for so long? What prompted him to change?

4. How does Lída hope and try to be different from her father? In what ways does she resemble him?

5. Lída, Tomáš, and Štěpán each want to honor Pavol's memory. What are some examples of how they try to do this?

6. What are Tomáš's, Lída's, and Štěpán's main hobbies and interests? What do these interests tell you about them?

7. Lída tells Štěpán, "We're your family now." How do the characters support each other in ways their families of origin don't or can't?

8. Pavol wanted to stay in Czechoslovakia and work for change within the country. The others choose different paths. How do their choices change over the course of the novel, and why? What do you think you would do?

9. Pavol suffered from depression and alcohol abuse. If he lived in your community today, how could his friends or family help him?

10. Lída, Tomáš, and Štěpán all consider themselves outcasts for different reasons. Who are the outcasts in your school or community, and how do you treat them?

AUTHOR'S NOTE

When I was a sophomore in high school, I signed up for a sociology class that changed the way I thought about myself and my world. I was an outlier in the class—a tenth grader among second-semester seniors, a high-achieving loner with weird obsessions that included memorizing the street grid of downtown Houston and sneaking off with a gay classmate to volunteer at a community radio station that the Ku Klux Klan had bombed off the air the previous year.

The sociology teacher was young and, to me, impossibly cool. He made no secret of his libertarian beliefs but encouraged us to form our own opinions and argue with him. As we made our way through the political theorists of previous centuries, I gravitated toward Karl Marx, socialism, and communism. I asked myself if I would've been better off under communism, where people were slotted into roles considered the best for the country as a whole and the State took care of everyone's basic needs. I longed to belong and to contribute to something larger than myself, but my lack of social skills or athletic ability kept me out of cliques, sports teams, and other organized groups. And having been tormented by bullies in my very conservative school in Houston at the height of the Cold War, I believed on some level that the enemy of my enemy was my friend.

I graduated from high school somewhat sympathetic to communism and at university devoured the works of twentieth-century Marxists. In the summer of 1984, I thumbed my nose at the Reagan Administration by visiting Nicaragua after the Sandinista revolution and serving as a part-time nanny for a family of Chileans exiled by the right-wing Pinochet regime. One of the Chileans who shared their house was a pilot trained in the Soviet Union, a key ally of the new Nicaraguan regime. I saw teenage soldiers carrying AK-47s and Russian tanks next to public buildings.

Eventually I found my place in the world as a librarian and magazine editor, and Marxism lost its attraction. I worked with Cuban exiles who described in harrowing detail the perils of living in a totalitarian dictatorship that controlled every aspect of life. One friend talked about his father requesting to sit facing the door in a restaurant so he could flee when State Security officials arrived. His future wife's parents sent her as an unaccompanied minor to the United States to keep authorities from shipping her off to the Soviet Union at the age of eight for training to become an Olympic swimmer—all because she showed early talent.

I realized that I would not have been better off under communism if I couldn't choose what to do with my life, if my life belonged to the State. The rules in a totalitarian country are strict and often incomprehensible, with draconian penalties for crossing invisible lines. I'd crossed lines throughout my life, with no worse consequences than being fired from a job. A dictatorship would not have been so forgiving.

In adulthood I was diagnosed on the autism spectrum and it answered a lot of questions about why I had trouble making friends, fitting in, and following rules. It also made me think about the experiences of people like me throughout the world.

In the past few years, I've also become aware of how easily

freedoms that we've come to take for granted can be snatched away, just as they were for the young people whose hopes for a third way between capitalism and communism—"socialism with a human face"—were crushed by the Soviet tanks that rolled into Czechoslovakia in 1968.

From these disparate origins, my character of Tomáš was born. In the course of researching for this novel, I discovered that a Soviet psychiatrist, Grunya Efimova Sukhareva, had identified the characteristics of what would become the autism spectrum a full twenty years before Leo Kanner and Hans Asperger—but Stalinism, World War II, and the Iron Curtain cut her work off from the others. I also learned of the Soviet-bloc abuse of psychiatry to punish dissidents.

In pursuing my obsessions as a high school student, I'd connected with other misfits—the model-train-obsessed sociology teacher, my friends at the radio station, a summer job coworker who'd dropped out of high school pregnant. After four decades, I haven't forgotten her asking, "Do you know what it's like to walk into a classroom and know everyone in the room hates you?" These outsiders became the inspiration for Tomáš's friends Štěpán and Lída.

At a time of growing hatred against the Other and mass support for would-be dictators in the United States and around the world, I hope readers will connect with three brave Czecho-Slovak teenagers seeking freedom, self-determination, acceptance, and belonging. I hope Tomáš, Štěpán, and Lída will help you to find your place in the world.

HISTORICAL NOTE

In 1969, Czechoslovakia was a young country with a tragic history. Carved out of the ruins of the defeated Austro-Hungarian Empire in 1918, it had become one of the few stable multiethnic, multilingual democracies of Central and Eastern Europe. Czechs and Slovaks spoke different but related languages, and while Czechs tended to be secular or religiously diverse, most Slovaks were Roman Catholics. Many German speakers lived in the Czech provinces of Bohemia and Moravia, while Slovakia was home to more than half a million Hungarians. The 350,000 Jewish people who lived in Czechoslovakia ranged from secular German speakers to Orthodox Jews who mainly spoke Yiddish.

After Adolf Hitler and his Nazi Party seized power in neighboring Germany in 1933, he eyed Bohemia and Moravia for their wealth, agriculture, and industry. He manipulated Western European leaders into signing the 1938 Munich Agreement, which forced Czechoslovakia to hand these regions over to Germany. No Czechoslovak delegates were invited to the negotiations. In March 1939, Germany invaded all of Czechoslovakia, turned Bohemia and Moravia into a protectorate under direct rule, and set up a collaborationist regime in Slovakia. The Nazis and their allies in Slovakia murdered 90 percent of Czechoslovakia's Jews and brutally suppressed all opposition. Those accused of supporting the

Resistance faced execution or deportation to concentration camps. Two Czech villages, Lidice and Ležáky, were leveled and their residents massacred in retaliation for the 1942 assassination of the country's Nazi administrator, Reinhard Heydrich, in Prague. Initially, most of the resisters were members of the Czechoslovak Army or students whose universities had been closed. After Hitler invaded the Soviet Union in June 1941, members of the Czechoslovak Communist Party (KSČ) joined the Resistance. Their leadership spent most of the war in Moscow, where they made plans to take over the country after the war ended.

After suffering abuse, deportation, and extermination at the hands of the Nazis and their collaborators, many ordinary Czechs and Slovaks welcomed the Soviet forces in 1945. The end of the war saw the forcible expulsion of hundreds of thousands of ethnic Germans and Hungarians from Czech and Slovak lands and the seizure of their property. In 1948, KSČ leader Klement Gottwald—an ardent ally of Soviet dictator Josef Stalin—ruthlessly eliminated all opposition parties to become reunited Czechoslovakia's supreme leader.

After Gottwald died in 1953, other hardline KSČ leaders took over. By the early 1960s, though, it became evident that Stalinist policies had led to low productivity and economic stagnation. After a very slow process of liberalization, the Slovak Communist leader Alexander Dubček became First Secretary of the KSČ in January 1968 and implemented the reforms of the Prague Spring—including freedom of speech and the press, the importation of books and music from the West, more worker input in the economy, and permission to travel outside the Soviet bloc. He called for "socialism with a human face," which granted freedom, rights, and power to ordinary people. Concerned that Czechoslovakia would break free from Communist rule and the Warsaw Pact military alliance, the

Soviet Union and three other Communist regimes—Poland, Hungary, and Bulgaria—invaded Czechoslovakia on August 21, 1968.

The new wave of repression that followed saw the withdrawal of freedoms, mass firings, expulsions from the Party, the imprisonment of dissidents, and the closing of the borders. When university student Jan Palach set himself on fire on January 16, 1969 and died three days later, authorities permitted a funeral attended by tens of thousands of people. It turned into a mass protest, leading the regime to suppress similar acts that occurred later that year, including the self-immolation of secondary student Jan Zajíc.

By the late 1980s, economic mismanagement led to shortages and a declining standard of living throughout the Communist bloc. While some Eastern European leaders loosened their grip on their populations, the KSČ maintained tight control of Czechoslovakia. A protest for the twentieth anniversary of Jan Palach's self-immolation resulted in the imprisonment of dozens of pro-democracy activists—among them the playwright and essayist Václav Havel, who'd barely survived a four-year prison sentence earlier in the decade. Protests within the country and international pressure led to Havel's release, at which point he became the face of Czechoslovakia's Velvet Revolution, the nonviolent mass uprising in November 1989 that ended more than forty years of Communist rule.

Havel became the first president of Czechoslovakia's first democratic republic since 1939. Right away he faced many challenges, including the Slovak parliament's demand for independence. Democratically-elected representatives from Czech and Slovak regions negotiated for two years, and on New Year's Day 1993, Slovakia became an independent country. As of 2022, both the Czech Republic and Slovakia are thriving democracies and members of the European Union.

I used a variety of sources to research *Torch*. My initial inspiration came from the three-part HBO Europe miniseries *Burning Bush*, which portrayed the aftermath of Jan Palach's suicide. Directed by Polish filmmaker Agnieszka Holland, it was released in 2013. I found valuable background on the diverse nationalities of Czechoslovakia in two books by Tara Zahra—*Kidnapped Souls: National Indifference and the Battle for Children in the Bohemian Lands, 1900-1948* (Cornell University Press, 2008) and *The Lost Children: Reconstructing Europe's Families After World War II* (Harvard University Press, 2011).

For the Soviet invasion and its aftermath, I consulted several works of fiction and memoir. Milan Kundera's *The Unbearable Lightness of Being*, translated into English by Michael Henry Heim, is a classic novel with a film adaptation. More recently, the Slovak novelist and screenwriter Viliam Kilmáček based his novel *The Hot Summer of 1968* (Mandel Vilar Press, 2021; translated by Peter Petro) on testimonies from exiles and his own remembrances of growing up in Bratislava in that period. Milan Šimečka, a professor fired for his support of the reforms and later imprisoned, writes about how the authorities used various forms of intimidation and terror in *The Restoration of Order: The Normalization of Czechoslovakia* (Verso, 1984, translated by A.G. Brain). For those who read Portuguese, as I do, *O "Socialismo" Que Eu Vivi* (*O Jornal*, 1984) is the memoir of Cândida Ventura, a Communist activist who fled Portugal's fascist regime and settled in Czechoslovakia; although she opposed the Soviet invasion, she admits she did not speak out due to fear of losing her job.

In addition, I watched various documentary films with footage secretly filmed in Prague during and after the Soviet invasion.

They were French director Chris Marker's film of the political movements of 1968, *A Grin Without a Cat* (1977); Brazilian director João Moreira Salles's *In the Intense Now* (2017); and Czech director Jan Nemec's *Oratorio for Prague* (1998).

Among the online sources I used were websites from Radio Prague and Radio Free Europe/Radio Liberty. Historical museums were a rich source of photos, documents, and interviews as well. In Prague I visited the National Memorial to the Heroes of the Heydrich Terror, the National Memorial on Vítkov Hill, the Museum of Communism, and the National Museum, in front of which is the memorial to Jan Palach and Jan Zajíc. When I traveled to Bratislava and Vienna, I saw the border region where forest was once razed to create the security zone.

ACKNOWLEDGMENTS

Torch had a long journey, and I am grateful to the many people who helped along the way. First and foremost my agent, Jacqui Lipton, sprung me from a five-year stint in Author Jail by taking on a manuscript that had significantly more words than it does now. She guided me to solving the pacing problem that had frustrated me through multiple drafts. At the time, she was with Storm Literary Agency, and Vicki Selvaggio worked with Jacqui and me to find the perfect home for this rebel of a YA novel.

I am proud to be with Carolrhoda Lab, the publisher of some of the boldest, most groundbreaking YA fiction to come out in recent years. Amy Fitzgerald understood and appreciated the multiple POV/collective protagonist narrative at the heart of the story, and she helped me to create even stronger bonds among my three main characters. Kim Morales's cover design perfectly captures the time, place, and mood. Thanks to the entire team for all their work.

I thank the readers who saw the potential in my early drafts and helped me to achieve it: Heather Demetrios, Cheryl Dishon, Michelle Hazen, Carly Heath, Tere Kirkland, Amanda West Lewis, Erin Makela, Shelly Nosbisch, Mae Pelster, Erin Phillips, Katia Raina, and past and present members of my VCFA critique group based in New York City—Katie Bartlett, Patrick Downes, Kate Hosford, Anna Jordan, Susan Korchak, Shelley Saposnik, Margaret

White, Anne Williard, Kathleen Wilson, Meg Wiviott, and Mary-Walker Wright. Julie Chibbaro, Linda Elovitz Marshall, and Ellen Yeomans shared their experiences of living in Czechoslovakia and the Czech Republic.

A key turning point came when I worked with an editor, something I'd missed in my many years in Author Jail. Bethany Simonsen not only gave me detailed notes on my characters and scenes but also identified my key subplot and how it connected to the main story. She offered this edit pro bono to a neurodivergent writer writing from lived experience, at a time when many of us were struggling to break into, or break back into, publishing. I also had the benefit of working with excellent authenticity readers: Andrés Pi Andreu, Elizabeth Bartmess, Peter Marino, and Alex Zucker. At this point, all errors are my own.

When I had what I considered a finished manuscript but no agent or pathway into publishing, Elana K. Arnold and Cynthia Levinson spoke with me and encouraged me to query agents rather than dropping *Torch* into a drawer on top of all my other unpublished manuscripts. I hope you feel you gave me the correct advice.

Finally, I would like to thank my husband, Richard Lachmann, for believing in me and keeping me going during all the years of disappointment. I know it wasn't easy for him to see me struggle against futility, my belief that every new project was going to be "the one," only to have my hope and my belief in myself shattered each year. He, too, was one of those early readers, and I wish he could have seen what this story ultimately became. I dedicate *Torch* to his memory.

ABOUT THE AUTHOR

Lyn Miller-Lachmann is the author of the award-winning YA historical novel *Gringolandia* and a translator of children's books from Portuguese and Spanish to English. Diagnosed on the autism spectrum as an adult, she is obsessed with history and building LEGO cities. Find her and her work at www.lynmilllerlachmann.com.